Child of My Time

MARK FRANKLAND

CHILD OF MY TIME

Chatto & Windus
LONDON

Published by Chatto & Windus 1999

2 4 6 8 10 9 7 5 3 1

First published in Great Britain in 1999 by
Chatto & Windus
Random House, 20 Vauxhall Bridge Road,
London SW1V 2SA

Random House Australia (Pty) Limited
20 Alfred Street, Milsons Point, Sydney,
New South Wales 2061, Australia

Random House New Zealand Limited
18 Poland Road, Glenfield,
Auckland 10, New Zealand

Random House South Africa (Pty) Limited
Endulini, 5A Jubilee Road, Parktown 2193, South Africa

Random House UK Limited Reg. No. 954009

A CIP catalogue record for this book
is available from the British Library

ISBN 1 8605 6022 9

Papers used by Random House UK Limited are natural,
recyclable products made from wood grown in sustainable forests.
The manufacturing processes conform to the environmental
regulations of the country of origin

Typeset by Plimpsest Book Production Limited,
Polmont, Stirlingshire
Printed and bound in Great Britain by
Biddles Ltd, Guildford and King's Lynn

Contents

I have only the key to the old times and the one for the new is denied me, and I cannot live in the new time anyway, because I belong to the old time, which is dead.

Bohumil Hrabal, *The Little Town Where Time Stood Still*

Prologue

A Dream of Disorder

Moscow, 1992

The sun woke me. At first I tried to ignore its heat on the back of my neck. There was no point getting up to draw the curtain properly, for the thin material offered scant protection from even the earliest rays of the midsummer sun. Usually I rolled to the furthest side of the bed, where I was safe in shadow for a little longer. In this way I sometimes managed to sleep through the noises that accompanied the insistent heat – the shriek of a tram as it escaped the deformed rails of its terminus, the amplified voice of a woman repeating the same nagging phrases that I had heard a hundred times but still could not quite make out.

This morning, though, the city would not let me sleep; the tram wheels were unbearably shrill, the woman's voice more than usually commanding. I got up and went to the bathroom to rub water on my face, but I did not shave or brush my teeth, knowing that the world waiting outside was indifferent to these daily disciplines. The doors of the lift jerked closed and the sour-smelling box shivered its way to the ground floor. In my hurry I tripped on a broken step in the hall and angrily pulled open the door into the courtyard.

There was little to please the eye in this house built of poor materials by grudging hands, but the yard had patches of grass, a few small bushes and, planted in military formation in a square of powdery soil, young trees whose dark green leaves freshened air that was already uncomfortably heavy. The peace of this limited oasis unsettled me. Why was no one else about? There was no sign of the cleaning woman who at dawn swabbed gritty water over the stairs and landings, no sign of the half-wild bitch which dozed all day outside her kennel of old boxes, or of the house watchmen who befriended her and had a hutch of their own by the car-park gate. Nor could I see Misha-Elektrik, the handyman who scurried about from early to late on ill-defined business, pausing only to bob his head when he saw one of the house's foreign residents.

I walked quickly through the car park and turned right, imagining I was the last creature to abandon the house, that every one else, even the mongrel bitch and her half-starved puppies, had set off in the direction of the sun and the nagging woman's voice. I no longer slept well in Moscow. It had begun ten years earlier when I moved into the flat. One night I lay down expecting sleep and my heart speeded up and I started gasping for breath. I went to see the doctor at the British Embassy. He showed no surprise at my symptoms and gave me pills that were a pretty yellow colour. They calmed my late-night anxiety enough to let me get to sleep, though still I often woke before dawn at that black hour loved by the arresting officers of secret police throughout the world. And the pills could not remove my feeling that I was living under siege. I told myself I was a thin-skinned foreigner, that I was not resilient like Russians, not protected by their pessimism. But Moscow was such a heavy city, with so few places to rest in, its streets as wide as rivers. The doors of public buildings, framed and studded with steel and bronze, were like old battle shields. Even the most innocent of them suggested that, once inside, escape might be impossible. Doctors said the atmospheric pressure of Moscow was bad for people with heart problems; they did not mention the pressure of its history.

I told myself there was no shame in needing sleeping pills in such a place and I had taken one last night when my heart began to race as soon as I lay down to sleep. When I was a child I had a recurring nightmare. It began with a white line running across a dark brown background. The line continued until it suddenly broke into violent movements like a seismograph recording an earthquake. At this point

I could smell the horror, a smell of burning rubber and of sealing wax as it melts under the flame of a match. That was the moment the terror reached its peak. The nightmare taught me that fear can exist without a recognisable object; and as I lay sweating in bed last night I had imagined all manner of horrors and disorder with as little recognisable content as that terrifying dream. I had woken without feeling rested, and this was my excuse for the panic that was now driving me away from the house.

It drove me past the Sevastopol cinema, which was showing yet another Indian musical. The low light of the rising sun blinded me and I stumbled where the road surface had collapsed, leaving tram rails exposed like teeth in an old man's mouth. Safe on the pavement, I stood to catch my breath by some railings round a patch of grass. The railings were hung with old clothes and the grass was littered with battered objects – saucepans, travelling bags, a pram, bundles wrapped in dirty check cloths – that seemed to have been abandoned in flight.

I turned left under a bridge and an engine drawing grimy green carriages passed overhead with such a stamp of metal I thought the structure was collapsing. Like a drum roll at the circus, the noise alerted me to the spectacle ahead. What I expected to see was this. To the right, the Kazan Station (disguised by its architect as a red-brick Kremlin) and beyond it a department store as unwelcoming as a prison; in a line on the left the old Customs House, the Leningrad Station, the Komsomol underground station and finally another station, the Yaroslavl, an art nouveau fantasy whose roof was shaped like a paper bag that has been inflated, turned upside down, and squashed.

But what I saw was a vast space occupied by a mass of people moving as slowly and incoherently as fish in a tank of water. Komsomol Square, the space into which they were crowded, was the shape of an inverted funnel, with the narrow end in the distance. The space between the buildings on each side was occupied by a wide road, parking lots and broad pavements, and it was here that the men, women and children were standing or sitting or performing their lazy movements. A woman carrying a plastic bag rested her back against the Customs House wall. Next to her a little girl held a white enamel bucket in one hand and a dog on a piece of string in the other. They had broad, pale faces and eyes of such faded blue that I thought for a moment they were blind. Most of the people in the square carried bags or bundles and some had enamel buckets like the girl's. All were lightly dressed, the women in cotton dresses, the men in short-sleeved shirts. They were summer clothes, of course, but also the sort of clothes you drag on when driven by disaster from your bed.

The soldiers added to the impression that a rout had taken place. They sat or leant on a parapet that separated the sidewalk from the central road, their uniforms unbuttoned, and stained with sweat and grease. The leather of their boots was torn. They had taken off their caps and were drinking cans of beer and smoking. The sun caught their fair hair, lighting up faces that were truculent but apprehensive. And, as in any rout, there were the bodies of those who had fallen by the way. I saw the first one when I went to inspect a knot of people gathered round a kiosk selling soft drinks. A pair of filthy trouser legs stuck out to one side of the queue. As people got closer to the kiosk, they stepped over the legs without looking down at the rough red face and matted hair of the man beneath their feet. A water truck had just cleaned a patch of tarmac outside the Kazan Station, leaving the surface as glossy as a sea lion's back. A little wagon made of a wooden crate and four ill-matched wheels stood abandoned on this shining surface while further on, where the water had not reached, lay what looked like another piece of wood but was a body with no legs. This human log was wrapped in clothes so foul they were as stiff and translucent as oiled brown paper. The face, swollen and bleeding, was turned towards the sky.

I was fooling myself into a fit of nerves. I knew quite well why these men and women were here. It was Saturday and the metallic woman's voice that nagged me so soon after dawn was the announcer at the Leningrad Station, directing people to trains for the suburbs, the destination of most of those on the square. Their bags and bundles held tools and provisions for a weekend's work in the gardens of country cottages, some of them no bigger than potting sheds. The fruits and vegetables grown there would be pickled and stored against the penury of winter, while the white enamel pails would carry the early harvest of currants and berries back to the city. The bodies on the ground were not corpses, just alcoholics and drugged or drunken cripples. It was a familiar scene, but I knew I had not conjured out of nothing the anxiety I felt around me, and that affected me, too.

Were there not omens of grief and disorder to be seen all over Moscow? A few days earlier I was walking along Tverskaya, the Gorky Street of Soviet times. I was opposite the central post office when I noticed the dogs. There were about a dozen of them. They had no collars, their coats were unkempt, and a couple were badly scarred around the muzzle. It was plain they were growing wild, and already paid no attention to the humans who had once domesticated them. They observed instead the discipline of their own pack. The lead dog took the rest of them into the middle of the street. Tails high, they loped down Moscow's main thoroughfare as though setting off to hunt in a wilderness.

Even in the old days, Komsomol Square had been a place of omen. A Russian friend came to see me soon after I moved into the flat in 1983. He had taken the metro to the square and the first thing he said when I opened the door was, 'What a sympathetic neighbourhood you live in.' Outside the metro station he had come across a tipsy peasant playing a *bayan*, a Russian accordion, and dancing to his own music. Such unplanned public revelry was rare in the censored Soviet city, but drinkers knew they could always find someone to split a bottle with in the stations round the square, even if they had to go about their pursuit with the stealth of secret agents.

In those years I sometimes walked down the funnel of the square on winter evenings when the snow reflected an ink-blue sky. I would escape from the cold into the station waiting-rooms, where the women sat, legs thick as young tree trunks in their black felt boots. They wore rough wool scarves over their heads and guarded sacks almost as big as themselves that were filled with loaves of bread and anything else they could find in the Moscow shops to take back to the needy provinces. They sat patiently, but there was a sense of threat in this unconscious display of endurance. Such women would out-sit any ruler, and any set of ideas about how the world should be ordered.

The square had accustomed me to such subversive signals, and there was no reason to be surprised by what I saw there during Communism's last stand, the attempted coup against Mikhail Gorbachev in the summer of 1991. One afternoon I took the metro home from Boris Yeltsin's headquarters at the White House. I could hear the music and clapping as I came up the escalator. The area behind the metro was growing wilder as the Soviet order weakened. The police no longer cleared away the alcoholics. Even at midday young drug addicts slept undisturbed under shady walls. A rough and dirty market traded in drink and food and smudgy pornographic magazines. The noise I heard came from a jazz band dressed in the remains of once smart uniforms. A crowd had gathered in a circle to listen to them, and as I arrived a little man in the uniform of the railways half-stumbled, half-danced, on to this makeshift stage. Although wearing sandals, he managed a few tap-dance steps before a woman who must once have been handsome ran into the circle. She took her first steps with her arms outstretched as though joining a village dance, but then her movements became ugly and she seemed determined to make herself and her collapsing body look as ridiculous as her drunken partner. This theatre of self-humiliation delighted the crowd. There were guffaws from men holding beer bottles in one hand and gobbets of dried fish (the drinker's friend) in the other. The women round the circle shrank away when the railwayman beckoned them to join the dance, but jeered at him when his back was turned.

These people knew what was going on at Yeltsin's headquarters, but they had no wish to take part or even watch, yet their drinking and dancing showed they felt the weight of power had lifted a little from them. They were like children whose school has lost its discipline and understand their unexpected freedom only as a chance to misbehave. Matters were more complicated on this summer morning two years later. This was no longer a temporary holiday for street rebels, but a collapse of order as Russia had for centuries known it. Even those who welcomed the collapse were disoriented, for they knew it was as momentous an event for Russia as the sudden suspension of some law of physics. In the past there had been two truths, order and submission to order, power and the submission to power.

Pushkin conjured up the Russians' vision of power when he imagined the equestrian statue of Peter the Great coming to life, and driving a harmless clerk mad by pursuing him through the streets of St Petersburg before jumping back on to its granite pedestal. The statue that came to life was, 'Neither beast nor man . . . nor this world's creature'. If you lived at the mercy of power like that, what happened if one day it returned to its pedestal for good, as now seemed to be the case? You were lost in uncertainty, and this new uncertain world was as shapeless as the crowd in the early morning square and as exposed to chance as the steppe to winter storms. The old Soviet future was not brilliant, but it had become predictable: it seemed unlikely to contain a return to the systematic murder practised by Lenin and Stalin. But now you could no longer predict your own, let alone your children's, future. The past was no longer a guide to who you were today, let alone who you might become tomorrow. Small wonder that when I first reached the square I took the men and women in their cheap, thin clothes to be refugees at a loss to know where to go next. They *were* refugees, not from war or natural disaster but from a time, once terrible, now less so, which had suddenly ceased to exist.

As I turned to walk home, I knew I was infected by the same uncertainty as the Russians around me. I had first come to this country thirty years before and much of what I did and thought in my life was shaped by my experience of it, just as the Western world I grew up in was shaped by conflict with it. I passed back under the railway bridge. There was more traffic now and I had to wait to cross the road by the railings which were hung with rags.

As I leant against them, I heard something rustle behind me, and turned to see one of the bundles on the parched grass move. A hand came out from under a blue check cloth and jerked it back to reveal the heads of a young man and woman. Their skin was the colour of old ivory, the colour of the covers of a prayer book made from cedars of Lebanon that my mother gave me when I was at school.

The couple sat up to consider their surroundings and smiled. They were gypsies, the only people I had seen that morning who looked at home in the city on the rack of change.

Chapter I

The Broken Chain

We are not born, my dear daughter, to pursue our own small personal happiness, for we are not separate independent subsisting individuals, but links in a chain.

Thomas Mann, *Buddenbrooks*

Gossip columnists called my grandmother the Gypsy Baroness. That was at the beginning of the 1920s when she had just come into her title. She caught journalists' attention by the unusual animals she took with her when she walked her dogs. Among them were a donkey, a crossbill hen and a goat, from which (the magazine *Eve* reported) 'Lady Zouche's cries of "Heel! Heel!" brought no answering obedience.'

There was certainly something gypsy-like about the old woman I knew, who lived in a house called Castle Mead on the edge of Windsor Park. Her hair was often tousled and she had a liking for large, circular ear-rings which she probably bought in Windsor market, where she shopped for many of her clothes. The cupboards in her bedroom held dresses by Worth and other famous designers of the 1920s and 1930s, but she never appeared in them. The most important item in her post-war wardrobe was the apron she wore throughout the day, a signal to her maid and cook and anyone else who happened to be in the house that she, too, was busy with chores. She was tiny – her children called her Little Mum – and remained very quick on her feet even when cataracts had damaged her sight.

She kept her gypsy-like closeness to animals into old age. There were never less than four or five dogs in the house and in summer the French windows in the dining-room were open so they could go into the garden whenever they wanted. This allowed the dogs to rush barking on to the lawn when planes came in to land at Heathrow Airport. My grandmother stopped whatever she was doing and ran after them, cursing and waving a gold-topped bamboo cane. They paid no more attention than the goat that had accompanied her forty years earlier. She exercised the dogs every day until her death at the age of ninety. These walks were also noisy adventures. She ruled that every dog in the house had to be a bitch and, naturally, often one of them was on heat. Neighbouring males led by the local policeman's dog waited to ambush this pack of females as they entered Windsor Park through a door in the garden wall, and had to be driven off by my grandmother with a riding whip. Animals occupied much of her time. She ate little, and her meals centred on a bowl she kept by her chair, into which she put the scraps from her own and visitors' plates; later she emptied the bowl's ripe contents on to a bird table outside the dining-room window. She was as restless as the animals she tended, or perhaps animals and mistress infected each other with their own restlessness. This community of old woman, dogs, birds and a half-wild cat called Appy, who lived in the boiler-room, was mysteriously democratic, and it was hard to tell who made its laws.

It was only after my grandmother died that I saw a photograph of her as a young woman. I was surprised by the big, heavy-lidded eyes, the full lips, and the slightly Roman nose, and by the way the front teeth pushed her upper lip forward. It was not a conventionally beautiful face, but it was a strikingly sensual one. She was twenty-five when Queen Victoria died, and almost forty when the Great War began and blew her aristocratic world to pieces, but I never heard her talk about those times any more than she talked about the glamour of her youth. And where her own house was concerned she might indeed have been some traveller who had wandered in one day and, finding it convenient, decided to stay. She showed no interest in its contents. She seemed not to see the portraits on its walls.

Her silence about the house puzzled me. Sometimes I would find her in the drawing-room, bent over a newspaper she was trying to read through a magnifying glass. In her permanent apron and nondescript clothes – even a boy could recognise the cheapness of her shoes and stockings – she might have been the caretaker of a theatre that had closed after its final production. Portraits of once famous actors and actresses hung on the walls around her. She even used some of the props they had used, though, as I was to discover, many more were hidden away and forgotten. But if she knew anything of the actors' lives or the stories they had played out she never mentioned it to me. There was no one else in the family to ask about such things, for her husband was dead and her children were as silent as their mother.

My first explorations were in the uncared-for grounds, which were as full of remains as an archaeological site. There were the remains of a garden of old-fashioned, sweet-smelling roses, the remains of a children's playground hidden in the remains of an orchard, the remains of a grass tennis court and of a kitchen garden, where the box hedges still smelled of spice when the sun shone but only a scrap of earth was under cultivation. There were abandoned greenhouses with broken glass and tanks of water that had turned a thick tropical green, and a summer house, which could still be rotated to face the sun but where no one sat, in the sun or out of it, and there was a long wooden box with hoops, balls and mallets for games of croquet that no one played any more.

As I grew older, I became more interested in what was inside the house. My grandmother and most of her possessions had left Castle Mead during the war, when it was requisitioned as an American Air Force officers' mess, and there was something austere and temporary about the arrangements of her return in 1945. It was as though a war had just started rather than ended. She closed the old dining-room, making a new one out of half of the old double drawing-room. The library and the billiard room were abandoned to the damp that took the house under siege after the central-heating boiler broke down and my grandmother refused to buy a new one. She put an anthracite stove in the drawing-room, where she spent most of her time, but to save fuel kept its doors shut, so it gave out little heat. In winter she dressed and undressed in her north-facing bedroom in front of a single-bar electric fire. She had the legs of valuable furniture bound with rags and string to protect them from the dogs, and did not think it odd that an Adam sideboard or a pair of oriental cabinets on Louis Seize stands should look like casualties from a battlefield. The servants' wing had the chill of an emptying prison. Its only occupants now were Mrs Woolner, the elderly cook who lived in a dark room on the ground floor, and her companion Susie, a black and white spaniel given her by my grandmother.

The portraits that most interested me hung on the main staircase, whose steps were painted green after the war instead of being re-carpeted. There was an auburn-haired Elizabethan admiral, one hand on his hip, the other on his sword. Next, and trying to look equally heroic, was Sir Cecil Bisshopp, a baronet dressed in white breeches and plumed helmet and riding a black charger. He was waving his sabre in front of the troop of yeomen cavalry he had raised (an inscription on the painting explained) to throw back Napoleon's expected invasion. The third portrait, a sombrely dressed young Victorian, had less obvious appeal for a growing boy. But he had quizzical eyes and, best of all, a pencilled moustache which a distant young cousin had given him and my grandmother did not bother to have removed.

All three men had different surnames. How were they linked to each other, and to my grandmother? They seemed to have led purposeful lives, so why was she trapped in this house whose restlessness was a parody of purpose? And why was there so deep a silence about her family's past that I imagined my grandmother putting gags on the men and women who observed her from the walls? I began to look for clues and discovered them in almost every drawer and cupboard, hidden under packets of flea powder and elastic bands, tins of throat pastilles, old bills, and countless pictures of dogs, horses and other animals clipped from newspapers and magazines. A dowager's will was muddled up with an invitation to dine with the Prince Regent at Brighton Pavilion and a recipe for walnut ketchup called Yatton sauce. There were portrait miniatures that no one had looked at for years: a swan-necked young Regency woman; an officer in the Foot Guards, cuttings from his auburn hair worked into a lozenge pattern at the back of the frame and the whole picture locked inside a red leather case. A watercolour carelessly folded into a torn envelope showed a party of two men and a woman taking a walk with some children and a dog. A little girl has just fallen into some bushes and only her shoes and the bottom of her crinoline can be seen. 'Miss Theresa Tufnell', someone has written on the back of the painting, 'as she [dis]appeared on Tuesday Jan 29, 1850.'

My searches took me to the abandoned library and billiard room. The library was used for a short time after the war by my grandmother's uncle, who came to live with her till he died. Each day he put on the black coat and striped trousers he had worn as chairman of the London County Council, but even he could not withstand the aimlessness of the life around him. He could only wait for teatime and the tomato sandwiches that were his old man's passion, and for the visits of young relatives, whom he tipped with five-pound notes, muttering that an old man was good for nothing more. His old study led into the billiard room. During the war homesick Americans had decorated both rooms to remind themselves of Hawaii, and grass-skirted girls danced and palm trees swayed on walls painted to represent a tropical sky and sea until the day my grandmother died. This was where she had chosen to dump the story of the lives out of which hers had grown. The Hawaiian girls, frozen now for lack of heating, performed their lonely dance in a room that was a bric-a-brac dealer's delight.

There was one pair of legs, very finely carved, from a billiard table. A Life Guard's golden helmet with a plume of white horsehair caught my eye. I put it on, but it hurt my head, so I took it off and did not play with it again. A later search revealed a breastplate that matched the helmet and two side drums of the sort that a cavalry horse wears across its neck. There were ancient trunks and suitcases, boxes big and small and tea chests that still had their lining of silver foil. One trunk painted with chocolate and brown livery stripes contained a baron's robes and coronet, both in fine condition in spite of their obvious age. Among the pieces of abandoned furniture was a set of decidedly theatrical chairs, their straight backs and solid seats covered in crimson velvet. The struts between the legs were made of twisted metal and on the back of each chair perched a pair of small bronze birds.

The disarray, the dust sheets and the garish walls combined to make objects that were still handsome or might again be useful look like junk. When local antique dealers called, my grandmother sent them to browse here among jugs and china basins that had stood on Victorian washstands, and a museum's worth of ancient household equipment: oil lamps, machines for grinding knives, a contraption for boiling eggs at the breakfast table. There was a Parliament clock, whose wooden case was black with age, and bronze candelabra decorated with coats of arms that were too heavy for a child to lift. A pair of Meissen pugs, each missing a leg and gold bells from their bright blue collars, led a long procession of similarly maimed porcelain creatures. Many of these abandoned objects had an exotic flavour, like the folding ikon made of brass and blue enamel found in the pocket of a Russian soldier who died fighting the British in a forgotten battle at the edge of vanished empires. There were drawings and watercolours of Middle Eastern characters and scenes, and in a disintegrating frame a brilliantly coloured Persian miniature of the great Shah Abbas entertaining the King of Samarkand.

Trunks contained too many old documents and packages of letters for a schoolboy to bother with, but some of the papers had spilled out and they caught my eye. A bill – made into a little book it was so long – listed furniture provided by the London cabinet makers Mayhew & Ince in 1781 for a house in Spring Garden, Whitehall. It was, I realised, my grandmother's furniture. The 'strong mahogany splat-backed chairs with wheat-ear carving' were the chairs we sat on at meals. The dishes of rissoles that Mrs Woolner called Kromeskis sat on Mayhew & Ince's sideboard with 'green and white fluted legs' and it was still kept company by the 'celeret' with brass partitions for nine bottles, and the two vase-shaped cutlery boxes 'japanned to look like porphyry', whose colour was now more black than purple. By what route had they got from Whitehall to Windsor? And who was the anxious Victorian father bombarding his son at Eton with letters and even a drawing to explain how to have his hair cut so he would look like a 'gentleman, and not a boy in a reformatory'?

If my grandmother knew, she did not care, or did not care enough to talk about such things to her children and grandchildren. Castle Mead was an orphan house; it had no future, it had forgotten its past. Many years later I recognised the same atmosphere when, travelling through East Germany, I came across an old town that had survived both the war and Communist reconstruction. It, too, had been left in the lurch by time. The purpose and the people it was built for had gone, and no one believed in the arrival of a prince who would kiss it back to life. The closest to a prince to appear at Castle Mead was an antique dealer with an expensive shop in Bond Street. My grandmother called him 'that nice Mr Parrot' and let him wander round the house and put anything that interested him on the long table in the abandoned dining-room. If no one in the family happened to come by and object, on his next visit 'nice Mr Parrot' wrote my grandmother a cheque and carried his forgotten treasures off to a new life.

There was one thing in the old dining-room the antique dealer did not touch, a portrait of my grandmother as a grave, Alice-in-Wonderland child with big blue eyes, fair hair down to her shoulders, and a straw boater in her hand. But why had she put such a charming picture in a room where no one went? And why did she hide away in the old stables another painting of herself, this time as a pretty teenager wearing a red tam-o'-shanter? It was as though some drama had ended before she had time to grow up – there was no painting anywhere in the house of her as an adult – and she felt her likeness had no right to hang beside the men and women who had been its protagonists.

Perhaps that explained her rages. To her grandchildren she was charming if a little distant, and always curious about the lives they lived in the great world beyond her forgotten little one. But the old woman who did not bother to heat her house properly was hard on herself, and harsher still to her servants. Mrs Woolner, as sweet-tempered and patient as her dog Susie, was reduced to tears by criticism of her cooking before guests had a chance to taste it. My grandmother's chief whipping-boy (it was her own expression) was May, the maid who worked for her all her life after marrying Fred the under-chauffeur when she was the pretty girl every butler and footman wanted to kiss. She now lived with Fred in a flat above the stables and though her voice was hoarse, her hands rough and her eyes often watery she was still beautiful. When I stayed at Castle Mead she brought early-morning tea with a plate of Petit Beurre biscuits, pausing for a moment to give me a thoughtful smile before hurrying out of the bedroom. She was always in a hurry, worried that 'M'Lady' would find some new reason to scold her. On the day before my grandmother's funeral May suffered a brainstorm and tore off her clothes in the flower room. Later she became delirious and began shouting, 'Don't beat me, M'Lady. Please don't beat me.'

I know of only one occasion when my grandmother acknowledged the past that was secreted throughout her house. A friend asked to explore the stables where lumber that could not fit in the billiard room was stored. She came across a portrait that had fallen against a rusty bicycle. A pedal pierced the canvas, slashing the face of a young woman who might have been attractive were it not for a too prominent jaw. 'Oh her,' said my grandmother when told about it. 'Everyone hated her. She was a terrible woman.'

That was all she said. A door swung open and snapped shut again. And yet she must have known a lot about the woman in the damaged painting because she was her grandmother.

Amelia Daniell was the daughter of a retired and perhaps not quite respectable director of the East India Company. While staying in Oxford with a relation who was a niece of the Regency dandy Beau Brummell she met and eloped with Edward Curzon, an undergraduate at Christ Church, Oxford. This marriage was the origin of a terrible quarrel between Edward, my grandmother's grandfather, and his elder brother Robert.

Robert, the young man in the portrait with the pencilled moustache, was swept away by disastrously romantic ideas of aristocracy. He enhanced his image of himself by travels through the East, where he picked up the exotic objects I often came across while exploring Castle Mead, and was later famous for the collection of early Christian manuscripts he acquired by charm and guile in the forgotten monasteries of the Levant and for the book he wrote about his manuscript-hunting expeditions. He was an antiquarian who revered his family as he revered all old things.

Edward, his younger brother, was a chronic, shameless plunderer, who exploited his family's pride for his own advantage. There was only one portrait of him in my grandmother's house, a drawing done in Dresden when he was sent there to study German. It shows a composed eighteen-year-old with the same large eyes as my grandmother, and a long face tapering through a pretty mouth to a determined chin. It is a face with trouble written all over it.

Sir Cecil Bisshopp, the baronet pictured at Castle Mead parading his troop of yeomen cavalry, was Robert and Edward's grandfather. He married a clever heiress (the Elizabethan admiral was one of her ancestors) and elevated himself into the peerage by claiming the Zouche barony, which had been in abeyance for over a hundred years. To become a lord he had to live like a lord. He spent more than he could afford both on his new house in London and on Parham, the old family home in Sussex: the cabinet makers Mayhew & Ince did very well out of him. His heir, also called Cecil, was the Guards officer whose miniature my grandmother hid away in a drawer. The swan-necked girl was the young soldier's wife, but she died before she could produce a child. Several years later the heart-broken husband was killed fighting the Americans in Canada. It was the end of the old baron's hopes and when he died in 1830 he was broke, bitter and a little mad. Because the Zouche title was one of the oldest in England it could pass through the female line and Robert and Edward's mother became the new baroness.

The 13th baroness was spendthrift, self-pitying, and a famous hypochondriac, to whom the king lent his sleeping carriage so she could travel prone round England in search of cures. Her husband was an unimaginative Tory MP with little more good sense than his wife. Under their management the family fortunes went from bad to worse. It did not help that they were frightened of Robert, their heir, whose dreams they could not understand, and that Edward – they called him Bunny – was their favourite. Bunny fell out of favour when they learned that he had run off with Amelia Daniell and married her in secret. They declared the family was disgraced and ordered him to become a clergyman and hide his shameful wife, whom they vowed never to receive, in the obscurity of a country parsonage. Bunny soon won them round. His father paid off his Oxford debts, which were large, and gave him money to become a lawyer. Amelia became pregnant. The baroness received her, and was won over.

Robert was in Smyrna, at the end of his first expedition to the Levant when he got his father's letter telling him what Edward had done. He was as mortified as his parents, but unlike them never forgave his brother and came to believe that Edward's reckless marriage was the cause of everything that went wrong in his own life. He watched in horror as Edward extracted money from their mother so his growing family could live like the rich aristocrats everyone supposed them to be.

Edward played on his parents' fear of family dishonour. He said the Curzon name demanded that he, his wife and children live in a certain style and that, if he could not pay the bills for it, his parents and elder brother should. He also refused to accept the role of younger son. It was his good luck to have been born into a family that was already an exception to the rules by having a woman at its head. Perhaps because she was a woman with no instinctive sympathy for the ruthless tradition of primogeniture, but more likely because she was foolish, the baroness did not feel obliged to preserve her property for her eldest son and heir. She let Edward's family occupy a wing of Parham, the house that would one day be Robert's and which he dreamed of re-making according to his romantic tastes. Edward advised his mother on the management of her affairs, with predictably disastrous results. The Life Guard's helmet in the billiard room at Castle Mead belonged to George Augustus, Edward and Amelia's eldest son and my grandmother's father, and it was of course the baroness, disregarding Robert's protests, who financed George Augustus's career in the most expensive regiment in the army.

Robert's sense of family would not let him cut his brother off completely. The charming watercolour I found hidden in a drawer at Castle Mead was done by Robert when he and Edward were staying at their father's house in Staffordshire. Some of the children in the picture are Edward's, but the young woman is Robert's future wife. Only Amelia is missing from this family scene and it was on her that Robert turned his rage. She was a moaner who quickly learned to manipulate her father- and mother-in-law, and when Robert's young wife died he blamed Amelia for driving her to an early grave by her constant financial demands. Relations between the brothers' families were poisoned beyond hope of cure.

The hypochondriacal baroness lived to a great old age and Robert survived her by only three years. In this short time he cleared Parham of his mother's gimcracks and tried to turn the Elizabethan mansion into a palace of dreams it never was nor could be. He removed floors to make rooms with soaring ceilings, and decorated them in a style that mixed the Renaissance and Middle Ages. He designed the theatrical bird-backed chairs I found at Castle Mead for his new dining-room (the birds were popinjays from the Curzon crest) and used the great hall, the one room already grand enough for his tastes, to display his collection of ancient armour. But he was already ill and haunted by the fear that he would die before his son and daughter were old enough to care for themselves. When his son Robin was away at school he bombarded him with nervous letters of advice, including the one explaining how to get a proper haircut. He took his daughter Darea on holidays to the seaside, though he felt, he said, like an ageing fly that struggles to climb a window pane knowing it will never reach the top. He had the family motto *Let Curzon holde what Curzon helde* engraved above fireplaces and on stained-glass windows, as though casting a spell to protect his children. It was not enough. Soon after Robert died the inexperienced Robin was manoeuvred into marrying the ravishing but unmanageable daughter of an impecunious Scottish peer. She was compulsively unfaithful, and after a mock-medieval tournament in which Robin and his wife's lovers dressed up in Parham's armour and fought battles she escaped on her horse to London and he divorced her. They had no child and he did not re-marry. Darea never married at all and brother and sister lived together in Parham as though not daring to break what remained of their father's spell. When Robin died Darea succeeded him, and when she died it was my grandmother's turn.

She took possession of Parham on a fine day in the spring of 1917. A housekeeper in a grey gown and white mob cap received her together with her daughter, my aunt, then a girl of eleven, and gave them tea in a long room with a low moulded ceiling. The room was crowded with furniture; family portraits and old paintings were hung in a double row around the walls. The windows looked south across a lawn to a neat church at the edge of a park, and beyond that to the Downs, which rose like a great green wave in the distance. The little girl stared at the strawberry-leaf decoration on the cups from which they drank their tea and breathed in the smell of candle wax, dust and old oak boards that permeated the house. That night she slept in a room with a strange wooden structure like a miniature stage below the window, and she stood on it to look across the garden to a lake and then parkland as far as the eye could see. The setting sun had turned the sky pink and gold like the pictures in her children's prayer book and a herd of fallow deer, among them a single white doe, spread away into the dusk.

A more seductive, and more poisoned, inheritance was hard to imagine. It had been plain for years that my grandmother would inherit both Parham and the title, yet she may not even have met her cousins, and certainly was never allowed to set foot in the house until that spring day in 1917. Darea had done everything in her power to cut my grandmother's inheritance to the bone. The two hundred ancient manuscripts that represented the greatest achievement of her father as a collector had been loaned to the British Museum on his death. In her will the spinster baroness turned the loan into a gift. Her meaning was plain: no descendant of Edward and Amelia was to be given the chance to profit from this part at least of the family treasure. She bequeathed what money she had outside the Parham estate to her mother's family. And when she knew she was dying and left Parham for her house in London, she took with her the gold plate that was displayed on what looked like an altar at the end of the dining-room, for under the terms of inheritance only what was in the house at the time of Darea's death had to pass to my grandmother.

The Parham my grandmother moved into was Robert Curzon's creation. The curious daïs in the room my aunt slept in that first night was built by Robert so his invalid wife could lie there on a chaise-longue and look out into the park. The pictures still hung in their double rows as he had arranged them. Almost nothing had changed since he dedicated Parham to romancing the past. There had to be an effort of memory, and a recognition of wrongs done, if Edward's heirs were to recover their links to the past, but there was neither one nor the other. The house's new owners were as careless as children about the origin and costs of the enchanting world that was now theirs to play in and enjoy.

There was one exception: my grandfather, who now makes his late, but fateful, entry into the story. Sir Frederick Frankland, 10th Baronet, of Thirkleby (as he would have wished to be introduced), had an interest in the past and a taste for old things. His own title had become separated from the family estates in Yorkshire at the beginning of the nineteenth century, and since then the baronets had earned their living as soldiers in unglamorous and inexpensive regiments. He fought with Rhodes in Matabeleland and took part in the Boer War, but failed to make a fortune in Africa, and hoped to acquire one instead by marrying my grandmother. He was not her choice. She fell for an Irishman, a well-known horseman of the time, but her father George Augustus, colonel of the 2nd Life Guards, thought a penniless English baronet the superior catch. Sir Frederick was a gambler, but marrying my grandmother was the safest bet he made. It was almost certain the Zouche barony and estates would pass to her on the death of her much older and childless cousins. Both title and property would eventually pass to any child of his, making up for the years the Franklands had spent as landless wanderers. He was a handsome man, not much taller than his wife but stockily built, with a heavy head and thick moustache. He dressed well and expensively and was entirely self-assured, just the person, it must have seemed, to take charge of the affairs of a young woman who had led a conventionally sheltered life and would one day inherit what remained of an old fortune.

During the Great War my grandmother turned Parham into a convalescent home for army officers wounded at the front. She invited her women friends to come and help entertain the young soldiers, and they seem to have enjoyed themselves. There was dancing in the great hall under the gaze of Robert's suits of armour. Copies of *La Vie Parisienne*, the nice people's naughty magazine, were kept in a chest so the children should not see them. Did she have affairs? Her children thought so. When the war ended she wore fashionable clothes to theatre first nights in London. She bought race horses, and watched them run in her colours of scarlet and yellow. My grandfather did nothing to regulate the family's spending. That was not his style any more than it had been Edward's, and of the two men it is hard to know who was the more dangerous. Sir Frederick was a snob and a stickler for correct behaviour in others. He was also a mythmaker who was happy to live by appearances, and in the management of appearances he showed something like genius. He wanted everything around him to be as good-looking and solid as he himself appeared to be, and Parham satisfied both his aesthetic and his social ambitions. He took the trouble to learn something of the house's history, going through the mass of old letters and documents in its archives in which no one else in the family showed any interest. He then extracted letters from Pitt, the Duke of Wellington and any other famous person whose signature he came across and mounted them in a handsome leather-bound album, which he produced to impress his guests.

It was not his style, though, to put up with shabby grandeur. The Parham estate had shrunk to fewer than four thousand acres by the time my grandmother inherited it, and its revenues accordingly. The house, like all big old houses, was greedy. It was expensive to run and had few modern comforts. There were just two bathrooms. Central heating was minimal. A tipsy old man carried copper cans of hot water to the bedrooms each evening, dribbling puddles as he went up the stairs. The house had its own electrical generator, but the billiard table still had to be lit by oil lamps, and candlesticks were taken to bed. There were damp, dry rot and a leaking roof. With no improvement to the Zouche income in sight, shabby grandeur was set to become ever shabbier and ever less grand.

My grandfather sold off what remained of the treasures Robert Curzon had spent a lifetime acquiring. What Sotheby's called the last great English collection of armour, two hundred and eleven pieces in all, was snapped up by New York's Metropolitan Museum and dealers such as Duveen. Among the books that went to auction was a Mazarin Bible and an edition of Shakespeare's poems with a rare portrait of the poet. When my grandmother bought a well-known race horse called Navana for her eldest and favourite son she paid twice as much as the Shakespeare raised at auction. And when my grandparents sold Parham and its estate, it was not to raise the resources to re-establish the family fortunes on a sound footing but to go on spending.

By some malign symbiosis my grandfather developed the worst traits of both Edward and Robert. Every bit as rapacious as Edward, he seemed as unable as Robert to grasp that the world he was intent on making could not long survive contact with reality. After selling Parham for the equivalent of several million pounds in modern money he bought Loxwood, a modern estate in Sussex with a large Georgian revival house and enough land for a herd of Channel Isle cows whose butter was stamped with the letter Z and a baron's coronet before being brought to the breakfast table. The garages were big enough for my grandfather's Rolls-Royce, my grandmother's Delahaye (the French Bentley), two MGs belonging to my father and his elder brother, and a Model T Ford shooting-brake. The house was usually full of guests, and the family seldom sat down to meals alone. When my grandparents did eat dinner by themselves they posted themselves at opposite ends of the long dining-room table, each with their dog at their chair. He was a generous but censorious host. Only men were allowed in the billiard room for a drink before dinner. The masculine drinks of port and whisky – he drank whisky at meals and port afterwards – were excellent, but the 'women's' wine was indifferent. If a woman started to smoke at a meal he would lean across the table, snatch the cigarette from her mouth, and break it in two.

He remained a gambler. Playing the stock market was a dangerous occupation in the 1920s and he was a notoriously bad judge of investments at the best of times. He sold Loxwood soon after the great crash of 1929 and took a lease on Castle Mead, the house at the edge of Windsor Park. The advantage of a lease was that it freed more of my grandmother's capital for spending. And as the new house was smaller than Loxwood he could also sell the paintings and furniture for which it had no room. Some of my grandmother's best pictures went to the auction room then, among them a Stubbs of Edward and Robert's grandfather, in which the old man is walking his favourite mare, and so proud of her that he steps out as elegantly as the horse. The move to Windsor had another advantage. It was close enough to London for Fred the chauffeur to drive him twice a week to drink and play backgammon at White's. The club's head porter established a rule: 'When Sir Frederick starts shaking the dice in his whisky glass I know it's time to call the Rolls.'

His wife may never have loved him, and I never heard my father or my aunt speak of him with affection. One night, sitting after dinner with his children and some of their friends, he talked about the hardships and disappointments of his life. He had drunk a good deal of whisky and began to cry. They were so surprised and so embarrassed by this display of emotion that later they could not remember a word he said. No one suspected him of sexual adventures. 'Mistresses!' my aunt exclaimed. 'The only mistresses he had were White's Club and backgammon.' But he squandered his wife's money to satisfy his self-esteem, and there is no evidence he cared about the damage he was doing to his family's future. He set about his work coldly. For all her ignorance of its past, my grandmother hated leaving Parham. She was invited back many times by its new owners but returned only once: to be buried in the graveyard of the little church she had seen on the first day she came to the house. No one remembers my grandfather sharing his wife's feelings about the ravishing house they lost.

His life's work was to undermine those customs and values he claimed to prize most highly, and which he would never have allowed anyone to challenge in his presence. His life was a hoax, but a hoax carried out with nerve, style and a craftsman's attention to detail, and he displayed all three in the last of the houses in which he spun the myth of aristocratic abundance. Castle Mead was a sprawling, red-brick, school-of-Lutyens place built at the turn of the century. A keen snooker player, the first thing he did was to build on a billiard room for the eight-legged Chippendale table that came from Parham (and only two of whose legs remained by the end of the Second World War). He then set about arranging the details of his new home with a sensitivity to modern needs surprising in such a boastfully conservative man. As always, he supervised the arrangement of furniture and the hanging of pictures. He had the eye for it, and could not pass a crooked picture or a table whose ornaments were badly arranged without putting them right. Perhaps he decided that if he could no longer have old grandeur he would enjoy the best modern comforts. He put in central heating. He had the window frames ripped out and replaced with the latest metal ones from Crittall's. Every door was given a heavy cut-glass door knob. He had the Zouche Z with its baron's coronet stamped into the lead joins between the gutters and the drainpipes, but at the same time elevated the internal plumbing to American levels. The three bathrooms on the first floor were tiled from floor to ceiling and fitted with massive heated towel rails. He had specially large taps made for the baths so that they filled quickly, and also matching plug-holes to allow them to empty no less speedily. He had the washbasins raised so there was no need to stoop over them and the lavatory bowls lowered because in Africa he had noted the advantages of a natural squatting position. He built a cloakroom off the hall that was a miniature of those then to be found in smart London hotels: a marble floor, a row of marble basins, two lavatory cubicles, mirrors (back-lit of course), and ivory hairbrushes, tortoiseshell combs and linen towels laid out ready for the next day's guests. He thought of the servants, too. China sinks were taken away and replaced with sinks and draining boards made of teak, so that if a careless scullery maid dropped a plate or a glass there was less chance it would break.

He dreamed of order. He did not like any little thing to be faulty or not working properly. He installed instruments to measure the rainfall in the garden, and patrolled its lawns and flower beds as obsessively as an ageing woman examining her make-up. When the head gardener was clipping the edges of the flower beds, Sir Frederick sat close by on his shooting stick to make sure he got the lines straight. He had a special greenhouse for carnations so he could have a fresh one each morning for his buttonhole. The garden had particular importance for him, for it was essential to the last myth he devised, the myth of the adored grandfather. He laid out the playground in the orchard for my brother, my cousin and myself, and decreed bantams should be kept so there would always be child-sized eggs when we came in to tea. He turned the top floor of the house into our nursery, putting in cork floors so that the noise from our games and squabbles should not disturb the grown-ups below and we did not hurt ourselves when we fell. And just as he gave names to all the bedrooms at Castle Mead, calling them after the woods and meadows on the old Loxwood estate, he also put names in gold letters on the doors of his grandchildren's rooms. My cousin slept in Pooh's House and my brother in Owl's. Mine was Rabbit's House and our bathroom was Pig Bush. Visitors were delighted by this evidence of grandfatherly love, and when the grandchildren were brought downstairs to be shown off to the guests and we put our arms round the old man's neck, kissed him, and called him Grandpa Darling their enchantment was complete. That was what he taught us to do. We did not call him Darling because we particularly liked him, but because he let us think that was his name. He smelled of whisky and cigars and his moustache prickled. He was no more dear to us than any other old man, and only slightly more familiar. Grandpa Darling was another hoax, but a hoax carried out with his usual style.

His only concession to reality was to give up the Rolls. This was one of my grandmother's rare victories and she celebrated it by buying one of those cheap pre-war seaside mementoes made of plywood with a motto burned into it. This one said, 'People on push-bike incomes shouldn't ride around in Rolls-Royces.' She put it in the hall at Castle Mead, where it rested against a set of brass Victorian postal scales. Somehow it returned to the same place when the war was over, causing me much puzzlement because by that time my grandmother did not have a car of any kind. Nevertheless, my grandfather still drove around in a big car, a Lanchester, whose doors were emblazoned with his wife's Z and coronet and beside it a red hand, the bloody hand of Ulster that was the symbol of his own baronetcy. He had a horror of being mistaken for a mere knight of whom, to his disgust, there were many living in the neighbourhood around Windsor.

He was consistent to the end. In 1937 he caught pneumonia. 'A short neck and too much whisky. He hasn't a chance,' said the family doctor, but my grandfather took to his bed with a smile and congratulated himself on his bravery in the face of illness. His children came home and waited in the billiard room, drinking with Fred and May, who got a little drunk on Gin and It. They were interrupted by the butler, who announced to my uncle 'Sir Frederick is dead, Sir Thomas.' They chorused back 'The king is dead. Long live the king,' but there was no more kingdom to rule over. The old man left nothing in his will apart from an overdraft, secured against his wife's fortune, of half a million pounds in the money of today. Not long after he died my grandmother discovered that two of her antique Chinese vases were replicas. Her husband had had copies made of them and substituted them for the originals, which he sold.

After he died, she seemed unable to believe anyone might be fond of her for herself. 'If I fell down in the street and was dying,' she would say to her friends and children, 'no one would bother to pick me up. I'm just a machine for writing cheques.'

Although I spent hours exploring the overgrown gardens and tattered rooms of post-war Castle Mead and loved the old woman who squatted there like a refugee, it is the house Sir Frederick conjured up that haunts me. A summer morning, and a cuckoo calls from somewhere far off and then flies across the garden towards the park. Even the cupboards in the nursery have been perfectly crafted, the doors open at the push of a silver button and fit so tightly that when I close them there is an outrush of air scented with mothballs and lavender. My grandfather is walking in the rose garden before breakfast. He wears a light-coloured summer suit, a bow tie and a panama hat. He walks with a cane and there is already a carnation in his buttonhole. His shoes are brilliant and are also polished on the underside. Croquet hoops have been set up on the lawn beyond the rose garden and as I stand at the nursery window I can feel the ribbed surface of the balls and smell the wooden mallets, their faces green with crushed grass.

This dream of bright order, the first such dream to put its spell on me, hung like perfume over the house in which my grandmother lived out her life. It survived winter days when the stone stairs were cold and the single stove in the drawing-room hugged its warmth like a miser. It survived each discovery of careless destruction, a Tudor miniature with the face wiped out, a finely carved picture frame snapped in pieces and thrown into the bottom of a cupboard. No wonder my grandfather was such a convincing magician when he was alive if he could still cast this spell from the grave. Thanks to him we grew up believing in permanence, although the evidence of dissolution was everywhere about us.

Some years after my grandmother's death I found myself in Windsor on a pleasant summer day. I came to the road that leads from the castle to the park, and then the side road, marked by a letter box in a wall, that turns off to the right just before the park gates. I walked down this road towards the entrance to my grandmother's drive, from where the red brick of the house could be seen. There was nothing there. A building site covered the ground where the house had stood and the garden that stretched beyond it. The stables were gone, and the greenhouses, and the wooden summer house that turned on rollers to face the sun. I looked at the line of trees that still stood where the garden had ended and wondered if a cuckoo might fly over them and into the park, but I heard nothing, and saw nothing, and I went away.

Chapter II

Nikita's Children – Innocence

> Let's drink, good friend
> Of my poor youth,
> Let's drink away our sorrow.
>   Alexander Pushkin, *Winter Evening*

Moscow, 1962

The press of people moved slowly up the marble staircase of the Kremlin Great Palace, their heads tilted back to catch a glimpse of the floor above them, from where they could hear a surge of voices overlaid by the sound of an orchestra. The musicians were playing the overture to *Ivan Susanin* (the Soviet name for the opera Glinka called *A Life for the Tsar*) and the triumphant melodies heightened the guests' anticipation of what awaited them in the room they were about to enter. At the top of the stairs they passed through heavy gilded doors, under a sculpture of St George lancing the dragon, into a long white hall whose roof was supported by tall columns and lit by golden chandeliers. Most of the men and women pushed their way towards long tables covered with white linen cloths, where there was a display of food so abundant and well ordered that even my grandfather would have been impressed. There were dishes of cold roast fillet of beef so tender and moist that the meat dissolved like snowflakes on the tongue; sturgeon from the Volga, smoked and fresh: Pacific salmon; Kamchatka crabs; silver cups the size of a giant's thimble containing a mixture of mushrooms and sour cream or a fricassée of wild birds; and in bowls pressed into crushed ice pungent red salmon roe and caviar from the Caspian, the fat grains glittering in colours from almost yellow to darkest grey. Bottles stood like sentries at intervals along each table, the vodka Russian, the brandy Armenian, the wines from Georgian Tsinandale and Mukuzani.

As the guests passed through the golden doors and spread out into the white space of the great hall, it was plain that two quite different sorts of people were invited to the feast. The men of the most numerous group were heavily built. Many wore uniforms of the curious bottle-green colour the Soviet Army had taken over from its tsarist predecessor, and their heavy gold shoulder boards emphasised their wearers' width. The civilian suits of the other men were as clumsy as the demob clothes issued to British servicemen at the end of the Second World War, and the dresses worn by the large-boned women who accompanied them had a similar look of austerity. The second and smaller group of guests in the hall were foreigners, suavely dressed and sinuous by comparison with the Russians. The chief interest of these diplomats and correspondents was not the food on the long white tables but a group of men gathered at the end of the room, who were protected by a barrier of tables laid with particular abundance. The guests of honour were here, too, a handsome, sturdy young woman who had just become the first of her sex to fly in space and the solid male cosmonaut who accompanied her, but the foreigners only gave them a fraction of their attention. Pressing as close as they could with propriety to the barrier of tables, they stood on their toes in their effort to catch each word and expression of a short, compact man with a bald head who was holding forth to a circle of respectful listeners.

Nikita Khrushchev was wearing a suit that might have been smart when it left the tailor's workshop but stood no chance against his barrel of a body. It did not matter. He could have worn a sack without people noticing because it was the face, and in that face the eyes, which held everyone's attention. Those little eyes conveyed a repertoire of attitudes and emotions. Curiosity, suspicion, glee, cunning, boastfulness and anger came and went and re-appeared, and by no means always spontaneously, for one sensed a calculating direction behind them. The finely dressed foreigners watched him as intently as children watch a Punch and Judy show. Power in the Kremlin had long worn a mask, yet here was a leader publicly delighting in his power, and taking pleasure in dazzling supposedly clever foreigners with the achievements of his space scientists, the brilliance of his Kremlin and the exuberance of its feasts. He was enchanted by his own story, the story of a little cowherd turned miner who was carried by revolution to the leadership of a country that, give or take a boast or two, was now America's military match and would also, he promised, soon produce more washing machines, cornflakes, tractors and butter than any other country in the world. He was also Little Pinya, hero of a story he liked to tell about an insignificant Jewish convict who lead a breakout from prison − in Khrushchev's case the prison of the Stalinist past − when others who thought themselves cleverer and stronger had funked it.

Khrushchev, his banquet and the splendour of his palace, created an image of sturdiness that any tsar would have applauded. Of course there were rumours that enemies were scheming against a Soviet leader who was too bold for his own good. It was whispered that the Army had been obliged to fire on inhabitants of a town in southern Russia, who had taken to the streets when food prices were raised. But Russia had always been a land of rumours. Rumours were parasites on the secretiveness of Soviet power, and enhanced rather than diminished it. The country the outside world saw was as solid as the gross skyscrapers Stalin had given Moscow and which now pinned the city to the earth like spears hurled by an angry god.

This appearance of solidity depended on two things − the heavy fist the Soviet state held up to your face, and the Soviet way of doing things, which newcomers at first found strange but soon accepted as inevitable. The rules of Soviet life were as inconvenient as they were inefficient, but they had the majesty of seeming beyond challenge. Foreigners were made to feel this the moment they stepped on to Soviet soil or, in my case, even before.

The first representative of this perverse majesty whom I encountered was a young man in a green-topped military cap and a greatcoat cinched so tightly I might have got my hands around his waist. This magnificent coat reached halfway down his calves, while his leather boots finished just below the knee. He appeared at the door of the plane within minutes of it landing at Sheremetyevo Airport and paused for a moment to look up and down the rows of passengers. He seemed displeased by what he saw, and when he came down the aisle to collect our passports he was frowning like a schoolmaster gathering homework he knows will be unsatisfactory: we had evidently failed our first Soviet test. It was February 1962, and a night colder than anything I had imagined possible. To leave the aircraft was to walk into a freezer perfumed with pine branches and cheap petrol. Unnerved by the disapproval of the frontier guard, I stumbled across the snow-covered runway to the airport building.

I was ill prepared for this adventure. I had learned something of Marxism-Leninism at university, but little of the Russian and Soviet history that held the most effective keys to the new world I found myself in. An interpreter's training during national service in the Navy gave me a good foundation in the Russian language, but no one offered lessons in the Soviet way of living, and that was what I needed most. For a start I needed somewhere to stay. The Intourist office in London refused to book me a hotel room because I was going to Moscow as the correspondent of the *Observer*. Their logic was irrefutable: as their name made plain they dealt only with tourists, while I was a journalist. Who could help me? Intourist did not know, nor did the press attaché at the Soviet embassy, who seemed offended even to be asked such a question. Before putting a foot on Soviet soil I had felt a tickle of the Soviet whip.

I did as Edward Crankshaw, the *Observer*'s wise man on Russian matters, had advised. I took a taxi and told the driver to take me to the Metropol hotel in the middle of Moscow. Packed snow covered the road and when the driver switched off the engine every five minutes to save fuel the heavy Volga car coasted along with no more noise than a sleigh. Our headlights picked out fir trees and clumps of silver birches with bark as vivid as a zebra's hide, and we drove miles in this curious way without seeing a light or a single house. The first lights, when they came, were a dirty yellow, and sparse, and even when the city proper began and large buildings rose up like cliffs on each side of the road the lights were still mean and grimy. There was little traffic on the streets and few people to be seen behind the parapets of snow separating the road from the pavements. The taxi driver parried my attempts to start a conversation and concentrated on his cigarette, a short roll of paper filled with powerful tobacco and fixed to a longer cardboard holder, which he grasped between his teeth so he could smoke it out of the side of his mouth. The ill-lit streets, where sound was stifled by the piles of snow, took on the aspect of ante-rooms in a dictator's palace that inspire awe and apprehension as visitors approach the centre of power. I searched for a sign of encouragement, but saw only an uninviting restaurant, the back of a statue in an empty square, a small neon sign announcing, simply, 'THEATRE'.

It was warm and bright inside the Metropol, but they would not let me stay. The woman at the desk was amazed that anyone could arrive at a hotel and expect to get a room without the help of Intourist or some other organisation of the Soviet state. She recovered, though, and taking pity on the young and foolish foreigner telephoned a friend at another hotel. Her voice turned coy and creamy, an unmistakable sign, I learned later, that a Russian was about to ask an illicit favour.

I went to sleep that night in a room that might have survived the Russian Revolution. A large oil painting of a forest by a river hung above an Empire-style chaise-longue. There was a veneered desk with drawers on each side, a mahogany dining table, and chairs with curved wooden backs also in the Empire style. A glass chandelier hung from the ceiling; most of the parquet floor was covered by a thick oriental carpet. The next morning I telephoned for room service. After a long delay there was a knock at the door. The young woman who came in was wearing a black dress and black stockings, a lacy white apron and a lace cap perched like a tiara on the front of her head. This vision of a maid from the bourgeois past revived my sense of being in a Russian time machine, but she spoiled the effect when she leant against the wall and murmured in tones of the deepest boredom, '*Slushayu Vas.*'

Galya was sexy. She had neatly curled hair that was silvery blonde and slightly pronounced cheekbones. Her eyes were grey and scornful and as she stood waiting for my order she rubbed one beautiful black-stockinged leg against the other. I studied Galya almost daily for the next three years. She taught me that in a country controlled by a single system of ideas you may learn something of how it works from just one small part of the whole, in this case Galya. Each morning I telephoned room service; each morning she appeared at my door after the prescribed delay. She leant against the wall, flashed her eyes and muttered, '*Slushayu Vas*', 'I am listening to you', the customary equivocal response of the Russian servant to the call of the master. I had the same breakfast each day – a glass of tea with lemon, a glass of *kefir*, black and white bread with butter and jam – yet I could neither order it over the telephone, nor persuade Galya to bring it to me as soon as I called room service. I telephoned, she made her grudging journey along the hotel corridors to my room, I gave her the order that she already knew, she retraced her steps, and then repeated the journey with my unchanging breakfast tray. The daily ritual bored us both but she would not, or could not, alter it. The only time she smiled at me was the morning I had a hangover of revolutionary proportions and after ordering just a glass of *kompot*, stewed fruit, asked her to leave out the fruit and bring me just the watery syrup.

I had never heard of a hotel called the Sovietskaya until the woman at the Metropol said she had found a room for me there. It turned out to be the Claridges of Moscow. Foreign heads of state stayed there, and the Soviet government used it for receptions. When Melinda Maclean followed her diplomat-spy husband Donald to Moscow in 1953, the KGB chose the Sovietskaya as the safest place to re-unite them. Rebuilt after the war as a Stalinist version of a Russian aristocrat's palace, it was decorated in ivory, pink and apple green, and had classical pediments, columns and a handsome marble staircase. The Soviet authorities wanted to provide the important foreigners who stayed there with the comforts they imagined foreigners were used to, and for which they, too, had developed a liking. Galya's antiquated costume and stately habits were part of the dignity assumed by the Soviet state to confront an often disrespectful foreign world.

The hotel's rituals certainly could not be altered to please someone like me, who had no right to be living there. I never dared ask why I was allowed into the Sovietskaya that night, but I know I was only able to remain there thanks to my first two Russian friends. Yelena and Irina ran the Sovietskaya's service bureau, an institution designed to be a shock absorber between foreign guests and the rough Russian world that lay beyond the hotel doors. Foreigners were supposed to have only limited contact with this world. The men who ruled over it knew all about its perils and discomforts and, partly out of shame, partly out of natural Russian generosity, were determined that visitors should be protected from them just as they, the country's powerful, took care to protect themselves. My two new friends inhabited the border land between the prim little world of the foreign visitor and the wide, wild Russia outside, and it was their job to mediate between them. Yelena was married, neat and bossy. Irina was large and overflowing. Like many women who grew up after the war's massacre of Russian males, she had never found her man. Her beauty was in rapid retreat but she still dyed blonde the hair she wore to her shoulders, and kept the habit of glancing downwards as though to draw attention to her impressive breasts. At weekends you could see parties of women like Irina in almost any Moscow restaurant, drinking and giggling and dancing together before going back alone to a little flat, or perhaps just a room that they shared with ageing parents.

This pair of middle-aged women found me *interesny*, 'interesting', in Russian a word rich in meanings, and they were sometimes more friendly than was prudent for people of the frontier like them. One day before I left for a holiday in London they beckoned me into their office and handed me a package wrapped in newspaper. It was for my father, they said, smiling at each other in anticipation of my delight. Inside were three fish that looked and smelled like flattened bloaters. *Vobla*, they explained, a fish from the Caspian that in this desiccated form was the greatest delicacy for the Russian drinking man and a rarity in Moscow. It was a token of intimacy all the more touching for being so ill chosen. The three dried Caspian roach made me queasy and when I got to London I did not dare even show them to my father.

The *Observer* knew that in spite of the changes being made by Khrushchev it was still not possible to report on the Soviet Union as on other countries. Khrushchev had abolished censorship only because he calculated that the self-censorship imposed by a journalist's reluctance to be expelled would be just as effective. In any case, correspondents had little access to officials. The telephone number of the head of the Foreign Ministry press department was a well-kept secret. My one permitted contact there turned out, when we met, to be a motherly woman quite as nervous and ineffective as the Wizard of Oz when he was at last tracked down by Dorothy. I spent many mornings reading Soviet newspapers, and soon the chaise-longue beneath my wintry painting was covered with envelopes stuffed with cuttings. Nevertheless, Khrushchev's was a new Russia. Stalin, genius of power and paranoia, had been replaced by a man who, for all his boastfulness and bullying, showed some remorse for the cruelties of the past. Khrushchev allowed young poets to recite brave verse to cheering audiences packed into the auditorium of the Polytechnic Museum, a stone's throw from the KGB headquarters. Economists dared to question the infallibility of central planning. There were signs of new music and new art, and literature was edging into formerly forbidden territory, like thaw water spreading out from ice in spring. Such developments had unusual significance in a country where the best of the intelligentsia had always tried to be truth-tellers at the court of the powerful.

Edward Crankshaw worked in Russia during the Second World War as a member of the British Military Mission. As a journalist his insight into Russian affairs so infuriated the Soviet authorities that by the late 1950s they banned him permanently from the country. Before I left London he gave me a lecture and two letters of introduction. Young Russians were starting to dress well, he said, and to make sure that I came up to their standard he persuaded the *Observer* to let me buy, at its expense, an overcoat that both looked good and would withstand the Russian winter. I thought I had found just the thing in Regent Street, a long double-breasted black coat with a collar of Persian lamb and a detachable lining made from black rabbit pelts. It had a look of Edwardian extravagance, and was as heavy as chain mail.

I put on this coat to walk to the offices of *Pravda* with Crankshaw's first letter of introduction. The illustrated magazine *Ogonyok*, part of the *Pravda* publishing empire, had on its staff a journalist whom he met on his last trip to Russia. He was, said Crankshaw, clever, young and just the person to give me an understanding of the new Russian world. I was shown into an office bigger than any in the *Observer*, where a man of about my age was sitting at a desk. He scowled at me, took the letter and, after a show of reluctance, read it. The conversation that followed was brief, and he made it plain he would prefer not to see me again. I put the overcoat back on (I was now beginning to be embarrassed by it) and walked home depressed by the ill-concealed hostility with which I had been met. The weight of the extravagant coat pulled me into the ground and by the time I reached the double doors of the Sovietskaya I was exhausted.

How was I to meet Russians? I wanted my own Russian friends, friendships made spontaneously and (I imagined) innocently outside the well-watched world in which foreigners were penned. I put great hope in the woman to whom the second letter of introduction was addressed. I knew little about her except that Crankshaw met her when he was in Russia during the war. I assumed they had been lovers but was too shy to ask him, though I doubt he would have minded. Certainly when I telephoned her and said I was a friend of Edward's she agreed at once to meet, and suggested a time and a metro station in the centre of the city. How was I to recognise her? She said – and she must have been smiling – that she would have no difficulty recognising me.

Vera Petrovna, to give her the proper Russian style of first name and patronymic by which I always called her, was plump and middle-aged and, at first sight, indistinguishable from the women I saw every day bulked up in hats, overcoats and boots on the winter streets. But she wore her unremarkable clothes with style and she spoke the most beautiful Russian I had heard. I listened, and imagined her looking, when young, like Tatyana Samoilova in *The Cranes Are Flying*, one of the first Soviet films allowed to show the heartbreak of the last war. Vera Petrovna controlled our relationship from the beginning. I had contacted her from a call box rather than from my hotel room, where I knew the telephone was, or easily could be, tapped. I still had no idea of the complexity of the calculations Vera Petrovna made before befriending me; that she did said much both for her courage and her affection for Edward Crankshaw. In some things she was careful. She never invited me to her home or introduced me to her family. She did not talk about politics: the Stalinist past and the promise of the Khrushchev present were equally taboo. We would meet at a metro station and she would show me the city's sights, at the same time coaxing me to speak better Russian, and to come to grips with the subtleties of the language. She spent much of one afternoon drumming into me the distinction between the two Russian words for imagination, a lesson I still sometimes repeat to myself on nights when I cannot sleep. It sounds staid, but that was not how it felt. I knew I was lucky to have these meetings with her because they opened a window into the Russia that was hidden behind the heavy scaffolding of the Soviet state.

Later, when I had my own car, we went further afield to look at houses and old estates on the outskirts of the city. She did not mind being seen in a red Volkswagen whose number plates clearly marked it as belonging to a British journalist. Nor, she told me, did she mind my telephoning her from the Sovietskaya. And as if to make that clear beyond doubt she came one evening to have dinner in my room. Galya brought us caviar and sturgeon Moscow-style, and stared hard at this dumpy Russian woman who had the self-possession of someone who dined tête-à-tête with a foreigner every night. I supposed Vera Petrovna reasoned that the authorities knew everything about her wartime link to the British. She may have suffered for it when the war ended (that was my guess, for she said nothing about it), but what could they do to her now she was almost an old woman? And times were different. Khrushchev was not Stalin. People were being let out of the Gulag, not driven into it.

Perhaps the reasoning was sound, but you still needed to be a cool character to act on it. No one supposed the Soviet state was less solid because there was now some room for its citizens to manoeuvre in. If Khrushchev delivered the abundance he talked about, the Soviet order would become more solid still. Revolutions happen when people realise there is nothing inevitable about the way they live, but Moscow was still the world capital of inevitability. The writer Kornei Chukovsky told me how not long after the Bolsheviks seized power he passed a door with the letters VKhOD written on it and for a moment wondered what they stood for, perhaps *Vyshy Khudozhestvenny Otdel Dipkurierov*, Higher Artistic Department of Diplomatic Couriers. The new rulers' enthusiasm for acronyms that promised an instant future was so compelling that Chukovsky failed to realise the sign meant only what it always had – 'entrance'. Even Khrushchev's most eccentric policies were protected by the inexorability that had long invested pronouncements from the Kremlin.

I observed the contortions Vera Petrovna made to bring me into a small part of her life without wrecking the rest of it, and to act like a human being in a system that at any moment might punish her for such folly. But I could never talk to her about such things. She was perhaps too old and too mindful of what she had lived through to comment with irony on her life. For irony I had to wait until I met Yegor.

I do not remember where I first saw him. Most likely it was with one of the Soviet affairs experts at the British embassy who, unusually for those days, had made some unofficial Russian friends. I am clear, though, about where my first proper conversation with Yegor took place. It was at the bottom of Gorky Street, outside a bakery where the smell of freshly baked bread hung over the pavement. I was walking in the direction of Pushkin Square; perhaps he was in the baker's, which was said to be the best in Moscow. Someone called my name and Yegor appeared in front of me. He was friendly. He had a nervous laugh, but there was real humour in it too. Slightly built, with slicked-back dark hair and a narrow face, he looked like a harmless rodent which had just climbed out of water and was prudently checking its new surroundings. That afternoon he wore a double-breasted suit made of an unpleasant reddish-brown pinstripe material. He preferred to dress formally and usually wore a tie, even if it shone with age. His father was Armenian and his mother Russian, but his education was entirely Russian, and if he spoke a word of his father's language it was a secret he kept from me. The Armenian roots perhaps made themselves felt in his ingratiating manner. His pessimism was as amusing as it was black: my new friend was a masterly performer on that 'Russian lyre' whose three strings, Alexander Herzen said, are sadness, scepticism and irony.

Yegor's was the first Moscow flat I saw and I never came across anything like it in all my later years in the city. It was a mixture of privilege and squalor that reflected his uncertain foothold on the middling slopes of Soviet society. It was on the ground floor of an old painted wooden house in a street off the Arbat. In those days the area round the Arbat was still little changed from before the Revolution, when its inhabitants were aristocrats and the grand intelligentsia. It was a charming place of crooked streets and not very grand Empire-style palaces built after the city burned down during Napoleon's invasion. The aristocrats had gone, or gone to ground, and the buildings needed paint and repairs but the intellectuals who still lived in the Arbat adored it as a spiritual home that had miraculously survived in the void of the Soviet city. A refuge in a harsh city, lilacs bloomed in its hidden courtyards and the snow stayed countryside-white in its quiet streets.

Yegor managed to live there because he worked for a publisher of children's books and therefore qualified as an insignificant member of the Soviet literary establishment. His white-painted house was sinking unevenly into the ground in a picturesque way and what he called his flat was no more than a room in a *kommunalka*, an old apartment divided up between several people who shared the same kitchen, bathroom, lavatory and (a sign of privilege, this, in the Moscow of those days) a telephone. The *kommunalka*'s shared rooms suggested a slum. The hall smelt sour and damp and was lit by a single light bulb so weak its filaments could be seen. Another dim light hung in the uneven passage that led to the tenants' rooms. The lavatory had no seat – I was discovering that in general Russians had little use for them – and if you stood still in the kitchen or bathroom you could hear the fluttering of the cockroaches that thrived in the muggy atmosphere. On my first visit, Yegor dismissed the unappealing hall with a wave of the hand and, opening the door of his room, paused to let me go in first. It was a summer afternoon and the sun came through two windows whose sills, because the house was subsiding, were almost on the level of the courtyard outside. Yegor had reconstructed a Russian past of his imagination. The star among the furniture was a gilded chaise-longue with upholstery of dark red silk. There were chairs, also gilded, a table with legs heavily carved in the style admired by old Moscow merchants, a pair of glass-fronted bookcases. The bed, piled with oriental cushions, could have belonged to a nineteenth-century poet just returned from adventures in the Caucasus. It was a room not so much designed to look old as a room that was naturally growing old. The little candelabra on the walls were missing several of their glass drops. The carpets were worn, the wallpaper faded and the gilt on the furniture had in places turned silver. Chair covers were as frayed as the knot of Yegor's ties and the cuffs of his shirts.

He gave a quick smile, asked me to sit down, and disappeared out of the door. He came back carrying plates and with the gravity of a priest preparing for communion laid them on the table, which he had covered with a linen cloth. There were cucumbers, the kind that are small and sweet; a can of *shproty*, bitter-tasting baby sprats; sliced sausage; half-loaves of black and white bread. From a cupboard he took two little glasses and a decanter of vodka, an eccentric touch of elegance in a country where most men thought bottles beautiful enough. He sat down opposite me and poured out the vodka so that it reached to the edge of the cut-glass sides and then bulged over the top, where it was held in place by a transparent skin. Yegor looked at me and nodded. He was as tense as though preparing to dive into an icy river. His hand trembled, but he got the tiny glass to his lips without spilling a drop. He sighed, bit into a piece of the moist black bread, and only then relaxed. He laughed when he saw I had spilt my vodka, and urged me to eat something. I had begun my first lesson in educated Russian drinking.

There was no nonsense about the vodka being chilled. Russians seemed not to mind at what temperature they drank it, and anyhow no one in the *kommunalka* had a refrigerator. In winter Yegor kept his groceries in the space between the double windows that looked on to the courtyard. Nor was there any worry about the quality of the drink: in those innocent days anything that came out of a bottle of state-made vodka was drinkable.

The same ritual was repeated whenever we drank in his room. The alcohol was always accompanied by food, in winter kebabs that he cooked up in the cockroach-haunted kitchen. Each time we started to drink the same mood of seriousness returned, as though he was scared that this communion celebrated with decanter and glasses might not liberate him from anxieties that remained unspoken.

Once when we were drinking he went into the kitchen for more bread and came back humming a song and I caught some words about Osip Mandelstam. I knew little about Mandelstam except that he was a poet and had died in Stalin's purges. The *Oxford Book of Russian Verse* that I brought to Moscow printed only four of his poems, and three of those dated from before the Revolution. As we drank together that day Yegor talked about Mandelstam as both genius and martyr, and told me some of the fantastic stories that were spun about the poet's final arrest and his disappearance in the Gulag, for no one then knew how he died, or where or when. He also told me about Mandelstam's poem on Stalin, which had a phrase about his 'cockroach moustaches' and imagined him forging laws like horseshoes, which he hurled at his people to cripple them. Yegor recited fragments from the poem, but he had never seen its full text, and I did not meet anyone in Moscow in those years who admitted to having read it. Even at this time, when Khrushchev had removed Stalin's body from the mausoleum on Red Square, Mandelstam was still a dangerous name and there was not a single edition of his poetry to be bought in the whole of the Soviet Union.

I guessed Mandelstam fascinated Yegor because the poet was such an obvious misfit in the Soviet world and, talent and courage apart, so ill-equipped to resist its iron pressures, for he was physically weak and famously incompetent in the business of everyday life. Hounded by literary officials and the secret police, he was a nervous wreck by the time of his final arrest in 1938, a twentieth-century version of Pushkin's horror story of the little St Petersburg clerk hounded into madness by the statue of Peter the Great.

Yegor was a little older than I, and must have been in his early twenties when Stalin died. While growing up, he would have seen those cockroach eyes and whiskers almost every day in newspaper photographs and cinema newsreels. How could he, how could anyone, forget them? I sometimes caught him looking at me with a mixture of wonder and irritation. Something I had done or said reminded him that I could never belong in the world he was introducing me to. Several years later I came across a full version of Mandelstam's poem on Stalin and when I read the opening line

– 'We live, without feeling the country beneath us' – I realised that that was how Yegor felt, even though by the time we met the dictator had been dead ten years. There was still a fear at the back of Yegor's mind that one day the earth might open up in front of him. The line described Vera Petrovna, too. Ever prudent in our relationship, she tested the ground at each step to avoid being trapped in old quicksands again. Yegor was less cautious, and that was why he was also more nervous.

He was a creature of limbo. Compared to the recent Russian past, the limbo he inhabited was not such a bad place. The hypnotic power that the word Revolution had exercised over so many Russian intellectuals no longer affected him. If he spoke it, or uttered any other cliché from the Communist vocabulary, he puckered his mouth as though tasting something bitter. Yet he belonged too much to the past to imagine a future very different from the present. He was content in a Soviet world where he did not have to bother much about money. There was no embryo consumer inside him. When I left Moscow he gave me a rare copy of stories by Pantaleimon Romanov, a writer who although already excluded from the canon of Soviet literature died a miraculously natural death in the purge year of 1938. I remembered Yegor saying he needed a new sweater and I bought him one in London. It was made of excellent wool and had a diamond pattern that was popular at the time, but when he put it on and studied himself in the mirror he made a face. I knew at once why. The effect was comic, even unpleasant, like a dog that has been dressed up in a bow tie. He thanked me, but I doubt he wore the sweater again.

Alek would have rejected the sweater outright, but on the grounds that it did not fit his idea of what was modern. He was loitering with some other young people around the steps of the Ukraina Hotel, where I had been having lunch, and they came after me, with Alek in the lead, as I set off for the nearest trolleybus stop. It was an inauspicious place to meet. The skyscraper of the hotel stood watch over us and the street was as wide as the nearby Moscow river, which glittered like gun-metal whenever the pale sun penetrated the heavy autumn clouds. I don't think Alek noticed the weather or the surroundings, for he had the knack of carrying his own world with him wherever he went. He was only nineteen; none of the others in the group seemed older and there was one boy who looked barely a teenager. They were bright and most of them were about to start some sort of higher education, but they did not speak the same Russian as Vera Petrovna and Yegor. They looked different, too. Alek wore his hair in a bad crew cut. He had a pair of grey suede shoes that were much too delicate for the slush of the early snow and, under a thin and unmistakably Soviet overcoat, an American-looking red plaid shirt. All the others in the gang had at least one piece of clothing that was obviously not Soviet, even if it was just a boot-lace tie. When Yegor first saw my fur-collared overcoat he laughed and said it was vulgar. Alek and his friends ignored it altogether.

The clue to these strange kids was in the first of the jargon words that Alek spoke. Did I have anything *shtatsky*, he asked, adding that anything that was *shtatsky* interested them. *Shtatsky* came from *shtaty*, meaning states as in United States, and Alek's gang were early members of an embryo Soviet cult devoted to the worship of America. The cult was encouraged, inadvertently, by Nikita Khrushchev. Confronted by American achievements, Khrushchev's reaction was to boast he could do better. He would tell the story of Levsha, the blacksmith who, when shown a mechanical flea made for the tsar by foreign craftsmen, outdid them by fashioning minuscule silver shoes for the insect's feet. Alek and his friends were not interested in the washing machines and refrigerators that Nikita-Levsha promised to make bigger and better than America. It was the idea of America that possessed them, the smell and manners and movement of a country that represented a modern world where anything was possible, and compared to which their own Soviet world was unbearably restricted and monotone.

I thought of Alek many years later when I saw pictures of Russian kids standing patiently in line to get into Moscow's first McDonald's. A hamburger meant for them what a piece of American clothing meant to him. Both were proof that a world of limitless possibilities existed out there beyond the Soviet border. Possession of a pair of grey suede shoes or a piece of meat in a sesame seed bun put a small piece of that world into their own hands. There was no mystical McDonald's in Moscow in 1963 and meeting my new friends in winter was an uncomfortable business. They were too young to have rooms of their own, there were queues to get into restaurants and the handful of decent cafés. So we sat in grim cafeterias and ate *sosiski*, imitation frankfurter sausages that Alek's crew liked because they could put them between pieces of bread and pretend they were American hot dogs. They had unfaltering energy for fantasies like this, and when there was nothing around they could imagine to be genuine *shtatsky* they chattered in a language that fitted American slang, or what they thought was American slang, into such rules of Russian grammar as they observed. My attraction for them was not unlike the *sosiski*'s. I was an ersatz American because I spoke English and could sometimes help them with American slang. My reputation increased when I told them I had spent a year at an American college; it reached a peak when I produced my Zippo lighter. It was the first thing I had bought when I landed in New York as a student, but my excitement then was nothing like theirs when I let them handle it and they lit and re-lit each other's cigarettes with a lot of clicking of the Zippo's magnificently heavy metal lid.

Meeting in summer was easier and I was less conspicuous without the overcoat I now kicked myself for buying. Alek took me to see an older friend who worked in a medical institute. This man's passion was jazz, which had been attacked after the war as Western bourgeois poison and was still not certain of its place in the Soviet authorities' good books. Alek's friend combined his love of jazz with his work, which gave him access to the old X-ray plates from which engineer friends made pirate copies of American records. He had a collection of their work and one Saturday afternoon we sat in a deserted laboratory listening to Thelonious Monk and Gerry Mulligan conjured up from images of broken Russian limbs. Later, it must have been in summer, he took me and a select group of his friends to an obscure park where, he told me, we would meet someone special. They giggled when I asked who this special person was. I expected a girl, but it turned out to be an unprepossessing man who handed Alek an envelope and disappeared. Alek led us deeper into the shrubs and trees where he undid the packet and passed its contents around. They were dirty pictures. Russian girls, Alek said proudly. Politeness obliged me to agree, but I did not believe him. The photographs were smudged and more blue and grey than black and white. They looked very like the antediluvian pornography that sometimes did the rounds in my public school and were as unerotic as imagining one's parents making love. But Alek had convinced himself the gloomy-looking women were Russian, for his purpose in showing them to me was to prove yet again that he could reproduce in Moscow the forbidden excitements of the Western world. The others echoed Alek. The girls were Russian beyond doubt, they assured me, and declared the outing a great success.

I was ten years older than Alek and keeping up with him was tiring. Luckily I made friends with others of Nikita's children who were more sedate, such as the married couple in their early twenties who spotted me as a foreigner in a shop and deftly started up a conversation. I thought of them as Ruslan and Lyudmila, the princely hero and heroine of Pushkin's poem, because they were so strikingly handsome and so self-possessed. They were a well-balanced pair, for she had the Russian gifts of spontaneity and directness while he was almost un-Russian in his reserve and tact. The secret of their unusual poise was Poland. They were Polonophiles. When they could, they took their holidays in Warsaw, where they went to the theatres and cabarets and saw how much bolder their Polish contemporaries were in exploiting the possibilities of the new world without Stalin. They came back exhilarated from their journeys, but were soon depressed by the contrast with what they saw at home.

Alek's imagination allowed him to recreate his fantasy America at any time and in any place, and at those moments he could forget he was in Russia. Yegor retired from unwelcome Soviet reality to the tired elegance of his room and the ritual of the vodka decanter. But Ruslan and Lyudmila had learned how Russia looked from the outside: they had seen their country through clever Polish eyes and it scared them.

They could see no escape but to hope that the changes begun by Khrushchev would continue, and that his noisy promises of better things to come were more than peasant boasts. Trapped between hope and doubt, Ruslan had begun to suffer from migraines. Their Moscow doctor said there was nothing he could do and they planned to look for help in Warsaw. We said goodbye in Mayakovsky Square. Something made me turn to watch them walk away and I was overcome by pity, because they were so young and so good-looking and yet they moved down the street with the heaviness of prisoners who have just begun to understand the meaning of their sentence.

There was no need to pity Misha, though I sometimes wondered if he did not pity me and all the other foreigners condemned by birth to misunderstand his country. I was going back one afternoon to my room in the Sovietskaya, the trolleybus was full and I was squeezed against other passengers heavily dressed against the mid-winter cold. I felt a tug at my sleeve and looked down to see a short, stockily built man of about my age. He asked if I was a foreigner. I could scarcely hear him for though the trolleybus made only a quiet hum he spoke softly to make sure no one else heard. In spite of the cold he wore nothing on his head, but his curly hair was as thick as the fur of my Astrakhan hat. He followed me when I got out and for an hour we walked up and down the snow-covered sidewalk that ran between the Sovietskaya and the Dinamo football stadium. He worked in a factory, he said, and held his palms towards me – he did not bother with gloves – so I could inspect a Russian worker's hands. When I told him I was a correspondent he became aggressive. He wanted to make me understand what young Russians were really like. Foreigners paid too much attention to untypical Muscovites who wore silly clothes. He meant the *stilyagi* who were regularly subjected to attacks in the Soviet press for wearing narrow trousers and other Western fashions, attacks that made Alek explode with laughter and brought an amused sigh from Yegor. Misha wanted me to know that there were plenty of young Russian men who would never think of altering the width of their trousers. Like him they wore them wide with pride, and to make the point he held out a foot so I could admire the generous cut of his trouser leg.

He sounded so serious that I suspected he was a member of the Komsomol, the Communist Party youth organisation, and had decided to enlighten me with an agitprop lecture. But when he said he would like to talk to me again and I offered to give him my telephone number he shook his head. Didn't I know how the authorities worked in his country? He knew very well, and if we were to meet again it would have to be arranged carefully. We would have a rendezvous, he said, at the Dinamo metro station at six o'clock every other Sunday evening. If one of us failed to turn up, the next meeting would take place in two weeks' time.

They were strange encounters. We walked on the streets whatever the weather. His lectures on the uniqueness of Russia and the impossibility of my understanding it were gradually replaced by long interrogations about life in England. He seemed to be testing the truth of Soviet propaganda. Did British people really get medical treatment without having to pay for it? Did the state provide free education? While I was doing my best to answer, his grey eyes did not leave my face, as though on the lookout for a hint that I was telling lies. Later he moved to more philosophical matters. He was particularly interested in psychology and, admitting for the first time that he understood some English, asked me to bring him from London a copy of Freud's *Introductory Lectures on Psychoanalysis*.

Misha said little about himself after that first declaration that he was a worker. He would not tell me the name of his factory nor what part of Moscow he lived in. It was only years later, when Russia had had more time to wriggle free from its Communist carapace, that I could identify this composed and distant young man. He was a Russian nationalist. He was ambiguous towards the Soviet state, which had made Russia powerful, and curious about the outside world he was determined Russia should not imitate. Our meetings, pre-arranged according to the classic rules of conspiracy, were hard to sustain. Contact was broken when I made a long trip to Eastern Europe and I knew no way to restore it. Much the same happened with Alek and with Ruslan and Lyudmila, for they all shared Misha's fear of telephoning me in my room and did not have telephones of their own.

Only Yegor did not mind. When I called him I took care to go out to a phone box not far from the hotel. He did not telephone me from his flat, but he was happy to call from any public place, though he never gave his name and sometimes put on a poor imitation of a woman's voice. This made possible something like the spontaneity of an ordinary friendship. He might call in the evening and ask me to meet him at a restaurant, where he was already having dinner with friends and as usual making jokes about people at neighbouring tables whom they found unbearably 'Soviet'. Sometimes he got tickets for a Svyatoslav Richter concert at the Conservatoire. The Moscow audience loved this pianist, who gave the impression of living in another Russia far away from Soviet reality, and even Yegor's darkest moods were lightened by hearing him play. He rang one winter evening when I was bracing myself to eat in the hotel restaurant, where a band played Soviet swing too loudly and out of tune, and I knew the menu by heart. He asked me to bring my car to the corner of Pushkin Square, where a shop called Armenia sold handicrafts, food and wine from the paternal homeland that he seldom talked about. I found him in the shop inspecting earthenware pots containing Armenian stews and fricassées. He made an expert selection, picked up some bottles of caramel-flavoured Armenian brandy and directed me to drive south past the Kremlin and across the river. When we went to see friends Yegor thought might be scared to meet a British correspondent he introduced me as a Latvian or Estonian because people from the Baltic were expected to speak imperfect Russian. There was no need for pretence that night. His friends from the Caucasus seemed delighted to meet a Westerner and we had a good party, so good I remembered little of what happened until I found myself driving a Volkswagen full of happy Armenians on to one of the main roads leading out of Moscow. It was about two in the morning and snowing hard. Where were we going? Someone said Tula, which was several hours' drive away, except that the police would have stopped my obviously foreign car as soon as it left the Moscow city limits. To the disappointment of my passengers I turned round and drove back into the silent city. It was later that day, when I ordered breakfast in the hotel and asked for stewed fruit but only the juice, please, that Galya rewarded me with her first brief smile.

Chapter III

Nikita's Children – Experience

This letter as it goes by the frigate *Clyde* I do not mind mentioning the above [the recent murder of Tsar Paul], but in future I must be careful as all Letters from Foreigners are opened at the post office.

Lieutenant Cecil Bisshopp to his mother,
from the British embassy, St Petersburg, 1802

One of the first signs of the fate awaiting Osip Mandelstam, the poet so admired by Yegor, came when literary Moscow began to talk about him as an 'inner émigré'. Spiritual flight from Stalin's Russia was as serious a crime as escaping physically across the border, and death was the appropriate punishment for both. Thirty years on many members of the Soviet intelligentsia were 'inner émigrés' to some extent, but there was no longer much risk in it. Like Yegor, these men and women were alternately repelled and amused by the falseness of so much of Soviet public life, and they pursued their private passions as far away as possible from the bullying official world. Alek tried to live in the America of his imagination, with little thought for the consequences, while Misha was only just setting out on his journey of dissent. In common with many Russians of her background Vera Petrovna had reached a prudent compromise between outward conformity and inner independence.

There was a price to pay for not making a show of support for the system, and the price mounted the more ambitious you were.

If you wanted a good career and a better standard of living, you had to conform with enthusiasm. Exceptions were made for stars such as the pianist Svyatoslav Richter. They were not expected to repeat official slogans, just watched to make sure they did not publicly contradict them. Ordinary people were expected to know the slogans, though there was no way of telling whether they believed them. Naturally the small number of Russians who were allowed to have contact with foreigners were supposed to be engaged in this way, and none was more successfully, though at the same time more ambiguously, engaged than a young man called Victor Louis.

One day in the late 1950s Louis walked into the newsroom of the *Evening News*, an undistinguished London newspaper chiefly bought by office workers for the racing results, and offered himself as the paper's Moscow correspondent. Russians of any kind were then rare visitors to Fleet Street; a Russian like Victor who acted as though he was a free agent might have been a creature from outer space. He still had the soft complexion of a boy and was of no more than average build, but his slow and slightly stiff way of moving gave him a solid, almost venerable manner. He was utterly self-possessed, and had a trick of holding himself quite still as he talked, while narrowing his eyes behind his gold-rimmed spectacles. Fluent though accented English spoken in a deep voice completed the impression of someone who deserved to be taken seriously. Louis offered the *Evening News* a deal they had no reason to refuse. They were to ask the Soviet Foreign Ministry to accredit him as their Moscow correspondent; he would ask for no money until they printed one of his stories. The paper began printing Louis's stories sooner than it expected, for this improbable young Russian turned out to be a scoop machine, predicting sensational events such as the removal of Stalin's body from the Lenin mausoleum on Red Square as though he had a direct line to the Kremlin.

It was outrageous, impossible, and exactly the sort of coup that Victor Louis delighted in pulling off. How did he manage it? In the first place he married an English girl who was working for a family at the British embassy when they met by chance while both sheltering from a rain storm under the portico of the Bolshoi Theatre. The Soviet authorities made it difficult for Western men to marry Russian women, but there was not a hint of an objection to Victor's wedding. Once married he was able to travel to Britain, where he stayed with his mother-in-law in Dorking, and equipped himself with a bowler hat and umbrella for journeys to London in the company of the commuters of Surrey. He discovered Harrods, and it interested him a great deal more than the British political system. Accreditation as a British correspondent gave Victor privileges beyond the grasp of most of the Soviet elite. Soviet citizens could not buy foreign cars, but Victor bought a Peugeot. He acquired an unusually large flat in a, by Moscow standards, smart new block on Leninsky Prospekt, close to where many foreigners lived. He also acquired a dacha in Bakovka, a settlement where senior Soviet officials had summer houses that bordered on the writers' colony of Peredelkino. It was one of the most desirable addresses in suburban Moscow, and out of the question for a foreigner to live there, let alone buy property. Louis's money for this came from one of his earliest and most successful enterprises, a directory of the foreign embassies, newspaper offices and businesses in Moscow supplemented by addresses and telephone numbers of restaurants, hospitals and Soviet government departments. There was nothing else like it in Moscow (city telephone directories were as rare as Mazarin Bibles) and soon almost every foreigner in Russia was buying an annual copy of *Information Moscow*.

Foreigners who knew Victor said it was obvious he had the blessing of the KGB for everything he did, yet they accepted invitations to his Easter parties, where his old nurse made piles of caviar and smoked salmon blinys that were eaten with sour cream and melted butter, and the meal ended with a magnificent *paskha*, a cone-shaped Easter cake of sweet cream cheese. In turn ambassadors invited Louis to their parties. His supposed KGB connections were more advantage than disadvantage here, for he could be counted on to turn up: other Russian guests often failed to show because some higher authority withheld permission at the last moment.

Many years later I came across a clue to Victor Louis in a novel called *A Place* that was short-listed for the first Russian Booker Prize. While I was drinking too much with Yegor and other friends, this book was only taking shape in the mind of its author Friedrikh Gorenstein, and even when he got it down on paper in the mid-1970s it was another fifteen years before it could be published in Moscow. Gorenstein's theme was, in his own words, that 'the first reaction to freedom and kindness of a man who has been crushed by injustice is not happiness and gratitude, but resentment and anger at the years he had to live in fear and chains'. The novel set out to destroy an illusion of the Khrushchev years: that Russia could be restored to normality simply by correcting the injustices of the past. Gorenstein's story of Gosha, a young man brought up in orphanages after his father was shot as an 'enemy of the people', suggested it was not as simple as that. The young man learns that the father he never knew was a general killed in Stalin's purge of the Red Army who has been posthumously rehabilitated, but this unexpected news does not bring him the place in society he now feels entitled to. Bitterness first pushes him into the anti-Semitic and proto-fascist underworld of Khrushchev's Soviet Union and then to the KGB, to whom he betrays his underworld friends. When his usefulness as an informer is exhausted, he declines into a respectable but utterly selfish middle age.

Like many Westerners who travelled to Russia in the Khrushchev years, I was not prepared for people like Gorenstein's hero. I supposed Russians who had suffered under Stalin were like invalids who only needed care and warmth to be brought back to normal health. Myself a citizen of a safe and orderly country, I supposed people were on the whole good, and that suffering could make them even more so. Had I read Dostoyevsky as thoroughly as I studied *Pravda* and *Izvestia*, I might have understood better the conditional nature of goodness, and that prolonged injustice is as likely to produce moral cripples as martyrs.

Victor Louis came from an educated, assimilated Jewish family that had its own burial plot in one of Moscow's oldest Russian

Orthodox cemeteries. He left university with a good grasp of several European languages and found work as an interpreter in the Brazilian embassy. This was a bad move because Jews, assimilated or not, were to be Stalin's last target and a young Jew associated, however legally, with foreigners did not stand a chance. He was arrested, sent to the Gulag, and only released, like tens of thousands of others, after Stalin's death.

Once out of the camp, his Jewish roots were perhaps more help than harm, allowing him to observe the world around him with a detachment ordinary Russians found difficult to achieve. He kept a distance from everyone and everything. His manner would have been unbearably chilling had it not been for his humour, though that was seldom far removed from scorn. I went on a trip with him and his wife to collect material for a travel guide they were writing about the Soviet Union. We inspected Vladimir and Suzdal, old towns that were ravishing but utterly neglected and quite unready for foreign tourists. Louis surveyed the decrepitude and squalor with his usual detachment. It was as though he enjoyed this evidence of disarray in a system that had made him suffer and that he was now determined to exploit so he should never suffer again.

His knowledge of the outside world may have sharpened his disdain for Soviet life, but it was not its cause. He distributed his cynicism equally among all powers, presidents and kingdoms, and trusted only what he controlled himself. He had an accurate eye for what people might be persuaded to do if sufficiently tempted. In the case of Russian workers he judged the threshold of temptation to be almost non-existent. When he needed heating oil for the house in Bakovka, he stood by a road along which tankers passed and flashed a vodka bottle at the drivers. It took no more to persuade them to make a detour and siphon some of their load into his private fuel tank. When fine old houses in Yegor's Arbat were pulled down to make way for an express route to the Kremlin, he took bottles of vodka to the demolition sites and returned with sumptuous fireplaces and panelling for his dacha.

Westerners in Moscow, speculating endlessly about how Victor was able to live as he did, gave him the rank of colonel in the KGB and when he was older promoted him to general. If anyone asked Victor about it, he made a joke or tried to embarrass the questioner for raising the matter. One night towards the end of a long party a British journalist said to him, 'You know everything there is to know about us, but we know almost nothing about you. Now's the time to tell us.' Victor was furious. He started to cry and rolled up his trouser legs to show what he said were scars from his years in the labour camp. It was humiliating for him, and he must have hated it, but he did not lose control and he gave nothing away.

What was there to give away? The nature of his bargain with the KGB of course, and as far as I know he never revealed that to anyone, perhaps not even to his family. Its outline was probably this: in exchange for acting as the Soviet Union's first spin doctor, releasing news both true and false that suited at least some of those in power in the Kremlin, and presenting it in the most effective light, he was allowed almost the freedom of a foreigner. Much more interesting, though, was the spirit in which he entered the bargain. He certainly did not work for the KGB out of conviction. Experience taught him convictions were worthless. Len Wincott, a British sailor who took refuge in Moscow after leading the Invergordon mutiny, was sent to the same camp as Louis. Wincott said Louis was an informer, a common enough way for prisoners to improve their conditions. Others said Louis simply used his wits to get the best camp job he could. When he got out of the Gulag he seems to have decided to put the KGB to his own uses while being of service to them. It was a twentieth-century Faustian pact and almost banal, but Victor developed it with the genius of a born entrepreneur and calculator of risk. He was careful not to be greedy, for he never forgot the old Gulag saying that 'greed killed the convict'. It was, though, a dangerous game and his special skill was to make it look like one of his own devising. He said to me once, 'I sit on top of the barricade. I just make use of Communism.' In fact he manipulated Western and Soviet worlds with equal agility, and the only side he was on was his own.

A Russian woman who was an old friend called Louis 'the nicest man with the nastiest character'. Paradox was part of his power. I have come across few marriages as successful as his. He was generous and loyal to friends, some of whom he met in the camps, and many with Jewish backgrounds like himself. They often came to him as petitioners because there was little he did not know how to get. When he went abroad he took a list of requests that ranged from urgently needed foreign medicine to amusing Western trinkets. He did not mind what people asked for; what seemed to count was that they depended for these favours on him. As he became more prosperous his staff grew. A cook, a driver, handymen and craftsmen became part of a self-contained economy insulated from the shortages and inefficiency of the Soviet world outside the padded door of his apartment and the dacha's heavy wooden gates. He treated these employees well but firmly. There was gruff encouragement, and also curses, but not a great deal of either, for he did not expect too much from anyone. When the cook ruined a curved grapefruit knife he had bought in London by straightening it out he was not cross because it made him laugh.

One November evening a group of Moscow artists belonging to a self-styled Experimental Studio of Painting and Graphics opened an exhibition in an out-of-the-way building on Great Communist Street. Thanks to publicity work by Louis, many foreign journalists and diplomats were there. Perhaps he did it off his own bat, or was it a piece of spin doctoring on behalf of some imaginative members of the KGB? The exhibition was an attempt by young Soviet artists to chip away at Soviet taboos on modern art. Louis had no strong feelings on the subject, but he was too intelligent to share the aesthetic obsessions of official Moscow. He was a friend of one of the exhibition's organisers, the sculptor Ernst Neizvestny, who had a famous public row about modern art with Khrushchev. He owned some of Neizvestny's work which he installed in the garden of his dacha and also bought paintings from other artists at the show. The chief enjoyment he got from them seemed to be watching the amazement of Western visitors, who did not expect to see such things in a Soviet house. It was always a pleasure to deflate a patronising foreigner.

If he used art to impress others, he had little time for literature. He did not care for novels. He could not see why he should bother to read invented stories. Art and literature had not helped him survive the camps or build a life that, had it been presented as fiction, would have been ridiculed as unbelievable. There was never a hint he shared the Russian intelligentsia's belief that art should be a moral guide in hard times (and when were times not hard in Russia?). What needled him was the suggestion that artists and intellectuals who criticised the Soviet government were morally superior. He particularly resented critics who came from the Soviet elite and enjoyed such luxuries as the system had to offer and yet had not suffered in the camps as he had. They lived better than most Soviet citizens (though not as well as he) and he could not see what they had to complain about. Louis was a cat: he always tested the ground in front of him and knew that in the world of moral judgements he would never be sure of his footing.

I saw him lose his self-possession only once. It was autumn 1964, just after Khrushchev was overthrown and no one knew what sort of regime would replace him or whether Stalinism was really dead. In his car, where we were safe from being overheard, he admitted he was as much in the dark as everyone else. He did not know what would happen to the life he had made for himself, and for a moment he allowed me to see he could still feel fear. His greatest horror was to be cut off again with no route of escape, as he once was in the camps.

Eventually he made a lot of money by 'smuggling' Khrushchev's memoirs to the West with the connivance of the KGB. He was also soon playing a part in a seminal KGB operation. In the summer of 1962 a little known writer called Valeri Tarsis was committed to a lunatic asylum for sending abroad the manuscript of *The Bluebottle*, a novel describing the difficult life of Russian writers. On his release Tarsis wrote an account of his experience in the asylum and smuggled that out too. After Khrushchev's fall the KGB hit upon a novel solution. They let Tarsis go to the West, calculating (correctly, it turned out) that he would make a few headlines and then be forgotten. Louis turned up in London as Tarsis's chaperone, and looked on impassively as the newly exiled writer gave his first press conference. Victor Louis was back in business fulfilling his part of the bargain, and there was no sign he regretted it.

There was certainly no regret on the face of the man who knocked one spring morning at the door of my room in the Sovietskaya. Its expression was defiantly louche, challenging me to show alarm, and ready to jeer if I did. The eyes were large and watery, the lips full and moist. A trilby hat and a camel-hair overcoat patterned with stains and cigarette burns completed the impression of someone got up as Laurence Olivier playing Archie Rice. I took his coat and hat and he sat down in one of my mock Empire chairs, pausing to catch his breath before he took a pack of cheap Soviet cigarettes from a pocket of his double-breasted suit. It was plain he would have liked a drink, but I had nothing to offer him. He caught me looking at his old Etonian tie, which was as grubby as the camel-hair coat, and the ribbon of the Order of the Red Banner, one of the highest awards of the Soviet state, which he wore in his buttonhole. He made a gesture with his hand that could have been in the direction of either ribbon or tie. 'I find it helps', he said, 'when asking for a table in a restaurant.'

It was the first time I set eyes on Guy Burgess.

There had been a recurrence of an old press rumour that he was on his way back to Britain. To Burgess's regret it was not true, but he enjoyed the alarm it caused in London, where he had been an embarrassment ever since his flight to the Soviet Union with his fellow diplomat Donald Maclean in 1951. The British authorities had at last tried to solve the Burgess problem by issuing a warrant for his arrest if he tried to enter Britain, and he had come round that morning to prove to me that he was still in Moscow.

In spite of his seedy appearance, he kept a good deal of the magnetism that his old friends, and even his old enemies, talked of. This was still an amusing and very clever man and he soon turned the conversation away from himself to me. He discovered we had belonged to the same Cambridge discussion society, whose members used a mock philosophical language to claim that their meetings took place in the 'real' world, while everyone and everything else were 'phenomena', mere appearance without substance. Burgess made neat use of this ponderous intellectual joke in a note he sent me when I was about to go on a short visit to London. He asked me to remind the society's president of Thoreau's remark that 'the place in a tyranny for a free man is behind prison bars'. By ordering his arrest, Burgess said, the British authorities – he referred to them as 'the phenomena' – had 'seemed to recognise this fact about *their* phenomenal world'. He hoped the president would agree with him, adding that he was already bucked by the way one eminent old member of the society, the philosopher Bertrand Russell, was challenging Cold War orthodoxy. 'I hope things will get worse', the note ended, 'and lead others to feel they should do the same [as Russell] to annoy the Established Phenomena, which I curse. Love to reality, Guy.'

It was just the sort of game he loved to play. His anger with the British establishment was sharpened by his homesickness for Britain, more accurately for those few square miles of Soho and London's West End where he spent the most enjoyable years of his life. It was clear after only a few minutes of our first meeting that he still lived in London in his mind. The airmail edition of *The Times*, which he read each day, and the London political weeklies and BBC broadcasts that supplemented it, were his parish magazines, for he knew most of the British public figures they reported on and many of them had been his friends. He was happy to gossip all day about this London world, but had much less to say about Russia. The only Russian memory he talked about with feeling concerned Kuibyshev, and the misery of his life in this provincial town on the Volga, where he and Maclean were sent to live when they first arrived in the Soviet Union. The two men were kept apart in separate houses. Burgess, who unlike Maclean had no talent for or interest in foreign languages, refused to learn Russian, and when he had no more English books to read roamed the streets, presumably sometimes looking for sex. It was a grim, rough town and he got beaten up, on one occasion losing most of his front teeth. After Stalin's death the British pair was allowed to settle in Moscow, though the KGB tried to hide them under new identities. Burgess chose the name Eliot after the novelist George Eliot, a hero of his. He still spoke almost no Russian and longed for people to talk English to, and about England with, and so made little attempt to avoid the British correspondents who were trying to track him down. It was not long before the only Britons in the Soviet capital who had not seen Guy Burgess were his former colleagues at the British embassy, who still blushed at the mention of his name.

He tried to construct an ersatz English life for himself. He thought it would be pleasant to live in part of the Novodevichy monastery, one of the most beautiful collections of old buildings in Moscow, but even the KGB could not arrange that. Instead they put him in a large flat in a block inhabited by senior army officers and security officials that was near the monastery and gave him a housekeeper who was a very good cook. They helped bring his library, which was large, from London and some of his furniture too, including a bed he claimed once belonged to Stendhal. His mother arranged for Fortnum & Mason's to send him provisions. The Russians were ready to equip him with a local boyfriend, but he insisted on finding one for himself, and installed him in his flat with impunity, although homosexuality was a serious crime under Soviet law. The Soviet authorities were patient with Burgess considering they had no work for him to do. Nothing worse happened to him after a drunken jaunt too many than a talking to from the KGB official who kept an eye on him and was, Burgess said, like the nicest sort of housemaster at a British public school.

His privileges did not make him happy and by the time he walked into my room at the Sovietskaya he was drinking himself to death. When the cognac from Fortnum's ran out he and Tolya, the boyfriend, turned to rougher stuff from Armenia. Tolya worked in a factory, played the Russian accordion and came from the old Tolstoy estate of Yasnaya Polyana, and after several years living with Burgess he had the appearance of a raddled Petrushka. Before another of my trips to London Burgess sent a hurried note asking me to buy 'expensive overcoat, expensive ties. You will know the hell there will be, domestically, if something for me, nothing for Tolya. Strychnine in your Vodka next time you come to lunch.' He enclosed a cheque for £50.

The storms in the Burgess household did not subside, one reason being that Guy still spoke such primitive pidgin Russian that he and Tolya could never even have a satisfactory quarrel. Lunches at the Burgess flat began well. The little housekeeper produced delicacies never seen in Moscow restaurants such as wild strawberries and fresh river trout, and served them on blue and white china made for the tsars which had belonged to Burgess's mother. By the end of the meal, though, Guy would be fighting a losing battle against vodka and brandy and it was hard not to feel sorry for a man who declined so rapidly from brilliance into grubby incoherence. One of the few things that cheered him up was the news in early 1963 of Kim Philby's flight to Moscow. While the world speculated on the former senior MI6 officer's involvement with Burgess and Maclean, Burgess said he just looked forward to having an old friend to talk to. He had quarrelled with Maclean and saw little of him, but he anticipated long conversations with Philby, in which they would return to the London that was still so vivid in his mind.

He told me, as he told every other visitor from Britain, that he never meant to escape to Moscow and only accompanied Maclean there out of friendship. He had never been a spy, he said, and this was the basis for his argument that he could go back to London if he wanted to (what he had done to deserve the Order of the Red Banner he did not explain). His only crime, he implied, was that he supported Soviet policy against a United States which, according to him, was dragging Britain into dangerous adventures. Many left-wing intellectuals in Europe at that time thought roughly the same, not least because Khrushchev's denunciation of Stalin and the reforms that followed persuaded them the Soviet Union was becoming a normal country again. Burgess's argument remained the same since he first presented it to the world through his friend the British journalist and Labour party politician, Tom Driberg, in 1956. Driberg wrote that the two former diplomats were nothing more sinister than freelance activists for peace whose job was now, as he put it, 'advising the Kremlin on relations with the West'. In his long conversations with Driberg Burgess did all he could to encourage this belief, insisting all he cared about was improving Anglo-Soviet relations.

I never heard him budge from that line, drunk or sober, and he spun it to me with particular energy when the Cuban missile crisis of 1962 seemed to push the world to the brink of war. I went to have lunch at his flat not long after the worst was over and we had hardly sat down when he announced that as former members of the Cambridge society to which Bertrand Russell also belonged it was our duty to send congratulations to the philosopher. Russell had accused America of 'madness' in the way it handled the crisis and had tried to broker an understanding between Khrushchev and President Kennedy. Burgess took a piece of paper and began a somewhat incoherent draft.

> We, the only two angels in Moscow, as far as we know [members of the society who had left Cambridge were known as 'angels'], have been thinking about your actions during the Cuban Crisis. One of us, Burgess, thinks you did everything you could and should have done. Burgess is very proud of you, not personally, but angelically intervening in a way angels should do, and could do, given the positions many of them occupy, more than all of them always do. Having lived here for 10 years in a constant attempt to do what you now try, I tell you that Communism [crossed out and replaced with 'Socialism'] does produce a beginning of an approximation to what we [here he wrote 'in the Society' before crossing it out] might hope things to be like.
> The other of us, Frankland . . .

The letter was never finished because I took it away saying I

would think about what I might write, a diplomatic way of hinting
I had no intention of adding a word. He must have understood
me, but did not seem the least offended by the failure of his
plan. Not long afterwards he was taken to the Botkin Hospital.
When he died there in the summer of 1963, most of the Moscow
correspondents were away in Yugoslavia, following Khrushchev as
he tried to restore relations with the prickly Marshal Tito. When
I got back to Moscow I learned that Burgess never did have the
meeting with Philby he wanted so badly. The KGB kept the two
men apart, not even allowing the MI6 man to visit Burgess when it
was plain he was close to death. That news upset me, and for some
time afterwards I quoted it as an example of the cold-bloodedness
of the Soviet security service.

Years later, after the collapse of the Soviet Union when KGB
men began telling their stories, I discovered it was all untrue. It
was Philby who refused to see Burgess, even when he knew his
old friend was on his death bed. Philby and Burgess were both
in Washington when the former learned that MI5 had identified
Maclean, then working at the Foreign Office in London, as a Soviet
spy. Philby sent Burgess to London to tell Maclean to escape to
Moscow, but made Burgess swear he would not go with him because
that would point a finger at Philby too. Burgess ignored him and
went to Moscow with Maclean (though why is still not clear) and
Philby, as he predicted, at once fell under suspicion himself.

Burgess fooled me as he seems to have fooled most other Britons
he came across in Moscow. He was never just an enthusiast for
better Anglo-Soviet relations who by some silly mischance became
trapped in Moscow. A master of the patrician trick of seeming to
be open while giving nothing away he talked amusingly, and often
scandalously, about everything except his spying for the Soviet
Union, into which Philby recruited him in 1934. One of his KGB
handlers called Burgess a 'rogue, but a phenomenally brilliant one',
and I suspect he enjoyed fooling me over the letter to Bertrand
Russell as much as he had relished all the other tricks in a lifetime
of deceit. He was drunk, he must have known he was dying, but

he could not resist another round of the old game, however trivial this last round was. Like the scorpion in the fable, it was his nature. His justification was belief in a world revolution of which the Soviet model, or so I imagine him reasoning, was an unsatisfactory first sketch, merely the 'beginning of an approximation' as he put it in the letter he wanted me to co-author. I suppose he believed the world revolution, when it came, would deal more kindly with the likes of Tolya, who when Burgess died was taken from the flat by the KGB and disappeared no one knows where.

I had to thank Vladimir for my proper introduction into the underworld of Soviet power. He was a tall young man, handsome and dark, more Latin in looks than Slav. He had got to know Sally Belfrage, a young Anglo-American writer who spent some time in Moscow in the late 1950s and wrote one of the first books about life in Khrushchev's Russia. One reason for their meeting was that Vladimir's American English was as good as his Russian. His father had worked in America, where he put his son through school in New York before returning to Moscow. Vladimir was said to have earned a black mark for his involvement with Sally Belfrage and when I met him he was working for Novosti, a new Soviet news agency assumed to have links with the KGB. I did not know him well and was surprised when he told me he had been talking about me to his old history professor at Moscow University and that the professor would like to meet me. I had not had the chance to meet a Soviet academic in what promised to be relaxed surroundings and I agreed at once.

A lunch was arranged at the Praga. It was a huge place, with restaurants on three floors and a winter garden, but when I gave Vladimir's name a waiter led me to a corridor in a part of the building I had not seen before. We passed several doors before he opened one and there was Vladimir with an older man, sitting at a large table spread with a fine white cloth. On the table were bottles of vodka and wine and dishes of *zakuski*, hors d'oeuvres, as rich as those at a Kremlin banquet.

Vladimir was taller by a head than his companion, but the smaller man was incontestably the more impressive figure. Strongly built, he had a short neck, heavy head and ruddy complexion. He seemed to me quite old, but I suspect he was only in his early fifties. Beady eyes, big teeth and a hooked nose completed the picture of a Russian Mr Punch who, given the chance, would very much enjoy using his cudgel. This was not my idea of how an eminent historian looked and I was not surprised that though we talked for almost three hours the subject of history was not mentioned once. Sergei Borisovich – he neither then nor later revealed his last name – took control of the conversation from the start. He asked me about myself and my views on international affairs, and questioned me closely on British politics. He had once, he said, met Lord Beaverbrook in the south of France and got on well with him. That was not hard to imagine, for Sergei Borisovich had a nice line in sardonic humour, and would certainly have withstood any attempt by the Beaver to bully him. He failed to explain what a Soviet academic was doing in the south of France or how the two men communicated, for at our lunch he spoke only Russian and gave no sign of understanding whenever Vladimir and I exchanged a few words in English.

The lunch took the usual leisurely course of meals in Moscow restaurants even though the waiters were unusually efficient, appearing promptly to replace the *zakuski* with *shashlyk* and fillet steaks (the only sort known to Soviet chefs). When we had finished the final course of ice cream and the waiters brought in Turkish coffee Sergei Borisovich produced a packet of American Kent cigarettes. They were a rarity in Russia in those days – I had never seen Alek smoking Kents – but Sergei Borisovich acted as though it was nothing out of the ordinary. Before we broke up he asked if there was anything he could do for me, but did not seem put out when I shook my head. He wrote a telephone number on a piece of paper and gave it to me. Ring it, he said, if something (he did not explain what that something might be) cropped up. Just ask for Sergei Borisovich, he said, and bared his long teeth in a smile. We collected our coats from the cloakroom. His was a thickly lined raincoat, as obviously expensive as it was foreign, and he took from its pocket what looked like an American golfing cap. Dressed in this un-Soviet way he walked off, but after a few steps turned and waggled the fingers of his right hand at me, the gesture of a grown-up saying goodbye to a hesitant child.

Something did crop up. The *Observer* wanted me to make a trip to Siberia and Tamara Mikhailovna, my timid contact at the Foreign Ministry press department through whom such journeys had to be arranged, made it plain she would not help. I rang the number Sergei Borisovich gave me. Official Soviet telephone numbers usually rang a long time before anyone answered but after only a couple of rings I heard the familiar voice. I wanted to see him? Nothing was easier. A lunch? In the Praga? A private room naturally. This time there was no Vladimir with his skill in Western manners to smooth the meeting, but the meal started off well enough and it was only towards the end that he asked me to explain my problem. He listened, and said he thought he might be able to help. There was, though, a question he had to ask me: was I in any way culpable before Soviet power? That is the exact translation of his Russian words which I have never forgotten, not least because of their archaic ring. He did not say guilty, but culpable, sinful. And he did not say Soviet law or the Soviet government, but power, *vlast*, a word that evoked the might of the Russian state throughout the ages. Of course I said no, but his little eyes were watching me and his lips were parted as if in anticipation of some rare delight.

Sergei Borisovich got me to Siberia and to places I never expected to see. In Yakutsk I was allowed to spend a lot of time with astrophysicists who had an observatory there. I flew in tiny planes to mining towns, where the only people with enough nerve to handle a foreign correspondent were the local Communist Party bosses who normally remained hidden from Westerners. I suspected before setting out on the trip that in Sergei Borisovich I had acquired some sort of KGB godfather; by the time I got back to Moscow I was sure of it.

I did not see him often. He sometimes telephoned to ask if I was going to some diplomatic reception marking an event the Soviet government judged important. He would urge me to attend, but when I caught sight of him there he just winked and waved his hand and vanished. There was another lunch when he asked me if there was anything I wanted to write that the *Observer* would not print. He was sure he could persuade some Soviet paper to take it. Naturally I would not have to use my own name; a *nom de plume* would do very well, he said with a grin that suggested it might be fun to practise a little deception. He was too much of an old trooper to be offended when I turned the offer down. What he had suggested was a well-known way of bringing a foreigner into the Soviet orbit. The secrecy and then the occasional payment could easily be made to look compromising and force a more serious involvement with the KGB. There were no more lunches with Sergei Borisovich after that. He did not scare me, but I disliked the feeling that he was observing me so closely.

And then something happened that did frighten me. I went down one evening to the restaurant of the Sovietskaya. Usually I avoided eating at the hotel, for the restaurant was full whatever the day of the week with partying Muscovites who ate and drank as much and as slowly as they could, and in the intervals bounced about the small dance floor to the music of the noisy band. It was fun to go there with friends, but a bad place for a quick meal on one's own. That evening a waiter showed me to a miraculously empty table, but a few minutes later came back with two men and two young women and asked if they could sit with me, as was the custom in such crowded places. The Russians were keen to talk, and were not put off when I told them I was a British correspondent and that I lived in the hotel which, restaurant apart, was out of bounds to ordinary Russians. They were a pair of out-of-uniform Air Force officer cadets with their girlfriends. The cadets said they came from the Peter Palace, a Gothic building just up the road from the Sovietskaya where the tsars used to stay a night before making their entry into Moscow. It was now the Zhukovsky Air Force Engineering Academy and among its many famous graduates were the aeroplane designers Mikoyan and

Ilyushin and the woman cosmonaut Valentina Tereshkova, whose Kremlin party I had attended.

I could not believe my luck. Here was a chance to talk not just with two young officers, which was rare enough, but with two future stars of the Soviet military elite. The Russians expressed horror that I was eating and drinking so little and set about ordering a large meal with wine and bottles of lemonade but no vodka, which surprised me. One of the men soon solved the puzzle by taking from an inside pocket a bottle containing a clear liquid. Why waste time drinking vodka, he said, when *spirt*, pure alcohol, was so much more efficient? He poured some into the bottom of a tumbler, added a dash of lemonade and held it out to me. It was the first of many toasts we drank in *spirt* and fizzy lemon. Perhaps I did try to get them to talk about how they, as young officers, saw the world around them. I do not know, because I remember very little of the meal and its aftermath. What I do recall is that it was decided to continue the party in my room. I also remember the five of us setting off towards the hotel lobby and the marble staircase that led to my room on the first floor.

Everything then went blank until I woke up late the next morning. I was lying on top of the bedclothes. Someone – I could not remember doing it myself – had taken off my shoes and undone the top button of my shirt, but otherwise I was still dressed. There was dried vomit round my mouth and chin and when I got up, which was difficult, I found more vomit on the bathroom floor. I had often drunk too much in Russia, but never before had I drunk myself into such a sordid state. Over the next few hours I tried to work out what had happened. At first I thought the Air Force cadets and their girlfriends had not got as far as my room. The Sovietskaya was organised to make sure that drunken Russians from the restaurant never penetrated the hotel proper, and certainly not to the rooms of its foreign guests. There was always a porter on duty in the lobby. I had to get the key to my room from a woman who sat at a desk on my floor. It was her job to turn back unauthorised visitors, and she had to be squared even when the irreproachable Vera Petrovna came to dinner in my room. There was no way she would let past a party of Russians high on pure alcohol. Yet someone had taken off my shoes and loosened my shirt collar. And after more thought I felt certain that I could remember the young Russians moving about my room, though I had no idea what they had been doing.

It was usual for Western diplomats to travel round the Soviet Union in pairs. This was meant to protect them against the KGB's trick of compromising diplomats, and any other foreigners they fancied, whenever the chance arose. It was harder, the calculation went, to put something into the drinks of two diplomats staying in a hotel in Minsk, and then photograph them in compromising positions, than to slip a Mickey Finn to one man travelling on his own. Photographs could be used for blackmail: drunken diplomat snapped in the company of half-dressed Russian women, or boys if need be; the KGB could arrange either. Sometimes the Russians made no use of the pictures, preferring to file them away in the hope they might come in handy in the future. Such incidents happened often enough to be a Soviet tradition. I was already beginning to feel Sergei Borisovich was playing with me. Was the time approaching when Mr Punch would produce his big stick and give me a swipe I might never recover from? And could it be that he and his colleagues were behind much of what happened to me in Moscow, had at some point insinuated themselves into what I thought was my private Russian life, and taken control of it?

I began to go over the events of the past two years and re-examine everything in the light of my new suspicion. Misha, the factory worker with the wide trouser legs and a secret interest in Freud – wasn't he too good to be true? I remembered the way he managed our first meeting, so discreet yet so self-assured, and his organisation of our future meetings – same time, same place, every other Sunday – along the lines of classic conspiracy. If he could not be trusted, what about Ruslan and Lyudmila? Surely their sophisticated knowledge of Poland sat uneasily with their pose as vulnerable innocents. They could have been just an act, and not even married. With Alek it would have happened differently. In my gloomiest mood I could not imagine him as an operative of the KGB, but he was vulnerable to their pressure. His passion for things American had turned him into a petty black-marketeer. He could have been picked up after one of his many meetings with foreign tourists and found in possession of a packet or two of American cigarettes or a pair of shoes. As for Vera Petrovna, she had a past, and she also had a family to protect. Wasn't there something too assured about the way she handled me, something too absolute in the way she excluded me from any contact with, and almost any mention of, that family? I could imagine her agreeing to report on me partly in a spirit of resignation, partly because she was experienced enough to know she could protect me as well as herself by reporting nothing that harmed either of us. That would explain why she sometimes treated me as though I was too much a child to be initiated into the realities of her world.

I could not bear to think about Yegor, for the truth was I always knew there was something odd about him. It was not that he was homosexual – he never said anything about that, I merely guessed it. The give-away was how we met: on the strength of one brief earlier meeting he had cheerfully hailed me outside the Gorky Street bakery where all the world could watch us. The British diplomat I had seen him with mumbled something about Yegor being a 'torpedo', someone controlled by the security service and aimed at foreign targets of interest. I had no doubt there was plenty of material for blackmail in Yegor's life, beginning with his sexual inclination. It would explain why his melancholy seemed infused with self-reproach, and why in surroundings that were superficially lively and carefree his gloom often deepened. My naïveté, and my British innocence, far from providing him with light relief could only intensify the darkness of his mood and thoughts. I do not think he meant me harm; it is possible he meant to protect me as I imagined Vera Petrovna trying to do. But she was an elderly woman while he was still young, and already trapped. It must have been painful for him – I hoped it was painful for him – to take part in putting the most tentative trap around me, for I believed our friendship was genuine.

I believed, but cannot know. Perhaps he was another Gosha, the maimed hero of the Gorenstein book that was to make such an impression on me many years later. Perhaps he was just looking after himself like Victor Louis, though of course without Louis's cool, let alone on his epic scale. It was not out of the question that he was as clever a deceiver as Guy Burgess. I was sure, though, that he was not a professional like Sergei Borisovich. It might have been better if he was. In that case I would not have worried about him any more, but now I could not help wondering when we met what sort of a trap he was caught in, and whether he was preparing one for me.

Leaving Moscow came as a relief. Depressed by the suspicion that contaminated my friendships I wondered whether the only way to make straightforward contact in this country was in the manner long practised by the Russians themselves. When in Yakutsk, courtesy of Sergei Borisovich, I had stayed at the town's only hotel and one night went alone to eat in its restaurant. I joined a table of young men and women who turned out to be construction workers. The noise and drunkenness was on a scale I had not seen in Moscow and the only thing to do was join in. It was easy enough, for the builders were drinking *spirt,* which was sold officially in distant parts of Siberia instead of vodka, and chasing it down with bumpers of sweet Soviet champagne. They invited me back to their dormitory, a military-style wooden barrack lit by a few naked light bulbs hanging from the ceiling and furnished with metal bedsteads and wooden boxes. There was more drinking; someone took up a guitar and sang. I had left in the early morning, as pleased with my fleeting friends as they seemed pleased with me, and trudged back through heavy snow to the hotel, where I had to climb over less-privileged guests who had bedded down on the stairs.

That, I told myself, was a good Russian experience, a short clean friendship launched by alcohol that caused no pain to either side. I had no right to expect more. And yet whenever I went back to Moscow in later years I could not help thinking about the friends

I had begun to doubt. They were imprinted on the city like scent on a handkerchief long put away in a drawer. I never shook off their presence, just as I never knew if I had been unjust to them. By remembering them in all their ambiguity I do them the best justice I can.

Chapter IV

P15/B

He has no name, but only a number and a letter – that is a custom among us.

Rudyard Kipling, *Kim*

Portsmouth and London, 1958

The foxy character in the window seat reading the *Daily Telegraph* looked up when I opened the door of the train compartment, and then returned to his paper. There was a folded mackintosh and a soft brown hat in the rack above his head. Memory suggests he was wearing a maroon cardigan under his tweed jacket.

I wondered if he was a plain-clothes detective, but did detectives travel first class? I had no way of knowing because I certainly never did. I was in this first class carriage now because the letter instructing me to take a certain morning train from London to Portsmouth enclosed a first class ticket. At Portsmouth Station, the letter said, I was to look for a small van and show my pass to the driver. The pass, which was attached to the ticket, was little bigger than a modern credit card, but made of thick, shiny pasteboard coloured in shades of grey and pink. It was numbered, and someone had written my name on it in an old-fashioned copperplate hand. There was no photograph, and no indication of what it was a pass to. I found the van without difficulty, but my travelling companion had got there first and was standing by the door, alert as a sheepdog at work.

There were six of us in his flock. Paul, in a gabardine raincoat, was an Air Force officer; George, who wore the same sort of belted mackintosh as my travelling companion, came from the Army. Harry, obviously the oldest of us, had a thick moustache and metal-rimmed spectacles. He was jovial and seemed at ease, unlike Anthony, a public-school type with a rugger player's build. Nicholas I knew from Cambridge, where he read Moral Sciences; we expressed our mutual surprise, or perhaps it was embarrassment, by a twitch of the eyebrows. Anything more demonstrative seemed out of place.

The van drove to the edge of Portsmouth and into the grounds of what appeared to be a fort built at the edge of the sea. We were shown to bedrooms in old army huts, and then assembled in a military-style mess, where a middle-aged man waited to address us. He reminded me of a schoolmaster who taught me history, the same slicked-back hair and horn-rimmed glasses, and the same theatrical manner. The schoolmaster scored a hit as Mr Collins in a stage version of *Pride and Prejudice,* but this man had a more dashing role. Welcome, gentlemen, he began, obviously enjoying occupying centre stage, welcome to SIS, the Secret Intelligence Service.

It is hard to believe it was the first time I heard those three words, but they were still innocent years. The government denied there was such a thing as a British espionage service, and the British were not encouraged to think about what spies were, or were not, doing on their behalf. Confidentiality ruled in all government departments, the Ministry of Agriculture and Fisheries as well as the Foreign Office. Kim Philby's escape to Moscow and the arrest and trial of the less senior SIS officer George Blake, two scandals that would remove the cloak of utter secrecy from the Secret Intelligence Service, were still several years away. James Bond – *Dr No*, Ian Fleming's sixth novel, appeared the year I went to Portsmouth – was still a character in fiction. New recruits like myself were drawn into SIS by a mixture of hints and studiously muddied explanations that avoided a precise job description. Not knowing what do with my life, I had taken the Foreign Office exam in my last year at university and at some point in the selection process was switched, without my knowing it, towards

SIS. One reason, I guessed later, was that in the summer of 1955 I had gone with friends from Cambridge to the Communist World Youth Festival in Warsaw, where we got involved in an impromptu operation to smuggle a young Pole to the West. Sometime after that a man who never said what part of government he worked for invited me and another of our Warsaw group to lunch in an ill-lit Hungarian restaurant in Soho. Later a Modern Languages don at my college whom I scarcely knew asked if I was interested in working for the government abroad, but not exactly in the Foreign Office. He left it as vague as that.

The result was an interview with a bluff man in a pinstripe suit, who sat in a remarkably bare office in Carlton House Terrace. This was followed by a medical examination by an expensive-looking doctor in Knightsbridge; and a final interview in a house near Hyde Park. Several men – I cannot remember a woman among them – sat round a large table and put questions to which it was often easy to guess the winning answer. Imagine you are taking a boat trip, one of them said, and you have plenty of books in your cabin. Would you stay below reading, or would you go on deck and get to know the other passengers? Get out and about, sir, I replied, though I doubted it was true. A telephone rang and I was handed the receiver. A voice at the other end of the line greeted me in Russian. We talked about the weather, the London theatre and foreign travel. After a few minutes the voice rang off, apparently satisfied with my less than perfect Russian conversation. There were no more tests after that, just 'positive vetting', a new and supposedly rigorous technique to find out whether candidates for sensitive government jobs had Communist leanings or what were known as character flaws. I had to supply two references. One of them, a Tory Member of Parliament who was once married to my aunt, asked how he was supposed to know if I was a Communist, but vouched for me all the same. Throughout the process of recruitment no one mentioned the Secret Intelligence Service or MI6, SIS's alternative name which I had heard of and understood to be an even more shadowy organisation than MI5. When I set off for

Portsmouth, I knew I had committed myself to something unusual, but the haziness of the enterprise did not alarm me. I think I was more curious than concerned.

The man who reminded me of my old history teacher wound up his welcome by saying that to accustom us to working in conditions of security we would use only our first names. We were to call him Noel. Anthony raised his hand. He had already unpacked his pyjamas (I imagined him putting them neatly under his pillow) and they were marked with his full name. It was unclear whether he was confessing to a mistake or suggesting a lack of foresight on Noel's part, for in those days the clothes of every former public schoolboy still had name tapes sewn into them. Noel ignored him. The game had already begun.

We were handed over to a series of nameless instructors who looked like Army NCOs but might have been old-fashioned criminals who had gone straight. One of them showed us how to pick locks, another how to start a fire so the flames burst into a fire ball in the quickest possible time. We were given an introduction to codes and demonstrations of secret inks. We wrote messages on a special paper that we then had to eat (it tasted like the rice paper stuck to the bottom of macaroons).

They also taught us how to use Browning automatic pistols: we were told the new C, the chief of SIS, was keen that all officers should know how to shoot in self-defence. The fort had a shooting gallery that was nothing like the ranges then used by amateur marksmen. It was deep rather than wide, and had wooden partitions painted to look like the walls of houses. Menacing cut-out figures appeared in windows and from behind the walls as we crept, one at a time, from the front of the gallery to the back. The idea was to shoot the cut-outs before they disappeared again. The instructor, surely this time an NCO rather than a reformed villain, taught us instinctive aiming, a method he said had been invented by two British policemen in Hong Kong. In an emergency there would be no time for the elaborate aim-taking of the marksman, or the uncomfortable, both arms outstretched posture used by the American police. When you see something you want to draw attention to, what do you do? You point at it with your index finger, and more often than not it is on target. You only had to remember to swivel on your right heel, bend the left knee and, to be sure of hitting the target, let off two bullets in rapid succession. It seemed to work, and we enjoyed advancing down the gallery, ready to aim our neat automatics at whatever cut-out appeared.

One day after lunch Anthony disappeared from the mess, returning later with the smile of the boy who has been made head prefect. He had remembered there was a shooting lesson, but did not fetch us so he could have the gallery to himself. Noel must have awarded him an extra mark for that, for Anthony seemed to have grasped the purpose of our training. We were not supposed to acquire the skills of burglars and arsonists: the lessons were too short for that. What was intended was to open our eyes to a world that officially did not exist. This world dealt in boyish tricks and thuggery, stealth and deceit. No one actually spelled this out, for the trick was to accustom us to this new world gradually and so break down what youthful inhibitions we still had. Sometimes Noel appeared, wrapped in a cloak, to watch our activities, but I doubt he realised the humour of that. He seemed to have lived too long outside the ordinary world, and hankered after the old days when C kept gold sovereigns in a drawer of his desk and handed them out to his men when he sent them abroad.

Our second and final week brought an unexpectedly academic interlude. We had to write an essay on 'the economic level of security'. Total security led to paralysis, for only if no one said or did anything could nothing be given away. Too little security led to disaster. Where was the golden mean? It was as good, or as pointless, a subject for debate as the medieval argument about how many angels could sit on the head of a pin. I cannot remember Noel or anyone else claiming to have a correct answer. Our final training exercises were meant to bring us back to what, in this place, passed for reality. We had to conduct a series of clandestine meetings on the streets of Portsmouth while avoiding the surveillance of the city police. I was

to meet my contact in the public library, but a plain-clothes detective
spotted me almost at once and took me off to a police station, where I
was received with polite suspicion and put in a cell. I stayed there for
what seemed a long time until the foxy-faced man, sly as ever, turned
up to spring me. The most elaborate game took place on our last night
at the fort. Dressed in gumboots, thick sweaters and woolly hats, we
set up signal lights on the beach outside the walls, and waited for an
answering light from a submarine that was to pick us up. Contact
made, we got into rubber dinghies and paddled out across a choppy
sea. We were a clumsy lot, but the sailors were too polite to make
rude comments, though one officer asked if we often did this sort
of thing. I smiled and shrugged. It seemed letting the side down to
admit it was our first time.

Our education switched to London. In a house not far from
Victoria Station we learned about the Service's organisation and
bureaucratic procedures. They were complicated. SIS headquarters
was at 54 Broadway Buildings, diagonally across from St James's
Park underground station, but other departments were spread around
nearby streets. Little blue vans carried files between them. They
looked easy to hijack, but in those days Whitehall felt secure enough
under its blanket of discretion.

We had one last exercise on the streets, but this was London, not
Portsmouth, and our opponents were the Special Branch watchers
who normally tracked foreign spies. We were supposed to shake
them off while moving from one part of London to another, but
– and this was the difficult part – without giving any hint we knew
we were being followed. I lost many points by getting on a tube train
and jumping off just as the doors closed. I left my watchers behind
all right, but gave myself away entirely. After it was over, we met
the men who chased us. I did not recognise any of them until they
reminded me about three workmen who for a few minutes stood next
to me at a bus stop discussing their next painting job. They produced
a photograph of us at the bus stop taken with a hidden camera. Their
talent for quick disguise was remarkable, but more striking still was
their tautness. They were short men, unremarkable to look at, but

even while talking they seemed to be straining at an invisible leash, like terriers keen to get back to the hunt.

One day during our lessons in Portsmouth the foxy man, who was our course mentor, came into the classroom carrying a tray covered with pieces of bric-a-brac. He let us look at it for a moment, then took it away and made us write down as many of the objects as we could remember. We were in the world of Rudyard Kipling's *Kim*. This was the game Lurgan Sahib's Indian boy taught the young Kim, boasting 'one look is enough for *me*', though the Indian boy's tray was covered with precious stones rather than the undistinguished oddments the foxy man showed us. 'Kim's game' is a good test of a certain sort of memory and I do not remember any of us doing very well the first time we played it, though like Kim we improved with practice.

It is hard to think of a rite of initiation with more resonance. Kim, the British boy, was being trained to take part in a secret war waged by empires with spies and thugs, some courageous, others depraved, but none of whom could be admitted into the company of the upright men of public power. In these unac-knowledged wars governments set aside the inhibitions of civilised statesmanship and surrendered to the pleasures of uncontaminated power. Small wonder they would not acknowledge the agents they used to conduct this dubious but necessary business. That was one thing we were never left in doubt about. You will get no public recognition, they told us from the start. We were to be assigned to the Foreign Office for purposes of cover, but could expect only junior positions when posted to British embassies abroad. We would never be ambassadors, and might not rise above the rank of first secretary. Whatever our achievements our highest decoration would be a CMG, the award given diplomats towards the end of averagely successful careers. The Foreign Office, we were told, looked upon our kind with distaste. British diplomats were no keener to be caught in our company than a married man with a hooker. We belonged to the world of primal urges in which respectable people indulged only in secret, and that was yet another reason why our new profession was not a proper subject for public discussion.

For once the British were being logical. Rather than try to justify an organisation which in terms of official public morality and international law was unjustifiable, the British chose to deny its existence altogether. No British government could admit in peacetime that it trained young men and women to eat secret messages, play Kim's game and handle Browning automatics so it could send them to scheme and spy abroad. There was therefore no such thing as a Secret Intelligence Service; no tip of amorality on which the moral world uncomfortably rested; and no need to trouble British citizens with an ethical puzzle that was beyond solution. Perhaps we, the new recruits, could take pride in our descent into the dark for the sake of those who lived their lives innocently in the light. As Chief Inspector Head says in *The Secret Agent*, 'There are things not fit for everybody to know.'

SIS headquarters in Broadway Buildings looked no different from most public buildings of the 1950s. Its Edwardian façade had seen better days and the doorkeeper in a navy blue uniform to whom I showed my pasteboard pass looked neither especially nimble nor alert. Inside it was shabby, with wooden partitions making irregular-shaped rooms, clumsy office furniture and a metal cage lift that did not even stop at every floor. I was P15/B, second assistant to P15, who controlled the production of intelligence from north Africa, a part of the world I knew nothing about. The large room in which I worked was sparsely furnished with just two filing cabinets and the double desk I shared with the senior assistant, P15/A, who treated me with the condescension due the new boy in school. Grey net curtains masked the windows, a precaution against prying eyes even though our room looked into a white-tiled internal well. P15 had a small room to himself, and his secretary, a cheerful, big-boned young woman worked nearby. There was more to the work of secretaries in Broadway Buildings than typing. P15's turned out to be the photographer with a camera hidden in her handbag who had taken part in our final exercise with the watchers.

My work was unexciting. SIS was only beginning to establish itself in the newly independent states of Africa, and was barred entirely from operating in members of the Commonwealth. We occupied ourselves with administrative chores; only Libya, where plots were being hatched against its ruler King Idris, provided occasional drama. There was a soft drink advertisement of the time that ran 'I drink Idris when I's dry', and I found it hard to worry much about the king, even though he was a British protégé and we were trying to keep him in power.

In these plain surroundings P15 glowed like a piece of radioactive material. He was short but quite solidly built, with a long face and thin, inquisitive nose. His hair was black and shiny under some sort of dressing and it straggled over the back of his stiff white collar. He dressed like any other senior civil servant, and took an umbrella and bowler hat when he walked across St James's Park to lunch at the Travellers' Club or the Reform, but anyone who studied him carefully should have seen he was an impostor. A KGB officer who ran Burgess and Maclean said the ideal secret agent should have a 'childish, gleeful, mischievous side to his nature'. That fitted P15, whose cheerful wickedness was seldom hidden.

An efficient administrator, he became another person when, in a mood to chat, he strode into the room where P15/A and I sat over our paperwork, and a conversation with him could be as instructive as our two weeks with Noel and his men in Portsmouth. P15 had an amused cynic's attitude to the world he spied on, and a view of human motives that shocked me, for I was still young enough to be a prig. In this he was only being true to the traditions of Britain's or any other country's intelligence services. All men have their price, a British secret serviceman noted at the end of the First World War and it did not have to be money – 'it may be a decoration or a Dancing Girl'. P15 had a sharp sense for all human weakness, but he put particular faith in Dancing Girls, and 'always look for the sexual motive' was one of his rules. Our little team scored a success when one of our men in the field got hold of an advance copy of the final document of a youth congress we thought important. Instead of praising the coup P15 wondered how his agent pulled it off. It was sex, he decided. 'Look at the fellow's face. Don't you think he's queer?'

SIS believed in the manipulation of events as well as human beings. During our training course we heard a pseudo-academic lecture delivered with considerable self-satisfaction by a bald-headed man in tweeds. 'Politics is power', he began, and everything that followed was a development of that theme. P15 taught me to search out the levers of power in any situation, a training as useful for journalism as espionage, and Broadway Buildings had a relatively new section called Special Political Action, whose job was to pull power levers in Britain's interests. SPA's greatest triumph so far was Operation Boot, launched jointly with the CIA to put the Shah of Iran back on his throne after the nationalist coup of 1951. Unsurprisingly Alexis Forter, the then head of SPA, had the same glow of mischief – or was it danger? – as my boss, but he was plumper and glossier than P15, his suits better cut and his hair better trimmed. His White Russian parents had escaped from the Revolution, and though he was brought up as an Englishman there was a Slav passion to his anti-Communism. He was also a convert to Catholicism, a suitable faith for a spy, for Rome knows as much about human fallibility as any intelligence service. Forter made his name in Iran by helping SAVAK, the Shah's security service, become feared and powerful, and claimed credit for the rumour that it kept a bear in its headquarters to let loose on uncooperative prisoners. Among his more light-hearted services to the Iranian monarch was arranging for him to travel to London airport in a Flying Squad car driven at high speed with its bell ringing, apparently long a royal ambition.

Most of the people I met in Broadway Buildings gave the impression they knew how to dominate others, and none more so than John Bruce Lockhart, the controller for Africa and nephew of Robert Bruce Lockhart, the British representative in Moscow after the 1917 Revolution whose book about his adventures made me sick with envy when I read it in the boredom of my room at the Hotel Sovietskaya.

Bruce Lockhart had the manner of a bullying games master, and a habit of stationing himself at the head of our stairs when we were meant to start work (the lift did not stop at our floor) so he could tick off the latecomers. I thought he lacked the subtlety of P15 or Forter, but he was impossible to ignore, for he was a big man and when he came into a room produced a shock wave like an express train rushing through a station.

The ability to dominate in ways either subtle or crude was essential to success in Broadway Buildings, for we were not so much spies as spymasters. The job of an SIS officer in the field was to recruit and run agents. P15 talked about agents as a philanderer talks about women. He could not live without them, but they also drove him mad. Agents always thought they were under-valued. They demanded emotional support. They worried about the future of their relationship with you, even though you were always thinking up ways to keep them happy. Flattery was one of the best. We were trying to recruit a police officer, but he kept jibbing at the last moment. He wanted proof we valued him as highly as he valued himself, and delivered an ultimatum to the local SIS man, who was coaxing him to sign on. He would only agree to work for us if C himself flew out to recruit him in person. Little did he know that nothing was easier to arrange. He had no idea what C looked like (I did not know, though I knew his name was Sir Dick White and that he lived in a handsome eighteenth-century house at the back of Broadway Buildings). A former SIS officer of suitably distinguished appearance was brought out of retirement to play the part of C, flown to Africa, and in conditions of ostentatious security introduced as the head of SIS. The policeman was enchanted, and another agent was added to the books of an amused P15.

To be a spymaster you had to be something of a sadist, but gentler gifts such as sympathy and patience were useful too, because agents might come to think of you as their best, perhaps only, friend, the one person who understood them. Had I paused to think, which I did not, I might have come to the conclusion that there could be few more unfortunate creatures than a spy whose happiness depended on being understood by an inhabitant of Broadway Buildings. Another question I did not ask myself at the time was why our little group of new entrants was thought suitable material for the profession. My desk mate P15/A had only been in the service three or four years but was already growing into the Broadway mould. He was self-assured and liked making his weight felt. It was easy to imagine him enjoying dominating agents, though harder to see him charming them. Anthony, our public schoolboy, would also have had problems with charm. He was energetic, and probably brave, but he lacked finesse, a quality Harry, late of military intelligence, and my Cambridge friend Nicholas certainly possessed. Harry, with his First World War moustache, had the suspect geniality of the police sergeant who knows all about the rough stuff that goes on in the cells on a Saturday night. He was assigned to R5, where tabs were kept on the KGB. This was the guts of SIS – governments do not always realise that the chief interest of spies is other spies – and Harry's appointment there suggested he was well regarded. I imagined him spending his life among the card indexes that stored the names of every suspected Soviet agent and KGB contact, and unwinding every Saturday night, as he told us he liked doing, in a pub off Trafalgar Square, where he downed enough pints of beer to send himself drunk to bed.

I was less sure about Nicholas. His suitability seemed to depend on him getting intellectual satisfaction from sizing people up, and balancing their strengths and weaknesses in order to make use of them. As for myself, I could not work out what the recruiters had seen in me apart from the escapade in Poland, which was unplanned and might have happened to anyone. Of the other students who took part in it, one became a philosopher, another a solicitor. There were also two real diplomats, a writer of thrillers and a teacher of English. What made SIS pick me out? Perhaps its recruitment was more haphazard than I supposed. There was only one incident in my past that might have made me a suitable candidate, but no one else knew about it. It was a moment of understanding I experienced when I was an eleven- or twelve-year-old boy at boarding school. We had a playing field from which the fresh mown grass was carried away in an open lorry whose back wheels had been removed and replaced with a roller so it could be used to prepare the cricket pitches. The man who drove this fascinating machine sometimes let us ride on it. There was room only for a couple of boys on the driver's seat, and the less fortunate sat in the back among the leaves and grass cuttings. I did not care much one way or the other where I was, until one afternoon during the usual scrum to climb on board I realised luck had little do with it. If I really wanted to I could find a way to sit beside the driver, which that afternoon I did. I discovered I was able, if I chose and exerted myself, to get my way with people; and I came to think of this as a trick I might perform or not, according to my mood. I also understood, even then, that I had no compulsion to behave like this, and that my newly discovered power to get my way conflicted with a natural laziness that I also enjoyed indulging.

What the recruiters did correctly see in me was a scarcely articulated readiness to become a soldier in the Cold War, which was what joining SIS meant. The Cold War was a fact of my life. I was at school when the Korean War began. We were scrapping over a tray of sticky buns in a break between lessons when someone shouted that the North Korean army had invaded the South. We soon understood it was a war some of us would grow up to fight in.

National service in the Navy began at Victoria Barracks, Portsmouth, with a lecture from the commanding officer on the coming war with Russia that was almost as blood-curdling as the film on venereal diseases that followed it. Newspaper sellers at Tottenham Court Road underground station called out the news of Stalin's death as our class of naval linguists returned home from a day's study at the School of Slavonic Studies. Relations with the Soviet Union eased, but could still relapse into tension. One day in Broadway Buildings John Bruce Lockhart called us to his office to warn of a plan to send NATO tanks to break a threatened Soviet blockade of the roads into Berlin. It was a crazy idea, he said, for it had to mean war. There was no sign of his bumptiousness then.

The younger self I struggle to remember accepted SIS as a

necessary part of this dangerous world. And although our training was designed to open our eyes to a secret world of licensed ruffianism we were assured that, whatever tricks SIS got up to, it did not carry out assassinations. (This had been true ever since Sir Dick White's appointment as C in 1956 with instructions to reform the service. Before he arrived in Broadway Buildings SIS had made plans to murder President Nasser, though they were never put into operation.) It seemed sensible to me that as SIS officers our names were flagged in Scotland Yard files so that if, in the course of duty, we had a brush with the police they would know who we were. In this protective atmosphere there were few inhibitions about whom SIS could enrol as agents; certainly journalism was not the forbidden territory it became later. Journalists working abroad were natural candidates for agents, and particularly useful in places such as Africa, where British intelligence was hurrying to establish itself. One of our station chiefs found an out-of-work British journalist he thought could be useful if he had cover as stringer for a London paper. P15 contacted the section that handled London operations, which sent an officer to call on co-operative newspapers, and in those days probably the only one that was not was the *Daily Worker*. A Fleet Street daily agreed to take the man on and a new agent was born.

My doubts about a career in spying took shape when I learned I was to be sent abroad. Till then agents had not been real, just codenames made up, like my own, of letters and numbers. I was not sure I wanted to deal with the people behind them, goading them into action, supporting them with sympathy, and all the time ready to cast them loose when the need arose. I looked into the pool of darkness and considered the 'things not fit for everybody to know', and I was too young, and still too prim, to accept that the good may be inseparable from the bad.

I jotted down arguments for and against resigning on the back of the letter summoning me to my first interview with a still shadowy SIS. They were a strange mix of the obvious and the obscure. My points in favour of Broadway Buildings were:

1 Security & salary & standard of living
2 Travel
3 Satisfaction of curiosity & 'public service' tick
4 Kick from work (?) whose subject intrinsically interesting

Points against included:

1 No recognition
2 No communication with others
3 Work versus private life
4 Committed to what principles by nature of the work?
5 Jealousy of Branch A [i.e. the real diplomats]

Number 4 bothered me most. It was a clumsy expression of my fear that, as a civil servant, I might be asked to carry out policies with which I passionately disagreed. This was not queasiness about SIS's black arts but a hangover from the 1956 Suez operation. I was at Cambridge then, and with some friends published an anti-war pamphlet seditiously advising conscripts to ignore their call-up papers. I always knew that if there was another Suez I would walk out of Broadway Buildings straight away.

I turned down the foreign assignment on the grounds that my mother, who lived alone, was chronically ill. It was true, but it was only a pretext, and soon afterwards I sent in my resignation. I still have the draft of the letter. It is repetitive, disingenuous, and only comes close to the truth in a brief reference to my lack of interest 'in the basic techniques and work of the Service'. The office was surprised. People said Africa was the wrong place to start me off in, that it would have been better for me to join Harry and his colleagues in R5 tracking down the KGB, but no one tried to talk me out of my decision. P15 raised his eyebrows when I told him I was going, but I am not sure he was surprised. I was sorry to say goodbye to him. There was something melancholy in his eyes and the set of his shoulders, as though he knew the price he paid for doing work his country did not acknowledge, and publicly condemned. I would not even be surprised if he felt tenderness for some of the agents in his life, as one may feel tender towards a lover one abandons and deceives.

I gave back the pasteboard pass, now worn around the edges, and returned, without any idea of what I was going to do, to the ordinary life of London. It was as though Broadway Buildings never existed. I had no more contact with the people there, and even my closest friends never knew exactly what I had been doing or where. Then a few months later, walking down the King's Road in Chelsea, I noticed three men sitting in a car parked in a side street. Even before I got a proper look at their faces their alertness made them unmistakable, and I could imagine their nostrils flaring for scent of their prey. They were the watchers against whom we had pitted our meagre skills in our last training exercise in London. I walked on as though I had seen nothing out of the ordinary. After that encounter I sometimes found myself looking closely at the occupants of discreetly parked cars, half-expecting to find traces of the secret game on all the streets of London, and I wondered whether it was as easy as I had supposed to walk out of Broadway Buildings and never be bothered with it again.

For a while nothing unusual happened. When I became a journalist I told my employers I had worked for a year in the Foreign Office, a plausible story since our cover was that we were diplomats. I never doubted the Soviet authorities would give me a visa to go to Moscow as the *Observer*'s correspondent, and I was not worried when Vladimir introduced me to the KGB in the person of Sergei Borisovich. But when he asked if I had sinned against Soviet power I was alarmed and I wondered if the KGB knew something about my year in SIS and were suspicious of what I was up to in Moscow, for they would never believe I had left the service for good. I thought about it, and then dismissed it as impossible. How could the Russians know what went on inside Broadway Buildings? Even if they intercepted messages between our office and stations in Africa and had broken the code, there was nothing for them to crack in the name P15/B. The 1951 flight to Moscow of Burgess and Maclean did not then seem to affect SIS: Maclean was a proper diplomat and Burgess had still not been charged with any offence. Even Kim Philby's escape to the Soviet Union at the beginning of 1963 did not bother me because he had been forced to leave SIS three years before I joined, and could not possibly have heard my name.

I was equally unworried by the earlier scandal concerning the SIS officer George Blake, who was sentenced to a mammoth forty-two years in jail in 1961, the year before I went to Moscow. Most of Blake's trial was held in secret, and no details were published of the charges against him. Had I known those details I would have been very worried indeed, because Blake worked in London for part of the time I was in Broadway Buildings. DP4, Blake's section, was housed a few blocks away and ran London operations such as recruiting British businessmen who travelled to the Soviet bloc. I could not remember meeting Blake, but perhaps I had. And even without meeting me he could have heard my name for, in spite of what Noel taught us in Portsmouth about using first names only, surnames were commonly used inside the office. Blake's posting to London was a rare opportunity for the KGB to identify SIS officers and it is likely he worked hard to satisfy their curiosity.

If I had understood the significance of Blake's trial, I might have given up any thought of working in the Soviet Union; and if I had knowingly taken the risk, that interview with Sergei Borisovich would have terrified me. But nothing could have helped me anticipate the cloud of suspicion that eventually fell upon me. One day not long after my return from Moscow I got a telephone call from a man who made a guarded reference to SIS and said he would like to talk to me about Russia. He suggested meeting at the Royal Academy, where the Summer Exhibition had just opened. We could have our chat, he said, while we looked at the pictures.

A man with an unusually heavy head and thick, dark eyebrows came up to me on the Academy's steps. He led me through the galleries, stopping every now and then to look at a painting. All he wanted, he explained, was for me to tell him everything I remembered about the Russians I knew in Moscow. I was expecting an SIS specialist in Soviet affairs but anyone could see this person was an interrogator.

I do not know if he was already suspicious of me when he came to the meeting. He certainly was by the end of it, not because of anything I said, but because of what I would not say. I wanted to go back to work in Russia, I explained, and would not be able to take up with my old friends there if I felt I was spying on them, even if, as was the case, there were only the most innocent things to report. I did not have to think hard before answering; the words came as easily as if I had rehearsed them. When I thought about it later I realised I was defending an abstract principle. If I did go back to Moscow, it was not certain I would find any of my friends again except for Vera Petrovna and Yegor; and if either of them knew what I had done supposedly on their behalf they would surely have shrugged their shoulders and told me not to be so stupid. Yegor would have laughed at my making a moral dilemma out of something any Russian would take in his stride. This was already becoming plain to me as we walked past images of an innocent England that no longer interested even my companion, for my mulishness had quite spoiled his enjoyment of the exhibition. I did not try to explain that, as a journalist operating in Cold War zones, I wanted to preserve an area of innocence outside the conflict. This was not because I thought both sides in the struggle equally to blame: I had lived long enough in Moscow to decide for myself that the Soviet Union was prisoner of a terrible inheritance. What horrified me was the idea of handling my Russian friends as an SIS officer was trained to handle agents. I did not try to explain any of this to my interrogator and he left me with a curt goodbye.

A few weeks later a letter, poorly typed on cheap paper, arrived from the Ministry of Defence asking me to report to a room in the old War Office. It was obviously not an invitation to be refused. Two men, I guessed from MI5, were waiting for me in a small room. They sat at one side of a wooden table, and I at the other. They repeated the questions I was asked at the Royal Academy. I repeated my answer, though this time I tried to explain myself more fully. They remained as unhappy as the man with the big eyebrows. At least, they said, you can look at some photographs and tell us if you recognise anyone. I agreed, perhaps because I was unnerved by their manner, perhaps because I really could not see the harm. I went through more than a dozen photographs, and picked out only two: Victor Louis (I would have been surprised if I had not found him there) and a pleasant-seeming man called Tolya Uglov whom I scarcely knew but who was one of the Russians licensed to hang around foreigners. To my relief there was no Yegor. It did not surprise me in the least that there was no sign of Sergei Borisovich, but I told the two men about him anyway, and gave them his telephone number too. He was the one person in Moscow I hoped never to see again.

I did not know why I had fallen under suspicion. Later, when more became known about Britain's intelligence scandals, I guessed someone decided the Russians, perhaps through Blake, had learned about my time in SIS, and 'turned' me while I was in Moscow. Perhaps I was suspect from the moment I left Broadway Buildings (how many SIS recruits resigned after only a year?) and the suspicion deepened when I showed up in the Soviet Union as a British correspondent. I arrived in Moscow only a few months after SIS recruited Oleg Penkovsky, the Soviet military intelligence officer who gave the West its best intelligence of the Cold War. Like all British correspondents in Moscow I knew Ruari and Janet Chisholm, the SIS couple who had the dangerous job of running Penkovsky in Moscow. I also knew the *Daily Telegraph* correspondent Jeremy Wolfenden, who was caught in a KGB blackmail trap and later married the Chisholms' British nanny. How were the chronically suspicious KGB watchers in R5 to disentangle the probable from the merely possible in such a sinister confusion of people and events? Shamed by the Blake and Philby affairs, and open to the charge of losing the irreplaceable Penkovsky by their own poor tradecraft (he was arrested by the Russians in October 1962 and shot the following May), it would not be surprising if SIS took no chances on me.

Ten years after the interview at the War Office I was asked to lunch with some other British journalists in Saigon by a young diplomat who, we guessed, was the embassy's SIS man. South Vietnam was near collapse, and the apprehension and excitement that gripped the city was affecting foreigners as well. It was one of those moments when people talked of matters they would in more ordinary circumstances keep silent about. The young SIS man came and sat beside me at the edge of his swimming pool, and when no one else could hear offered a confession. He had found his few conversations with me interesting and would have liked more of them, but for one thing: I ought to know that London had forbidden him to have any dealings with me. There was, it seemed, an indelible black mark against my name.

In 1982 I went back to live in Moscow as the *Observer*'s correspondent without any objection from the Soviet authorities. In 1985 Mrs Thatcher expelled fifteen Soviet diplomats and journalists from London for spying and I was one of fifteen Britons thrown out of Moscow in retaliation. I did not link this to my time in Broadway Buildings until the *Observer* colleague sent to Moscow to replace me told me about a conversation with a Russian journalist who had unusually close links to the Soviet leadership. They had an uneventful talk about foreign affairs, but when my colleague got up to leave the Russian said he had a question: was it true Mark Frankland worked for British Intelligence?

When I heard that, Sergei Borisovich sprang back into my mind, baring his teeth and ordering me to confess my sins. It was, of course, only to be expected that the KGB was as much the prisoner of suspicion as Britain's SIS.

Chapter V

Mr Loc's Apprentice

We had forgotten everything: mother Au Co, father Lac Long
Quan, the shared womb from which we had sprung. A more
beautiful legend had never been told.

Duong Thu Huong, *Novel Without a Name*

Saigon, 1968

The metal grille on the front door rattled, and then rattled again as
though someone was sending an urgent message. When I opened
the door the man standing on the step trotted past me and was
in the middle of the living-room by the time I turned round. He
stopped there, but it obviously cost him effort to stand still; the
smallest gesture from me, even a breath of wind, might have set
him in motion again. Not much more than five feet tall, and thin
but wiry, he wore dark trousers and a short-sleeved white shirt with
pens clipped into the breast pocket. He looked at me expectantly,
tilting his chin, the most pronounced feature in the long face, in my
direction.

It was an important day for Mr Loc. I had just taken him on as my
assistant and we were about to set off on our first trip together. An
American correspondent had introduced us and at that first meeting
Loc said there was nothing he liked better than travelling round the
country. He assured me he had contacts of all kinds all over South
Vietnam, and to prove his point in the most dramatic way possible

undertook to arrange a meeting with the Viet Cong. There was to be a ceasefire in the war between the Communist-led guerrillas and the Saigon government at the end of January 1968, when the Vietnamese celebrated Tet, their New Year holiday. Loc said it was the perfect opportunity to travel out of the city and see the Viet Cong on their home ground.

He reported back with a plan that seemed foolproof. We would leave Saigon on the eve of Tet and, unhindered by the soldiers of either side, get to our rendezvous in a rubber plantation north of the city before dusk. We would spend the night there with our Communist hosts and return the next morning. It sounded more like a picnic than a serious expedition and I went off to gather supplies for our evening meal – Portuguese sardines and La Vache Qui Rit processed cheese from a Chinese-run *épicerie française*, US Army combat ration tinned fruit from the black market – while Loc brought sandwiches for the journey. Later, but only when he knew me better, he admitted making other preparations too. He had called on a well-known fortune teller to enquire whether the heavenly signs favoured an adventure such as ours. Apparently they did, which perhaps explained why he was now so impatient to be off.

He helped me wheel my Suzuki motorbike out of the living room, which served as its garage, and into the little alley in front of the house, where his own Honda was parked. As we turned into a street that took us along the side of the presidential palace, someone let off a string of firecrackers that was hanging from the roof of a house. They sounded like rapid rifle fire and I must have looked startled for Loc, who was driving beside me, laughed and shouted that it was only Chinese boys celebrating the New Year early. The firecrackers were supposed to drive away evil spirits and the approach of Tet certainly seemed to have calmed the usually irritable and restless city. The quarrelsome Saigonese were briefly united in preparing for a festival that was all the sweeter for taking place in a country at war. Diligent families moved their furniture into the street before cleaning their houses and restocked their larders, in the hope that abundance at the start of the year would ensure twelve more months of plenty. Shops were selling the holiday delights of sugared lotus seeds, candied coconut and ginger, and sweets made from custard apples. The better-off had decorated their houses with little mandarin bushes covered with fruit, with water narcissi and young plum trees that miraculously burst into flower on the first day of the New Year.

Loc never hinted that he regretted leaving Saigon at such a special time. He had not yet told me he had a wife and children even though we drove close by his house as we left the city, heading for the new highway that would take us to Bien Hoa and the plantations beyond. I do not believe he thought he was making any sort of sacrifice, for he was a man who loved movement. We did not drive fast – our little machines were not built for speed – but when Loc bent down low over the handlebars and the wind flapped in the sleeves of his shirt he might have been a modern centaur, for his Honda was in perfect scale with his slight body. We passed the American army base, which was the size of a small town. Loc waved a proprietorial arm in its direction and grinned. He respected the Americans for their energy and efficiency, but they often puzzled him and the grin suggested there were limits to his respect.

We stopped to eat our sandwiches at a small roadside café. They were excellent – slices of finely ground and pressed pork that the Vietnamese called *cha lua* inside crisp French bread – and it was only when I complimented him on them that he admitted having a wife and that she had made them. The café owner brought us glasses of black coffee and we dawdled over it, for we did not want to arrive at the plantation before the appointed hour of four o'clock. Loc took out a pipe and smoked quietly for a while. I came to recognise this peacefulness that fell upon him at moments of rest during a journey. He could never manage such tranquillity when sitting in Givral, the old French café in the centre of Saigon which still made *bûches de Noël* each Christmas and where Loc gossiped with other Vietnamese journalists who worked with foreign correspondents. He had to force himself to sit still while the others swapped rumours of political intrigue and military disaster. One of the regulars in the group had the delicate, pearl-pink skin of an old opium smoker;

another man, who looked as though he had just bitten something sour, would turn out to be a senior Viet Cong intelligence officer. They had far better sources in the government than Loc, but while he admired their knowledge he shook his head over their reluctance to move out of the city. Saigon with its rumours, which were usually malicious and often false, confused him, but travel cleared his mind. It let him feel he controlled events, while in the capital he was at their mercy, driven erratically from point to point like the ball on an old-fashioned bagatelle board.

He knocked out his pipe. '*On y va?*' It was more statement than question and he was out of his chair before I replied. We drove on under a clear sky through the sort of scrubby landscape that could have hidden the soldiers of either side and reached the plantation according to schedule. It was a relief to escape from the heat of the open country into the shade of the rubber trees, which stood as tall and smooth as the columns of a great cathedral, the cleared ground between them adding to the impression of order and space. It did not look like guerrilla country, and my doubts increased when we drove past a large house with a swimming pool. It was a handsome establishment, the terracotta walls and roof of heavy brown tiles setting off the purple and white flowers in the hedge of bougainvillaea that surrounded the garden.

Somebody was living there, either the French plantation owner or his manager, and they would not be pleased to see us on their property. I had another reason to be wary. Alexis Forter, the dirty tricks specialist whom I had met in Broadway Buildings, had told me he was spending the Tet holiday with a plantation owner, and I wondered if he was somewhere behind this hedge, lounging in a rattan chair and enjoying the light of approaching evening. Forter had arrived at the British embassy in Saigon a few months earlier and as soon as he saw me asked me to lunch. His house was protected by a high wall and when I pushed open the gates made of heavy metal sheeting I saw Forter getting ready to dive into a tiny pool, his face very red and his little pot belly quite white. The sturdy young woman in a flowered dress who waved at me with more politeness than warmth was P15's former secretary, the one who had taken my photograph with a concealed camera at a bus stop. We sat in the garden and ate *salade niçoise* and drank white wine and I knew I was under observation. He took me out to dinner several times after that, choosing out-of-the way places run by old French refugees from Algeria from whom he ordered couscous and red wine as thick as treacle. One evening when it was late and we were drinking brandy he began reciting some lines of Alexander Blok in their Russian original

'And drunkards with the eyes of rabbits
"*In vino veritas*" cry out . . .'

Perhaps he thought the alcohol would make me open up, for that was when he warned me to stay out of trouble. He did not explain what sort of trouble he had in mind – it was as though I was supposed to know – but described in detail the unpleasant things the Saigon security police did to their suspects. The later it got, the more he talked as though we were enemies on different sides of the barricades. That was the expression he used: 'When the chips are down you and I will be facing each other across the barricades.' The prospect seemed to excite him. I could not make out the reason for this melodrama and it was only later, when the young MI6 man told me about the black mark against my name, that I understood what he was talking about. Forter thought I was a Soviet spy.

No one came out of the planter's house, and we drove without incident through the calm plantation until we reached a settlement of some thirty workers' cottages with cream-coloured walls and tiled roofs ranged each side of a dirt road. The overseer was waiting for us in his house, which was set a little apart from the others. He smiled knowingly as we drank the acrid tea he had poured into dusty glasses. The tiny house was dirty too, and his wife, a Tonkinoise with blackened teeth, looked exhausted. The youngest of their twelve children tugged at one of her elongated breasts as she complained that they had to deal one day with the government troops, and with Viet

Cong guerrillas the next. The peasants, she said, were helpless, like an empty barrel rolled backwards and forwards between one side and the other. Her long complaint made the overseer fidget and he sent one of the older children to look out for the Communists, assuring us they would certainly come that evening. Loc seemed equally confident. He had arranged the meeting through a trade union official in Saigon and, perhaps to impress me with his experience as a fixer, acted as though it was nothing out of the ordinary. I was excited and a bit scared. After almost a year in Vietnam I had come to think of the Viet Cong as a magical creature who was ever present but seldom seen.

Dennis Bloodworth, the *Observer*'s great expert on the Far East, had given me an introduction to a left-wing Saigon politician, an old Trotskyist. But he shied like a nervous horse at my questions and all I got out of him was the advice to 'listen carefully for the elusive voice of the Viet Cong'. Dennis also sent me to Lucien, an old Vietnamese friend of his who ran a paint business from a strangely quiet office in the centre of Saigon. There was much that was unusual about Lucien, his name for a start. His father was a rich southern landowner who became a French citizen when the South was still France's colony and gave French names to all his large family of sons and daughters. Although the family was Catholic, two of the older brothers played important parts in the Viet Minh's war of independence against France. One of them, Gaston, eventually became a senior official in Hanoi's Foreign Ministry while Albert, better known by his Vietnamese name Pham Ngoc Thao, although once a Viet Minh intelligence chief, rose to the rank of colonel in the South Vietnamese army. In fact he was still working under cover for the Communists and three years before I arrived in Saigon had launched an unsuccessful coup against the military government of the day. He was arrested, interrogated and done to death by strangulation of the neck and testicles.

Lucien was said still to have contacts with the 'other side', as people careful to burn none of their bridges called the Communists. At our first meeting he was composed and polite, sucked at his pipe and said nothing very much, which did not surprise me, given the delicacy of his position. Not long afterwards, though, he invited me out for an evening with his younger brother Gabriel, who owned a garage and was plump and, unlike the reserved Lucien, rather jolly. We made an erratic journey through the city's restaurants and bars as though trying to avoid surveillance, ending up at a back alley nightclub I was never able to find again. Here we drank whisky with an unremarkable-looking man whose importance was obliquely suggested by the haziness of Lucien's introduction. Bar girls moved around us like butterflies, and a band played sad but noisy Vietnamese songs. Listen to him carefully, Lucien said, but the man spoke so softly, and in such heavily accented French, that I made little sense of anything he said.

After the fiasco of that evening, Loc's idea of meeting the Viet Cong on their own territory seemed simplicity itself, but where were they? The overseer's wife was still chanting her complaints and there was no sign of the boy we had sent to be our lookout. Loc shifted in his chair and I was not surprised when he got up and said we should go and look ourselves. We walked down the dirt road surrounded by a pack of children, from whose chatter it was obvious the Viet Cong entered and left the settlement as freely as birds. Then we turned round and saw them. Fifty yards away two men dressed in black and carrying carbines were walking up the road towards us as casually as on a country hike. Loc quickened his pace and then crouched and broke into a half-run, half-walk. He was smiling, and making cooing noises that I took to be a signal of respect. The men remained impassive. Loc, still crouching a little, introduced me to the smaller one, who was the leader. He offered an extraordinarily strong handshake for such a slip of a man, for he was shorter than Loc and had the features of a gothic elf, with pointed ears, a small pursed mouth and a sharp little chin. His neck was as slight as a child's, and were it not for that handshake and the lively eyes I would have judged him to be exhausted.

The others arrived just before the punctual tropical dusk, when the smooth trunks of the rubber trees were immersed in a golden light and the settlement children were playing volleyball as though they had never heard the sounds of war. Loc and I watched unbelieving as the road between the houses, quite empty the moment before, was suddenly occupied by two dozen young men and women, who appeared from behind hedges and the walls of houses. They wore a strange variety of clothes, shirts and trousers that were black, khaki, green and even blue, with wide-brimmed bush hats and sandals cut from old motor tyres. They carried a mixture of Soviet and American weapons, some with red cleaning rags tied round their muzzles. A tall young man whose hat was embroidered with blue and white flowers frowned at us, but the others walked by as though we did not exist.

That evening we were called to a meeting in an office at the back of the barn where the raw latex was stored. The guerrillas had lit the room with oil lamps and made a poster out of a cement bag, which listed the Viet Cong's achievements in the past year. The elfish man poured us tea from a tin canteen and offered biscuits and sugared coconut wrapped in a screw of newspaper. This painstaking hospitality as much as the truculent answers to our questions about the war made me think of countless meetings I had had in Russia. It was the unmistakable Communist way of simultaneously dealing with and fending off the enemy, and quite unlike my ambiguous encounters in Saigon. Yet there was tension, too. For one thing, we had an audience. Throughout the hours we talked faces came and went at an open window close to where we sat. Children levered themselves off the ground to stare at us and giggle, while Viet Cong soldiers, themselves little older than schoolboys, leant against the window frame, gravely conscious of their military dignity. The most attentive member of our audience was the overseer's wife, her face a caricature of curiosity and apprehension in the uneven flame of the oil lamps. She listened to our conversation as though hoping for a revelation and then, disappointed, slipped away.

The elf's defiance of the Americans, and his insistence that the Viet Cong would fight until victory, interested Loc a good deal less than the story of the guerrilla leader's life. He was thirty-seven and had joined the war against the French when he was nineteen. He stayed in the Maquis after Vietnam was split in two in 1954 so he could help 'liberate' his native South and had not seen his wife and children since then. He paused to suck up noisy mouthfuls of tea and to pull the smoke of his cigarette deep into his chest, Loc lighting each cigarette for him, and eventually taking over the host's duties and pouring him fresh glasses of tea.

When after several hours the guerrillas left us, Loc marvelled at this story of endurance. He could admire it because it did not scare him. 'I'm a poor man,' he said. 'Why should I be afraid of the Communists?' It was true he was not well off. The *Observer*, I remember with shame, paid him rather meanly. His only luxuries were his Honda and the large refrigerator that stood in the passage of the little one-storey house into which he somehow fitted with his wife and seven children. I doubt he was much more interested in material things than the elf who revealed an ascetic's pride when, at our urging, he showed us the few possessions that he carried on his back. Watching our faces to catch any expression of surprise, he laid out on the desk a toothbrush, toothpaste, a razor, a hammock made of string, an ingenious little oil lamp with its wick set in an empty cartridge case, a US army spoon, anti-malaria pills, a piece of plastic sheeting for lying on and a wretchedly small cape against the rain. Loc followed this performance as intently as a child watching a conjurer take rabbits from a hat, and when it was over shook his head with what I took to be a mixture of admiration and approval.

We opened some of our cans of food, and soon after midnight two guerrillas came to take us to the house, where the Viet Cong were giving a Tet party for the plantation workers. This was when Loc's mood began to change and no wonder, for I have never attended an occasion so moving yet so chilling. About ten older men from the settlement sat at a long table in the middle of the room, while a handful of women cradling young children in their arms occupied a bench behind them. The guerrillas stood or squatted along walls that had been decorated with patriotic slogans and a large Viet Cong flag. The overseer came in after Loc and I sat down. He had changed out of the grubby shorts he had been wearing into a long black *ao dai*, the traditional dress for a man in authority. He was still smiling, but it was now the smile of someone desperately anxious to please. A few minutes before one in the morning the elf turned on a big Sony portable radio. We heard the voice of an announcer in Hanoi and then the chimes of midnight (the guerrillas observed Hanoi time, which was an hour later than Saigon's). There was an explosion of firecrackers echoed by static on the radio and a man read out a poem about a new spring bringing a new victory. Ho Chi Minh, Loc whispered. Like everyone else in the room he looked as attentive as a model pupil.

Then the guerrillas stood up and sang songs. A young man performed a piece in the style of the traditional Vietnamese theatre about South Vietnam's sufferings under the anti-Communist President Diem, murdered by his own generals five years earlier. A seventeen-year-old, the youngest in the unit, blushed and hid his face in his hands after getting through a song about a buffalo herdsman driving a truck with military supplies to the South. Another lost his step and disappeared into a trench dug at the back of the room as a shelter against air and artillery attacks. One of the two female guerrillas, a dark blue scarf wound into a turban round her head, stood up to sing and Loc whispered a translation of her words.

> I go to the market to buy material for a handkerchief, and with some red thread I shall embroider it with flowers and two swallows and give it to my soldier-lover. When he uses it to wipe away his sweat, or after eating his rice, he will think of me.

The elf would not let us talk to the male soldiers, but he left us alone for a few minutes with the girl in the blue turban. Did she know who she wanted to marry? A soldier, she said at once, because soldiers fought hardest against the Americans. And what was her favourite colour? Black, the preferred colour for the guerrilla's clothes, but when peace came, all colours.

I had never come across such a powerful mix of patriotism and the private passions of youth. I remembered a phrase from a poem the Americans discovered in the notebook of a dead Viet Cong soldier, part of a mass of captured material they translated in an attempt to understand the secret of their enemy's resilience. The dead soldier was writing about his sandals, the same crude rubber sandals made out of old tyres that our entertainers wore, and he praised them for being 'long-lasting, and supple, like love'. When Loc and I left at two o'clock in the morning the guerrillas were still singing their songs that plaited love and war into one single strand of suffering and sacrifice.

Many years later a North Vietnamese writer remembered the soldiers who, like him, had fought with such passion in the South. We were then, he wrote, seeming hardly able to believe his memory, 'young, very pure, and very sincere'. But if that description fitted our entertainers, it was quite wrong for the elf and his second-in-command, and that was why the evening left Loc in such a troubled mood. While the young soldiers were revealing their hearts to us, their two commanders were performing theatre of a different kind that had nothing to do with spontaneity. Neither sat down, but stood all night behind the table where the village men sat, refilling their glasses with tea and handing round plates of biscuits, sweets and candied coconut. In soft, humble voices they entreated the villagers to eat more, and as they talked they bent low – as Loc had bent low when greeting them – as if to say look, this is our true nature, we are only the people's servants.

It was a sinister show and the overseer, whose smile became so forced it was painful to see, certainly knew it.

The atmosphere of the evening was unexpectedly re-created the next morning. We had just got up from the tables on which we slept, Loc rising with the lightness of smoke and restored to full energy after rubbing his face with a damp flannel that he kept in an envelope of plastic. I was envying the simplicity of this toilet when the elf came to say goodbye. He had brought coffee and a traditional Tet cake, shaped like a roly-poly pudding and made of sticky rice wrapped round sweet lentils and a core of pork lard. He took off the cake's banana-leaf wrapping and was cutting it with a piece of string when one of the plantation workers who had been at the party appeared holding two small boys by the hand. They were his sons, whom he had brought to offer New Year good wishes to the Viet Cong. Wearing pyjamas obviously bought for the holiday the boys were coaxed by their father to step towards the elf, put their hands together and bow their cropped heads. It was the theatre of the night before but in reverse, this time no longer a dishonest pantomime but a true expression of subservience and respect that was hard to distinguish from fear. For all his show of humility, the elf was master in this village. He was equally the master of the young men and women delivered to him by emotions too intoxicating to be within their control. Their lives were at his disposal, and during our conversation he made plain what he was ready to do with them. The American GI, he told us scornfully, valued his life and therefore wore a flak jacket, but the Vietnamese soldier considered his life to be as nothing. He himself had given up everything a normal man most values in life, so what reason did he have to regret the sacrifice of lives that had barely been lived?

We watched them leave. They formed up in single file between the little houses and then moved off at a brisk pace, the sandals that perhaps really were as supple as love rustling the dead rubber-tree leaves that lay scattered on the ground. They followed the road where it swung left, and without turning back to look at us or the village disappeared into the plantation.

I doubt many of them were still alive by the end of that week. We could hear gunfire as we drove back to Saigon that morning and the next day the Communists broke the ceasefire completely, launching attacks all over the country. The elf had boasted that the Viet Cong, like God, were everywhere, and for two or three days it seemed true even in Saigon.

Loc and I manoeuvred our motorbikes through streets littered with empty shell cases and here and there corpses that looked so much like dummies it was hard to believe they had once been living creatures. One day at a police checkpoint we came across a young peasant guerrilla who had been sent into Saigon armed with a single home-made grenade. It was his first time in the big city and he had got lost and given himself up. His commanders had told him the inhabitants of Saigon would rise up against the Americans as soon as they saw the Viet Cong, and he would be able to take all the weapons he wanted from surrendering government troops. The elf would have told his guerrillas exactly the same, for it was what the Communist leadership believed would happen all over the country. It was a fantasy, and once the Americans and Saigon's army recovered from their surprise they wiped out the lightly armed guerrillas, who often charged straight into their guns.

The Communist leaders made a terrible miscalculation, but they still had the wind of history in their sails. The scope and daring of an offensive that carried the Viet Cong into the United States embassy in Saigon destroyed America's confidence that the war could be won. And the destruction of the southern Viet Cong, who at least shared the same language and culture as the southerners they fought against, forced Hanoi to send its army of northern regulars into the South to continue the war. South Vietnam was trapped between an increasingly reluctant ally and an enemy from whom little understanding or mercy could be expected.

The Tet offensive also brought about the disappearance of Lucien. I had bumped into him at the French grocer's the day before Loc and I set off on our expedition; I had gone there for sardines, he was buying cognac and *marrons glacés*. A few days later Loc spotted Lucien's name on a list of members, all well-known southerners, of a new front organisation set up by the Communists to exploit the military success they expected the Tet offensive would bring. When that did not happen Lucien had no choice but to remain in the Maquis, returning only at the end of the war to a Saigon renamed Ho Chi Minh City that was too dogmatically Communist for his taste.

Loc regarded Lucien with the cautious curiosity a dog has for a cat. Lucien was one of those privileged Vietnamese instructed by

French education in the disciplines of rational thought and scientific enquiry that underpinned the power of the West. Freed from the passivity of tradition and superstition, the Luciens of Vietnam turned their new knowledge against their European teachers. But what might have been a national, almost private, war against the French was twisted into something infinitely more malign when the Communist and Western worlds decided they had an interest in the conflict's outcome. As a result Vietnamese nationalists who feared the Communist Ho Chi Minh were forced into a humiliating alliance first with the French, later with the Americans. Nationalists of Lucien's sort could not stomach that, and had no choice but to co-operate with the Communists, who exploited them, and then squeezed them to extinction.

Like many Vietnamese, Loc was secretive about his background, perhaps because years of colonialism followed by a war fought in people's minds as much as on the battlefield taught the Vietnamese that only dimwits are trustful. His full name was Tran Ba Loc and he was born in Vinh, a North Vietnamese town not far above the border with the South. His family were Catholics but not well off. He had only secondary schooling and learnt his imperfect French during compulsory service as a quartermaster in the French army, an experience that did not seem to mark him one way or the other. When France accepted defeat in 1954 and Vietnam was split in two, Loc's family joined hundreds of thousands of Vietnamese Catholics who fled to the South to escape from Communist rule. Loc was twenty-nine.

These few facts suggested a man who was carried along, as most people are, by events, and it was as an Everyman that he became for me a precious, if sometimes unconscious, teacher.

They were barren years, the years after the Tet offensive, when the Communists had sunk their hooks into the South but for a long time the South did not realise it, and mistook its flapping and wriggling for signs of life. Loc was a tireless observer of this sad though sometimes comic spectacle. He was a journalist himself and, like most Vietnamese who wrote, had a *nom de plume*, Minh Huy, which meant Bright Intelligence – when it came to pen names there was no point in false modesty. He never showed me anything he wrote, but he was a brilliant oral reporter. He would arrive at my house, rattle the grille on the front door as he had on the eve of Tet, and like a clockwork toy that had just been wound up pour out the gossip and rumours told him that day until there was nothing more to say and the spring ran down. No wonder many of the actors in Saigon's intricate but pointless dramas found him a useful go-between. Loc brought about some strange connections in the ill-functioning brain of South Vietnam's body politic, shuttling one day between an astrologer and a disgraced but still ambitious general, the next carrying messages from a Catholic bishop to a politician claiming to command a Buddhist peasant sect in the Mekong delta.

He would talk to anyone, and was ready to like anyone. True, he had a slight prejudice against the Americans, but only because they baffled him and this was hard to bear for a man whose favourite expressions were *Moi, je connais!* and *Moi, je sais!* He chuckled when the elf mocked American soldiers as 'flesh targets' because they were so big and easy to hit. And he quoted with approval a remark of the Roman Catholic archbishop of Saigon (for whom he also ran errands) that South Vietnam should not oppose the Americans, but should not follow them either. He liked the subtle obstinacy of that, for helpless though he might have been against the tide of events he could not bear being bossed about. That made me wonder what sort of a Catholic he was and several times I heard him talk as though the Pope of Rome had no claim on him. Certainly he was fascinated by magic and omens. One of his favourite stories was about a woman who procured diamonds for the wives of army generals. She made a fortune because (Loc said) she possessed a magic rouge which when rubbed on her lips enabled her to convince anyone of anything. This was how she diddled even the notoriously sharp-witted mother-in-law of a contact of ours who was both Saigon student leader and Viet Cong agent. Whether Loc believed the story, or just enjoyed telling it, I never made out.

He particularly liked stories about omens and famous people. We were travelling on a country bus when he noticed a story in the paper the man next to him was reading. It was about a horde of large insects invading the village where South Vietnam's President Thieu was born. Was it a good or a bad sign, I asked. Bad, said Mr Loc, and both he and his neighbour laughed loudly. He was doing nothing unusual when he consulted the astrologer before we made our trip to the rubber plantation. If you visited the house of any well-known astrologer in Saigon, you would be sure to find a queue of army officers and civil servants or their wives all anxious to know their prospects for promotion. Even Thieu was said to have consulted an oracle about whether he should stand for re-election. The visible world of the South Vietnamese was so unpredictable, and so often beyond their control, that it made some sense to take a supernatural shortcut to understanding.

Loc remained enough of a Catholic to get on with Catholic priests. When we travelled in the countryside he usually persuaded them to give us a bed or a meal, and most of them had interesting information to pass on. Some had brought their entire parish south to escape the Communists after 1954, and their settlements were easy to spot. A real southern village spread like a creeping plant along the sides of waterways or country tracks. The Catholic refugees reconstructed the villages they had abandoned in the North, and their carefully laid out houses with thick protective hedges were like military camps on the alert against attack. Loc admired the stubbornness of these priests, whom experience had taught to trust only in themselves and God, and probably in that order. They wore soutanes so old they were turning green and in places shimmered like mother-of-pearl and lived in comfortless, dusty rooms whose only decoration was a plaster statue of the Virgin Mary. Their only relaxation seemed to be the water pipe they produced when we sat down to talk, loading it with a bullet of rough tobacco and reducing it to ashes in three or four great puffs. 'Firing the canon,' they called it, an expression that came well from such pugnacious men of God.

Perhaps Catholicism contributed to Loc's uprightness, though there was also much of the traditional in his virtues. He could be wily and was outraged when the government, desperate to collect elusive tax revenue, sent survey forms to every Vietnamese household. It was unconstitutional, he insisted, and refused to fill it in. It was one of the rare occasions I saw him in a bad mood. He certainly had chances to make money illegally, but as far as I know he never took them. Once a Saigon businessman asked him to smuggle in dollars from Hong Kong. On another occasion two Chinese asked him to approach a powerful general with an idea for a gambling racket that would make all of them rich. He disapproved when his younger brother, an Air Force pilot who flew opium into Vietnam from Phnom Penh on the orders of his flight commander, went into drug-running on his own account. And Loc was prudish about sex. A member of the South Vietnamese parliament went into hospital after a trip to Japan: rumour said he was being treated for 'shrinking bird disease,' a complaint in which the penis was believed to shrivel as a result of too much intercourse. When the MP made his first speech on coming out of hospital, he made as if to drop his trousers to prove the gossips wrong. Most people laughed, but Loc thought it disgusting.

What particularly bound me to Loc was his affection for the South and its inhabitants, for this was not common in northerners. The history and geography of the two parts of Vietnam were different in many ways, and North and South grew further apart when they ended up on opposite sides in the Cold War. Southerners cursed northerners as abrasive, carpet-bagging 'Yankees'. Northerners mocked the South as feckless and lazy. There were grains of truth in these stereotypes. When middle-class northerners fled to Saigon after 1954 they swallowed their pride and rebuilt their fortunes by opening soup shops and engaging in the meanest sorts of trade. That was not at all the southern style, as some southerners were the first to admit. These differences, though, did not bother Loc and he never seemed happier than when setting off on an expedition to the deep South. At dawn we would breakfast in a hut at the edge of Saigon on finger-shaped Chinese doughnuts and *café au lait* made by dropping an inch of condensed milk into the bottom of a glass and topping it up with dark-roasted coffee from the highlands. The buses that began their journey there held only two dozen passengers but were crewed by a driver and two boys, whose job was to lean out of the back and side doors and shout and gesture at slower traffic to get out of the way. Loc leant forward in his seat like a jockey as though to urge the bus on, and these hours of movement punctuated by horn blasts and the cries of our ragged conductors seemed to calm him. He modified his accent when we travelled South. Northern speech buzzed like an angry insect, but once in the countryside Loc mimicked the accents of the southern people we talked to, a sound as soft and liquid as the lapping of the delta's chocolate-coloured waters.

The soothing effect of these journeys soon wore off and by the time we were back in the city he would be tense again, puzzling over the confusion of stories we had heard, evidence of a society eaten away by an endless war. One day our return trip took us through a village where we had spent a night during the Tet fighting in a ruined pagoda. The village was peaceful now, its crooked lanes smelling of baked mud and the heavy-tiled houses scattered among the trees like mushrooms. We scarcely recognised the pagoda. It had a new roof of corrugated iron and its biggest room, empty when we saw it before, was taken up with beds made of slats of wood, with cooking pots and bags of food beside each bed. People were sitting or lying on the beds, most of them women, but there was one old man and a much younger one, a policeman they said, who seemed to be in a state of shock. One of the women had a chain round her leg and her gentle-faced husband sat beside her holding its other end in his hand.

We had come across a sanctuary for the spiritually wounded. The old man, a patient himself, explained that so many soldiers had been killed, and their souls not laid to rest by proper burial, that the countryside was full of wandering spirits. These unhappy ghosts were looking for a resting place and sometimes found it in a living body. The men and women in the pagoda had been possessed in this way and the cure was exorcism, a process that looked simple. The patient lay down on a bed and the exorcist, sitting at the head, recited prayers and tapped out a rhythm on a brass bowl and a coconut shell. Each session ended with a fiery explosion caused by the exorcist blowing a mouthful of rice alcohol through a candle flame held above the patient's face.

The grave young monk who ran the pagoda said it was hard to find people who were fit to perform the cleansing rite. The back of the monk's shaven head ran in a straight line down to his neck, making him look like the Buddha as he appeared in popular Vietnamese prints, but he did not consider himself ready for the work. An exorcist had to be completely pure, and such people were now rare. The pagoda was nothing like a madhouse. There was an informal order about it that seemed to calm the patients, and when someone gave the withdrawn young policeman a flute he squatted on his bed and played it beautifully. Even the woman with the chain, who the day before had escaped on to the roof, was quiet now, and as Loc and I were leaving she stood up and bowed down low in front of us.

No one could ridicule the old man's image of a country haunted by its dead soldiers, for few Vietnamese had not lost a member of their family in the long war and what are memories of the dead but ghosts that live in our minds until we ourselves die? Others might have been depressed by such a place, but Loc was not easily downcast. The monk and his patients were doing much as he did in his own life, coping by the means they had at hand. He could not understand people who gave in to pessimism.

There was an opium den near where I lived. It had nothing exotic about it, but was merely a tropical version of the sort of broken-down London pub that no longer exists, sad and shabby but scarcely sordid. It was across a courtyard at the back of a cinema which showed Kung Fu movies, and you entered it through a room where the patron's children slept in bunks under pictures of Jesus Christ and the Virgin Mary. The regular customers who lay dreaming or quietly talking among themselves were vicious only in the sense of being addicted to an illegal drug. They were mostly schoolteachers, melancholy middle-aged men who had given up the struggle of life and justified themselves with remarks like

'We are bringing up our children to be even more unhappy than ourselves.'

I cannot imagine Loc saying such a thing. One night he invited me to dinner at his house and before we sat down to eat he brought out his children from the back rooms to pay their respects to me. Five girls and two boys, the eldest a teenage girl, the youngest still almost a baby, lined up in the small, bare living room dressed in clean pyjamas. The biggest boy was unmistakably Loc's son, with the same stroppy jaw and sticking-out ears. The children put their hands together and bowed to me in the same way the two little boys had bowed to the guerrilla leader in the rubber plantation. Loc frowned as he watched them, and only allowed himself to smile when he hurried them back to bed. I do not believe he ever doubted he knew what was best for them, or that he would always be able to take care of their future.

I was in Tokyo at the beginning of March 1975 when the North Vietnamese army began what was to be its victory offensive. I had just got a letter from Loc, in which he predicted nothing out of the usual in the weeks ahead. Perhaps his surprise at the Communists' advance (a surprise shared by most people) explained the enthusiasm of his greeting when I returned to Saigon, for when he caught sight of me on the street he ran forward, put an arm round my shoulder and called me 'brother' Mark, a Vietnamese expression of friendship he had never used before.

The city that had been spoilt and protected for so many years was now in a state of panic, for nothing seemed able to stop the North Vietnamese. Pharmacies made a fortune out of sleeping pills and tranquillisers. 'Can't you tell me a miracle is going to happen?' a friend asked, and he was only half joking. Loc's eldest daughter, now a student at a teacher training college, said her friends had wept for days before deciding to enjoy themselves while there was still time. People did not know what to expect from the Communists and so they expected the worst. There were exceptions. A young politician who still hoped a neutral South might be salvaged from the ruins of the war said he would not leave, though his wife was badgering him to. But even he wanted reassurance. 'You won't abandon us, will you?' he asked when we said goodbye after a chance meeting on the street. As for Loc, he neither asked for nor, if I guessed rightly, needed reassurance. I cannot remember us talking about even the possibility of his getting out of Vietnam. His attitude had not changed since the day we set off to meet the Viet Cong on our first outing together: he knew the Communists well enough, and as a man of few means had nothing to fear from them. As if to prove his point he took me to see an old acquaintance, the head of the Dominican order, who was another model of calm. This time, he said, there would be no repetition of the Catholic flight from the North in 1954. Every parish and priest would stay. You have to understand, the Dominican concluded, allowing himself a smile, that the Catholic church sleeps with many masters but in the end cuckolds them all. Loc laughed and nodded. I think it was pretty close to his own recipe for survival.

It was decided that an *Observer* colleague, Colin Smith, would stay to cover the North Vietnamese entry into Saigon while I took one of the last helicopters out of the city to report on the ignominious American evacuation. That day I got up shortly after dawn, a moment when Saigon briefly recovered its old beauty in the kindly first light, and you understood why the French thought they had built a perfect city, an irresistible child of the tropics and Provence. But all I remember are the faces of the people who watched us leave, some reproachful, others quite blank as though they could no longer see us. I had not been able to announce a miracle to the friend who asked for one, and in spite of the young politician's plea I was abandoning him, and many others too. The only person I left with an easy conscience was Loc. I do not even remember anything remarkable about our last goodbye. As usual he had somewhere to hurry off to and I was sure, because he had convinced me of it, that he of all people would be all right.

Four years later, when I was back in London, a letter arrived from Thailand.

Dear Sir,
My name is Tran Ba Phuoc. My father is Tran Ba Loc. Many years
ago he worked with you in The Observer. Do you remember? Now
I am in Songkhla [Thailand]. I have nothing. Please you help me. If
you see, you can know how we lived at here.

Phuoc, Loc's eldest son, was twenty now, but I recognised him at
once when I saw him in the refugee camp on the beach at Songkhla
for he seemed little changed from the boy who paid his respects to
me when I had dinner at his father's house. The young woman whose
hand he held as he came to greet me was Lan Phuong, his wife. It
was plain from the way he told his story that he had his father's
truculence and grit. His chances of getting higher education in the
new Vietnam had been destroyed when he failed an enquiry into his
family background known as the 'three generations' investigation'
and was judged lacking in 'party spirit', a mischievous concept
borrowed by Vietnam's Communists from the Soviet Union. He
was left with two choices, both grim: to work under labour camp
conditions reclaiming the wasteland of a so-called New Economic
Zone, or join the army and fight against Vietnam's latest enemies,
the Khmer Rouge of Cambodia. Determined he would do neither,
he went into hiding when he got his call-up papers and in April
1979, after a terrible quarrel with Loc, who did not want him to
take the risk, escaped in a fishing boat with the girl he had just
married. Their plan was to go to America, where relations of his
mother were already living. It was a common enough story, for by
that time more than one hundred thousand South Vietnamese were
fleeing their country each year.
    Within weeks of Phuoc's letter another arrived addressed in a
familiar neat hand, but this time with an Indonesian postmark.

My dear Monsieur Mark
Here I am in Indonesia, in the village of Letung Jemaya on the island
of Kuku. I was forced to leave my country in spite of my good will. I
have left my wife and seven children [in fact six after Phuoc's escape]
in Saigon.

It took several more letters before I understood how this man of 'good will' had become so frightened that he abandoned not just his country but his family too. Like many others, Loc was excited by the first appearance of the North Vietnamese soldiers in Saigon and the promise they seemed to bring of peace and reconciliation. He knew he was likely to fall under the Communists' suspicion because he had worked with Western journalists, but he thought he could disarm them by the modesty of his life and his readiness – naïve perhaps, but nonetheless genuine – to accept the new order. He nevertheless took the precaution of acquiring a little plot of land outside the city, calculating he could grow food there for his family and at the same time keep out of the authorities' way. Nothing went right. A landmine exploded while his younger son was helping him clear the land and blinded the boy. And as the Communist regime tightened its grip on the South it changed, as we had sensed our friend the elf could change, from smiling liberator to stern master. In 1978 the police arrested Loc on charges of collaborating with foreigners. They let him go after four weeks of interrogation, but ordered him to report once a month to police headquarters in Saigon. In May 1979, just a month after he failed to stop Phuoc's escape, friends tipped him off that the police were about to round up everyone on their list of suspects and send them to a re-education centre. 'The real word for these places', Loc explained, 'is concentration camp.'

This man who could not live without movement panicked at the thought of losing his freedom and decided he had to escape at once. I do not like to imagine how he said goodbye to his family, and how savagely he reproached himself for his inability to take care of them. He made his way to the Ca Mau peninsula, the southernmost tip of the country, where 'thanks to the generosity of fishermen, for I had no financial means of my own' he was crammed with thirty-four other people into a thirty-foot open fishing boat. During a month at sea they were robbed by corrupt Vietnamese coastguards and then by Thai pirates. Driven away from the Malay coast by the Malaysian Navy, they put ashore on an Indonesian island so small it shows no bigger than a nail clipping on a map of the South China Sea. They were lucky because thousands of Vietnamese died while trying to escape their country. Loc asked me to let his wife know he was safe. 'Make as though to write a letter to me,' he instructed, 'and in that way put the Communist police off the scent. Just say that Monsieur Thanh Thai is in perfect health – Thanh Thai is my pseudonym.'

He was in Paris by Christmas, accepted as a refugee by the French government, and I went to see him there. I was in my room in the Hotel Louisiane when the receptionist rang and said someone wanted to see me. The Louisiane is a cramped place with a narrow curving staircase leading to the front door and as I walked down a man I did not recognise rushed up the stairs towards me. He wore a dark jacket and a dark polo-neck sweater and had lustrous black hair. It was Loc of course, but dressed as I had never seen him and with his old pepper and salt head returned to youth by hair dye. When we went across the street to have lunch at the Restaurant des Arts, the contrast between the man sitting opposite me and the Loc I knew in Vietnam was painful. The restaurant was a simple place popular with students, but it was obvious he felt uneasy, for he was fidgeting and looking around him and sometimes seemed not to hear what I said. It was as though he knew the clothes and the hair fooled no one and least of all himself. He was a man of fifty-five who belonged in Vietnam and nowhere else.

He let on then that he had a sister and another brother in Paris, though he was not close to either. The brother was a monk whom I never saw, but he took me to meet the sister, who was a widow and lived in a comfortable flat in Neuilly. She was Loc's height but plumper and with his energy. She told me she liked betting on horses and lectured both of us on the psycho-sexual benefits of animal placenta as a restorative food for middle-aged men. 'It raises their morale,' she said, and giggled. Loc looked as uncomfortable in her bourgeois world as he had in the student restaurant.

His dyed hair and a work permit proved little help when he started looking for a job because all the people who offered him one wanted to avoid paying his social security by not declaring him. One day I got a letter from Dijon. With 'my persistent patience', he wrote, he had at last found legal employment as a night watchman at the university. 'I eat at the university restaurant – 6.30 Francs a meal – and have rented a room for 260 Francs a month. I bought a bike to get to work on . . .' He recorded those details just as he used to pass on bits of information he picked up on our travels – the price of rice, the amount of traffic on the roads – in case they came in useful. I took it as a sign of improving spirits, but he still felt he was unwanted in France, and was painfully grateful for the help that I and some other correspondents and our newspapers had given him. 'A scrap of rice given to someone in distress', he wrote in one letter, 'is far more precious than the tea of Emperors when it is offered at a time of plenty.'

He sent me a New Year card at the beginning of 1981 and it contained only bad news. His eldest daughter, the one who cried and then made merry before the fall of Saigon, had died after stomach surgery in an ill-equipped hospital. Loc, too, had been in hospital for several weeks. 'My dear Mark – in spite of my energy I have been feeling a little weak, above all since my daughter's death.' When I next saw him in Paris he seemed recovered; he had found new and less tiring work as a bookkeeper and was staying with his sister. His hope, of course, was that his family would be able to join him in France. It might eventually have been possible to arrange their legal departure from Vietnam, but Loc's wife took matters into her own hands and made her way with the five remaining children to the seaside town of Vung Tau. It was a well-known route of escape, but something went wrong with her plan and police fired on their party, either when they were still on the shore or in their boat. No one was able to discover exactly what happened but she was killed and so were some, and perhaps all, of the children. I never learned who buried them, or where, and for Loc the calamity was intensified by his powerlessness to look after them in death. He died not long after, aged sixty-one.

The following year I got a letter from Phuoc. He and his wife had settled in Texas and he had changed his name from Tran Ba

Phuoc to the shorter, and simpler for foreign ears, Phuoc Tran. His purpose in writing was to tell me he no longer needed help.

> We appreciate you very, very much but please understand me. I dont want to receive any more helps while I dont really need. I mean I can take care myself now. I want to make my life by myself with my ability. I am working for Texas Moulding Inc and when I feel I have enough english I will study again in night class as some Vietnamese did here. So dont give me money any more.

Mr Loc would have approved. He had given his son a name that means 'happiness' in Vietnamese, and the young man who reminded me so much of my old friend was now building something new out of a family in ruins.

Chapter VI

The Family of Books

> We rear our children, guide them and advise them, but each child finds his way to a library, which is a world totally independent of us. There total strangers compete with us. So what can we do?
>
> Naguib Mahfouz, *Sugar Street*

In February 1968 I was getting ready to fly to Hue when the elderly messenger from the Saigon PTT brought the telegram with news of my mother's death. I heard the whisper of his bicycle wheels on the dusty concrete of the alley and the scrape as he rested the machine against the wall. When I opened the door he was standing on the step in his pith helmet, his face impassive but not unkindly, a suitable mask for the bearer of news in time of war. It was the second week of the Tet Offensive and there was a big battle in Hué, where the Americans and South Vietnamese were struggling to drive the Communists out of the city. I could have flown back to Britain, but when journalists are caught up in great events they easily believe they are a necessary part of them. It is not true, of course, but the illusion makes it easier to be a passive witness to the suffering of others. In my case it worked so powerfully that I knew at once I would not go home for the funeral.

There was another reason for my decision, though I scarcely admitted it then. In my mind my mother was already dead. I do not know when she died. It was not sudden, but a slipping away from life that may have begun when she was very young, but certainly there was no escape from it once she fell in love with my father. I think she knew quite soon what was happening to her. She might have been aware of it for more than half of what others called her life.

I have a photograph of her taken by the society photographer Lenare just after my elder brother was born. He sat her in a favourite pose, the young mother gazing in adoration at her baby, knowing that these unholy imitations of Virgin and Child were expected to look glamorous. He made my mother ravishing. She sits almost in profile, her head tilted back so she seems to be looking at her baby from under lowered eyelids. Portraits such as these suggested women too conscious of their own glamour to bother much with the children they seemed to worship, but in my mother's case the cliché was wrong. She was never a beautiful woman; she was pretty. Beauty may be dangerous and calculating; prettiness as sweet as my mother's is vulnerable and rarely wise. She had naturally curly fair hair (which Lenare tried to straighten out) and her nose turned up slightly at the tip. She giggled a lot and my father's friends thought her 'great fun', innocent and something of a dumb blonde. They loved playing tricks on her because she took them so seriously. When they were driving somewhere and there was a man in the party known to be a bottom-pincher (MTF, Must Touch Flesh, in their jargon) they would put her next to him so they could enjoy her squeaks and protests.

Neither family liked the marriage, and there are no photographs of the wedding, which was attended only by a mutual friend of the bride and groom and my father's sister, on whose help he had relied to escape earlier entanglements but who would not let him get out of this one. There had already been several engagements, for women liked him as much as he liked them even though, his family's titles notwithstanding, he was not a brilliant catch. At Cambridge he drank too heavily to get the cricket blue he deserved, and spent so much time partying with richer friends that he only just scraped a pass degree. As a younger son he could expect little money from his family, and he seemed unlikely to make a fortune in the City, where my grandfather found him a job.

My mother's parents knew all this, but her stubbornness defeated them. She was their eldest child, and made her own way round social London. Her father, a broker on the Baltic Exchange, was a philanderer with an uneasy laugh. My grandmother, from whom my mother took her prettiness, dealt with his infidelity by claiming a weak heart and spending many hours on her chaise-longue. My mother's name was Elizabeth, but her parents called her Betty, a little girl's name she swapped for Eve when she went into society. The re-naming signalled her separation from a family for whom she seems never to have felt much warmth.

She must have known what other people said about my father, and she had plenty of other boyfriends who were more desirable from almost every point of view, but he was the one she picked and stuck to. Of course she saw in him what others saw, a tall young man with smooth dark hair and aquiline profile, and so naturally elegant that when he was at Cambridge tailors made him suits for nothing because he was such a good advertisement for their clothes. There was something else that only she saw, or thought she saw, for no other woman loved him as she did. She decided her life depended on having him and that was the trouble, for it was a drowning woman relying for salvation on a man who could scarcely swim himself.

They set up house at 7 Cathcart Road, on the western borders of Chelsea. Today it is a millionaire's white stucco *palazzetto*, but in 1930, when smart people still lived in Mayfair, it might have been Bohemia, which in a way it was, for there were artists' studios just round the corner. When my father's friends came to visit they kept their taxis outside with the meters running for fear they might otherwise not get back to civilisation. I doubt if my mother had more than a brief spell of happiness in Cathcart Road, for my father was soon making breakouts from the marriage. He would set off one night in evening dress and come back two or three mornings later in the same clothes, to find a wife in tears and his mother-in-law lying on a sofa in the drawing-room as though she was the centre of crisis. No one summoned my mother's father. One evening when my parents were out together they spotted him in white tie and tails spinning a young blonde round the dance floor of the restaurant at the Ritz. To do my somewhat mysterious grandfather justice I never heard that he tried to give his son-in-law moral lectures.

My parents soon moved to Wellington Square, a more fashionable part of Chelsea almost on the borders of Belgravia. My brother and I lived on the top floor under the care, as was the custom for children like us, of a nanny and a nurse maid. We were not supposed to see much of our parents, though we might be taken down to the drawing-room at our bedtime when they were having drinks before dinner. My mother did not object to this system of family apartheid, and nor did she feel the need to compensate for her unsatisfactory husband by getting closer to her children. I do not think she ever thought we could be substitutes for him.

The other photographs of her that survive from before the war were taken at the seaside, where my father's mother rented a house each summer. One dates from 1939, the summer we saw British warships gather in the Channel while playing with our buckets and spades on the beach. In this photograph my parents are sitting side by side on a lawn. My brother and I are between my father's legs, while my mother holds a black Scottie dog. They are both tanned, and screw up their eyes against the light to look at the camera. Is that the only reason they seem so far from smiling? My mother's left hand, which could easily have been on his shoulder or arm, lies empty on her lap as though paralysed.

Nanny did not smile much either. Nannies were often known by the name of the family they worked for, but Nanny Moreland kept her own and deserved to, for she was an independent source of constancy in the house. She was Liverpool Irish, dark-haired, a little sallow, and too serious to be pretty. For many years it was a mystery to me why she vanished each Sunday morning: it was thought improper for us to know that she was Catholic and went to mass. I cannot remember loving her in an obvious way for she was not a woman who invited hugging, but I seem to have understood that I needed her, and the quickest way to make us behave was to threaten that Nanny would leave. It must have been a lonely life, observing the frantic unhappiness of the adults who lived on the floors below and yet always behaving as though nothing was wrong. I suspect she was too proud to gossip about such things to other nannies, and neither then nor later, when I was in my teens, did she let slip what she knew or thought about my father and mother. She connived in just one act of clandestine nursery resistance. For reasons of class prejudice, not nutrition, my parents forbade us to eat Heinz's tomato ketchup. Nanny ignored them, and smuggled ketchup into the nursery, where we ate it with bacon and fried bread for breakfast.

As war approached, my brother and I became old enough for toy soldiers and family and friends pressed them on us. The cork floor of the nursery at Castle Mead was a fine place to drill and send them into battles where we bombarded them with howitzers that fired steel shells as thick as my thumb. We had our own military uniforms. The earliest had a pantomime look, but about the time of our last seaside holiday my father's elder brother had a tailor make copies of his regiment's walking-out dress. There were dark blue trousers with a stripe up the side, dark blue jackets studded with brass buttons (my brother's with sergeant's stripes, mine with only a corporal's), peaked caps and swagger sticks that we had to hold correctly under our right arm, grasping the stick's silver knob between the thumb and forefinger.

I was five when real war came and I cried, but only because my father got his call-up papers when we were at the seaside, and, trying to please me when he said goodbye, sat me on top of his car. The sun had been shining all day and the bonnet was hot and burned my bare legs and I burst into tears.

Tears were the appropriate overture to a war that destroyed what hopes my mother still had for her marriage. My father was in the Air Force and we followed like obedient dogs as he moved from airfield to airfield, but we were always a little behind him and he escaped us for good when he was posted to Malta. My mother moved us six times in four years, sometimes to stay with relations but more often to rented houses. I do not know how she coped, for she was a tidy person for whom everything had to be in its place. I dreaded the times she took me to buy school clothes and made me stand for what seemed hours while she pulled and tweaked at a jacket or a pair of trousers, turning me round and round until she was sure the fit was right. When she packed our suitcases for boarding school she used tissue paper to wrap even our vests and football socks. Her meticulous habits had been early causes of quarrels with my father, for she kept him awake by checking the weekly laundry in their bedroom late into the night, folding and re-folding the dirty shirts and towels until they lay in the laundry box as neat as new.

Perhaps she was able to cope with the disorder of moving and new houses that can never have been clean or tidy enough for her because she believed that one day she would catch up with my father and win him back for good. She had nothing else to believe in. They did have meetings, mysterious occasions such as the time my mother took us to spend the night at a hotel in London and when my brother and I went to her room in the morning my father was there and she seemed happy and he embarrassed. Sometimes my brother and I saw him on our own and once he took us to lunch at Quaglino's, where I was enchanted by an omelette made from dried-egg powder. Mostly, though, my father was not there, and one evening when he did turn up while we were staying with my grandmother and he came to see me in bed I cried and told him to go away. I cannot remember my mother crying. Perhaps Nanny, believing children should not catch sight of adult emotions, took care that I did not.

What haunts me is the thought of my mother's loneliness. She only had Nanny, who never let her down, but Nanny was dour and perhaps unwilling to bear the secrets of others. My brother went away to boarding school and, though I enjoyed a younger son's unearned privilege of being the favourite, I did not feel particularly close to my mother. I played on my own out of the house, and when we lived in Norfolk bicycled for hours through the fens and along river banks with piles of sour-smelling beet that sailing wherries would carry to the sugar mills. At nine I was sent to boarding school, but I cannot remember crying for my mother, or even missing her.

She stood no chance of getting my father back. He was a ground controller in Fighter Command, where many of the pilots were friends he had known in his amateur flying days before the war, and for the first time in his life had work that absorbed him. Affairs were easy in wartime, and so were excuses for not coming home to a family he would rather not have had. I was twelve when Miss Pike, the only woman teacher in the boarding school, called me out of class and told me about the divorce. She was Irish, with red hair and a liking for green dresses, and I suppose a Catholic too, which might explain why she looked at me not unkindly but with pity, as though I had just developed a terrible disease.

It was characteristic of my parents to have someone else tell their children that their marriage was over. They were not callous, but it saved them embarrassment, for my father felt guilty and my mother helpless. They believed they were doing the best for their sons by sending them off to boarding schools from which we would emerge after nine years like cakes baked according to a tested recipe, and resembling our ancestors as much as possible. It was still not plain that the war and its aftermath would destroy the world in which my parents had grown up and when my father sent his sons to Charterhouse, his old public school, he thought he knew what lay in store. There would be enough education to get us into university, plenty of exercise and organised games, and school chapel every weekday and twice on Sundays.

The formula might have worked for me if I had not decided to learn German. German beginners were sent to Mr Iredale, whose red face and pure white hair made him easy to spot as he moved around the school grounds on his bicycle. Though he smiled a lot and had the figure of a paunchy teddy bear, boys were nervous of him, and behind his back called him nothing worse than Harry, which was his real name. The purpose of Harry Iredale's introductory German classes was to weed out boys who did not really want to learn a language which, he constantly told us, was difficult and no fun at all. For weeks he rubbed our noses in the nastiest places of German grammar until the last of the faint-hearted were gone, each departure greeted by Harry with a smile of triumph.

Not long afterwards he invited the remaining rump of the class to the bachelor rooms he rented in the house of one of the school chaplains. The sitting-room was obviously a schoolmaster's, with comfortable old armchairs, framed reproductions of Italian Renaissance paintings, and one wall covered by books. There was also a large radiogram, which he called the Groaner and was the purpose of our visit. That day he played records of Schubert songs to show us the beauty of the language he had done his best to dissuade us from learning, and perhaps also to apologise for what he had put us through.

A boy who was older than me and a poet gave Harry a facsimile edition of Blake's poems when he left the school and wrote at the front a few lines that perhaps applied to both teacher and poet:

> The cliché-blind eye
> Lifts lids that can't pass
> Blue sky, green grass.

In some things Harry was as conventional a schoolmaster as his room suggested. He went on walking holidays in Switzerland. He was a practising Christian, but in a quiet way and he never preached God to boys. He spent other holidays with a sister who was married to a clergyman in Suffolk, where he bicycled round the countryside looking at old churches. He wore tweed jackets and grey flannel trousers and the only hint of the unconventional in his appearance was his dark-coloured shirts and woollen ties, but from the way other masters and some of the older boys talked about him you would have thought he was a Bolshevik. Harry did not always respect the conventions on which public schools were built. He made fun of the character-building powers of team games, and would not treat the school as a microcosm of an adult world in which order and authority had to be maintained at all costs. He was nothing like a Bolshevik but he was bolshy, and the clue to that was also in his sitting-room, an oil portrait painted at the end of the First World War of a young army officer whose hair has turned prematurely white.

I never heard him talk about the war or what he did in it, but I believe it taught him never to trust authority again. He criticised all powers and princes, though it was hard to predict the direction from which his attacks would come. He fell out with Britain's new Welfare State because he thought it ignored the crumbling condition of the country churches he loved, and cared only (as he put it in a letter) about 'that horror Westminster Abbey, which it finds handy for circuses and gets the use of free'. It was hard to pin his politics down. He admired the governments of the Swiss Cantons that he visited each year; he said they knew how to look after old buildings and still keep public life running smoothly. I never heard him mention Karl Marx and if he sometimes seemed sympathetic to Uncle Joe, as he called Stalin, it was because he would not take on trust what any British government told him. He was something like a Christian Socialist, but with a hard edge, for he was unsentimental about human nature.

In 1950, when I was sixteen, he gave me a copy of *News from Nowhere*, William Morris's 1890 vision of a utopia whose citizens are equal, love their work and are all blessed with the author's aesthetic sensibility. It is the only book I have kept from my schooldays, and though now it makes me smile, it excited me then. It is the story of a man who falls asleep one summer night in his house on the Thames at Hammersmith and wakes up in a future Britain that has no prisons, no slums and no private property. Since all government is at the local level and the business of every citizen, the Houses of Parliament are not needed and have been turned into 'a storage place for manure'. That 'horror' Westminster Abbey has been restored to beauty by the removal of 'the beastly monuments to fools and knaves' that William Morris detested as much as Harry did. There are no rich, no poor; and also no criminals because all men and women are free and equal, and human nature can no longer be the cause of conflict. Everyone works, and everyone's work is beautiful.

It was an odd book to give a teenager in 1950, when George Orwell's *1984* had just appeared and utopias were more likely to be understood as nightmares than lovely dreams. I do not believe he expected me to understand it as a blueprint for the future, even though he did share the fable's egalitarianism and aesthetic vision. He wanted to infect me and others like me with the belief that change was necessary and possible, that life could be lived differently, and that there was nothing inevitable about the world we were growing up in. He incited us to question school tradition for the same reason that a bird gets its chicks to exercise their wings while they are still in the nest. He teased the boys who were promoted up the hierarchy of school power, and nagged and encouraged what he called the 'bad' boys who showed signs of independence.

It was the 'bad' boys he most often asked to tea, a mix of schoolboy feast and donnish seminar. There were always oatcakes and Swiss black cherry jam, which he brought back in tins from his walks in the Alps. The jam was eaten from the tin and butter or margarine (depending on the state of his ration for we still lived in post-war austerity) from their wrapping of grease-proof paper. Harry ignored the difference between them and called both 'smear', a scholarly joke about *smör*, the Swedish for butter with its roots in Old English and German. Another of his quirks was to pronounce foreign names as though they were English, making Beathoven out of Beethoven, taking the t out of the usual 'tz' in Mozart, and turning Goethe into Geeth and sometimes (there was a linguistic reason but I have forgotten it) Kédé. The meal ended with a Fuller's cake, sometimes chocolate but more often walnut, and he gave us Lapsang Souchong tea so strong it smelled like tar-paper.

Not all the conversation was high-minded. However much Harry made fun of Charterhouse, it was his world and he enjoyed its gossip as much as boys did, even if he always kept his darts of scepticism at hand. The meal ended with a recital on the Groaner. Harry sat in his armchair under the portrait of the young lieutenant with puzzlingly white hair, smiling as he listened to the music and sometimes beating time with his hand. He believed in the moral power of beauty, and his recipe for a well-lived day was to read a poem, listen to a piece of music and look at a reproduction of a painting.

He had an unacknowledged ally in subversion in the school librarian. The library, a mock-medieval hall lined with dark bookcases, was heated by a great double-sided stove whose glow suggested a magic force of which the short-sighted Mr Evans was the Celtic guardian. He kept an eye open for boys who showed an interest in books. 'Have you read this?' he asked, pushing across his desk a novel by Aldous Huxley or D. H. Lawrence, as though he had conjured it out of nothing. He particularly liked the Russians. 'I think you might try that,' and there was *Crime and Punishment*; 'I've always liked that,' and he slid across Turgenev's *Fathers and Sons*, the title alone enough to whet my appetite. He did not have to say more, for he knew what hooked a teenager. He also brought out for me books written by my grandmother's great-uncle Robert Curzon, a contemporary at Charterhouse of Thackeray, who fictionalised the school as Slaughterhouse. I had not yet come across them in the jumble of my grandmother's house, and the discovery that someone in my family had written books that were clever and amusing excited me.

In those days, when public schools had changed little for decades, you did not have to do much to be thought a rebel. I decided I was a conscientious objector and refused to take part in the school cadet corps. When I was made captain of my house cricket team and had to choose the players for the next match I scribbled the names on a piece of plain paper instead of the usual house writing paper with its embossed blue letterhead. This was thought disrespectful of cricket in particular and school tradition in general. Harry chuckled when I told him, but I was disappointed that George Turner, the headmaster, seemed more amused than angry when he called me in to calm the storm.

A little man, Turner achieved the dignity expected of headmasters by holding himself very straight and gliding rather than walking, as though his tiny feet were shod with wheels. He knew his good points were a shapely head and silver hair, and was particularly proud of his tenor voice. When he thought the school was not singing well enough in chapel he would smile, throw back his handsome head and produce notes so pure and loud they could be heard above the voices of six hundred boys.

He was, though, less conventional than he chose to seem. He never questioned in public the school's belief in the character-building powers of team sports, but he remarked to boys he thought would understand him that team spirit might be learned just as well, and perhaps better, by singing in a choir or playing in the school orchestra. There was something adolescent in Harry Iredale's rebellion which made him all the more attractive to boys who saw themselves as rebels too. The headmaster was entirely adult, but knew the adult world did not always deserve to be taken as seriously as it demanded. His favourite rebuke to my storms of teenage intolerance was 'to be fastidious is un-Christian', but he smiled as he said it, as though he thought a rebel or two was no bad thing in a school as conventional as his.

The school tolerated Harry because it believed he could do no real harm, but boys who were thought too much under his influence were slow to be appointed to positions of authority. In the end the wily headmaster spoilt my rebel glory and made me a school monitor in my final term. Monitors were subalterns in the pyramid of power, close to the school rank and file but responsible to the masters. I did not like the job and to judge by his final report, which I found in my father's desk after he died, I sometimes tried even the headmaster's considerable patience.

> As a monitor, Mark suffers from being more interested in the theory than in the practice of discipline. He will understand by and by that a school must to some extent reflect as well as serve the larger society of which it is a small part, and is not a suitable field for social experiment, beyond narrow limits.

The handwriting and the grammar were as precise as everything else about him and if he showed me understanding and even affection it was because he was sure it was he, not Harry Iredale, who knew the ways of the world and that 'by and by' I would accept them too. It would have shocked him to know that Charterhouse, far from turning me into an almost-adult my parents could recognise, drove me apart from them. I am less sure what Harry thought about that. He was a gentle man, but he was an agitator too and like all good agitators had enough anger in him to be careless about the consequences of his words.

The growing gap between myself and my parents did not matter much for my father. After the war he married a woman whom he loved a great deal more than she loved him and at last had order brought to his life. It was different for my mother. When the war ended everyone's life was meant to start afresh and be better than it was before, but how could that be for her when she had lost my father? For her children's sake, perhaps, and surely because she was lonely, she remarried too. A friend saw her just before this second wedding and said, as people do, that she hoped she would be happy. 'I shall never be happy again,' my mother replied, as though it was a fact so obvious everyone should be able to see it.

She married a good man, but the wrong one. Olof Wijk, brought up as an English gentleman by an anglophile Swedish father, was a captain in Winston Churchill's old regiment, the 4th Hussars, when the war broke out. Captured in Greece in 1940 he spent the rest of the war in a German prisoner-of-war camp, where he got a letter from his first wife saying she was leaving him. When he came back to London his body was covered with eczema and he spent months in hospital before it cleared up. He was highly strung and in spite of British schooling and years of cavalry life still inclined to bouts of Nordic gloom. He needed a strong and cheerful woman, and he got my mother, a winged bird trying to disguise that it would never fly again.

Both were still only in their thirties, and they made a fine-looking couple: 'like a pair of greyhounds,' a country friend said, watching them set off on a walk together. But apart from having known each other before the war, and finding themselves wretched and lonely after it, they had little in common. He left the Army and joined an old-fashioned wine merchant's in Jermyn Street whose chief customers were the officers' messes of rich Army regiments and Oxford and Cambridge colleges. They lived in Medmenham, a village on the Thames, and he took up gardening, just one of the enthusiasms he pursued to keep his gloomy demon at bay. He liked to cook, and bought *French Country Cooking*, Elizabeth David's second book, as soon as it came out. He was child-like in the kitchen, always demanding applause for the sole in white wine and the water ice made from young blackcurrant leaves that were his most successful dishes. He was a dandy, too, wearing neo-Edwardian suits with narrow trousers and cuffs on the sleeves several years before they became a fashion. He had read a lot in prisoner-of-war camp and also developed a taste for music. He played me my first Mozart piano concerto on the radiogram at Medmenham.

I came to hate that house. It is humid in the Thames Valley and I felt imprisoned during the oppressive months of long summer holidays. The house's mood was set by my mother as she tried in the only way she knew to keep control of her life. The meticulousness with which she dressed herself and her children, and managed the ordinary business of life, like the laundry lists she tormented my father with before the war, turned into obsessions and made living with her torture for a careless adolescent. When she washed dishes they had to be rinsed first, then washed in soapy water, rinsed again and at the end polished, not just dried. We had two dogs. She doted on them and developed complex rules for the regulation of their lives. She would take the train to London to buy them fresh horsemeat and when the horse butcher in Praed Street, conveniently near Paddington Station, was closed went to another shop in Chelsea and carried the heavy bags back across London with blood from the sickly smelling lumps of flesh leaking through the newspaper wrapping. She boiled the meat in a cauldron, each night cutting it into little pieces that had to be of identical size, mixed it with dry biscuits broken up with similar care and finally added a moistening of water that only she could gauge. It took an hour to feed two small dogs and if we went away, which she became increasingly reluctant to do, she took bags of dog food with her, for she would not trust the kitchen of even another animal lover. She was almost always late because her rituals, to be performed correctly, needed frequent repetition. When we did go out together we waited, for what to a boy seemed hours, while she did and then re-did her hair, or brushed and brushed again her skirt to get rid of lint and hairs that only she could see.

She still had light moments. She would sing songs that were popular before the war or during it, the sentimental ones of course but funny ones too, like the song about Mussolini we heard the landgirl sing when she delivered our milk in Norfolk. 'Oh what a surprise for the Duce! He can't put it over the Greeks . . .' She did not know all the words and would break off singing and giggle and that is how I imagine she was when she met my father. Her face had changed little since then, even if she was now forcing herself into a prison of her own making. There are photographs from a holiday in Devon when she and Olof played golf with my brother and me on links looking over the sea. She is dressed in a sweater and skirt, the collar of an Aertex shirt showing over the top of the jersey. Her hair is short and curled but a little wind-blown, which she must have hated for she could not bear anyone or anything touching her hair. She is frowning slightly in one photograph, but in another she smiles and her face is pretty and sweet, but it is still not happy. She had a social smile that she put on when she met an acquaintance out shopping, or if someone called at the house. It made me shudder for even then I suspected it was a mask that hid feelings I did not want my mother to have: fear, shame, and above all emptiness. She straightened her body, became attentive, and smiled as sweetly as an untroubled child, but when the postman turned away or the acquaintance had gone on down the street she sagged, for she was not sure that there was anything inside her. But she wears a different smile in this picture taken on a Devon golf course, the smile of someone watching a boat with a precious cargo sail away, knowing she will not see it again, and all that is left is to turn round and meet the approaching emptiness.

She could not save herself. She did not have any simple dis-
tractions. She had once played golf and tennis well, but I cannot
remember her playing after the war, apart from that holiday in
Devon. Olof took her canoeing in France when they married, but
she never wanted to repeat it. She was not interested in the garden.
Scarcely educated, as was the custom for her sort of girl, she had
no taste for reading and seldom came to the cinema in Marlow, the
nearest town, where Nanny took me once a month, and amazed me
by crying when Garbo-Karenina threw herself under a train. Nanny
got romantic novels from Boots' Library but I do not think my mother
looked at them. For my confirmation she gave me the prayer book
whose cedar-wood covers the colour of worn ivory I unexpectedly
remembered many years later in Moscow, but Christmas and Easter
were the only times she went to the village church, even though it
was opposite our house. God hid himself from her as she was hiding
herself from her family and everyone she knew. She had no passions,
my father in his carelessness had seen to that. All she had were her
obsessive rituals, and because other people would not fit into them
they were a solitary occupation that only deepened her loneliness.

Her greatest torment was visits by Olof's mother. When he was
a young soldier he had kept by his bed a picture of her so striking
that people supposed it was his girlfriend. She was no less striking
as an elderly woman, handsome but chill and self-assured as a judge.
She spoke English with a Swedish intonation that made her sound
always aggrieved and, to the particular horror of my mother, she
was both knowledgeable about food and greedy. Olof chose the
menus for her visits and my mother, who learned her cooking
in the war and had not got far beyond austerity bacon and lentil
pies, was put to work preparing Elizabeth David's recipe for *Turbot
à l'Espagnole* ('poach a fine whole turbot in a *court-bouillon* . . .').
When we sat down to dinner Olof, who was as ingratiating as
his mother was haughty, presented the oval plate with the great
fish and its red robe of tomatoes. The old lady nodded approval,
and ate heartily but I doubt my mother cared. She was scared,
simply, by the intelligence and solidity of an older woman measured

against whom she seemed to regard herself as a creature without substance.

I do not know when she became a compulsive drinker. Some friends said she drank too much before the war. It was not hard to do in the world she lived in and certainly my father gave her reason. Others disagreed: of course she lived among people who drank a lot, but she never did, and at the most got tipsy in a mild and giggling way. I discovered she was drinking heavily when I came home on a weekend's leave from national service in the Navy and she was lying on the kitchen floor among the ruins of one of her bacon and lentil pies. She must have dropped the dish as she was putting it in the oven for our lunch, and collapsed on top of it. Olof, it turned out, had left and gone to London.

Soon after that they sold the house in Medmenham and moved to London, where Olof hoped to find someone to treat her, though she still did not accept anything was wrong. She drank, of course; there was no secret that she drank. Olof often brought home wine from his office, but they were expensive bottles he wanted to sample and drink sparingly. There was usually a wooden keg of the local brewer's beer in the kitchen at Medmenham and my mother often had a goblet of it by her side. She would not admit, though, that she drank too much. If she collapsed, it was because she was tired. If she refused to go out, it was because there was too much to do in the house.

There was little public discussion of alcoholism forty years ago and 'alcoholic' was more often a term of abuse than a clinical diagnosis. Trapped between the polite, intolerant world she believed she ought to inhabit and the nothingness into which she felt herself vanishing, how could my mother say she was alcoholic? After many battles Olof did persuade her to see a leading specialist in addiction. My mother withstood the attacks of this forceful woman until one dreadful afternoon she brought together Olof, myself, my brother and my mother's sister to plead with her to start a course of treatment. The specialist, dressed in her usual stern suit, chain-smoked cigarettes through a holder while we shouted at my mother and even cried, and she stared at us like an animal who knows it is trapped but will still not let itself be broken.

She agreed in the end, but no amount of explaining convinced her that her alcoholism was no fault of hers, just an illness triggered by a faulty metabolism that locked her in addiction. She was too obstinately conventional to let anyone absolve her from the shame of drinking, and I wonder now if she clung to her shame because it was a last piece of the identity she knew she was losing. She could not stop drinking, but at least she could hate herself for it. And what was left to her if she did, by some miracle, stop? We did not ask that question because the advantages of her stopping were so obvious from our point of view, but they were not obvious to her. Olof could do nothing for her. Her sons were grown up. And my father was by then just the ghost of a memory, less a continuing cause of pain than part of the void into which she was being drawn. She was treated with drugs and electric shock therapy, started drinking again, and had more treatment. She came to like her specialist, who was gentler than her appearance suggested, and even to depend on her, but it was not enough to stop her drinking. Aversion therapy put her off gin and the next time she turned to whisky. Olof could take no more, and they were divorced. I was angry with him, but it was chiefly because I did not know what to do, and I was scared.

She moved into a block of flats off the Earls Court Road, where she could be an anonymous middle-aged woman who smiled charmingly at anyone who met her in the corridor and was always polite but made no friends. She still had furniture and pictures from her marriage with my father and the sofa and chairs with Jazz Age patterns I remembered from visits to the drawing-room in Wellington Square, but in spite of them the flat was as dead as a demonstration room in a furniture store. In her sober months the bed looked so smooth and the kitchen so clean that no one seemed to live there; when she was drinking the rooms appeared abandoned, the ashtrays full of Players' butts and every space in the kitchen covered by dirty pots and plates. She bought her drink in half-bottles, partly because money was scarce but also, I guess, because she was ashamed to ask the off-licences for larger amounts. I suppose she called at several shops and collected a discreet half-bottle from each. Perhaps at first they did not notice anything unusual about her: she was thin from not eating enough, but she always had the pretty smile and her clothes though old-fashioned were still neat. That is the most painful thing to imagine, the middle-aged woman who dressed so carefully even when she was unsteady on her feet, checking and re-checking in the mirror the hood of the plastic mac she wore when it rained, and if on her way out she met a neighbour, smiling as she once smiled at acquaintances at a pre-war party, and all the time determined to buy her drink even if everyone saw through her pretence.

When she got the bottles home she hid them under the cushions of the sofa, among her clothes in drawers and at the backs of cupboards. They were never hard to find for there are not many secret places in a small modern flat, but she was hiding evidence from herself as much as others. We cleared the bottles out each time she became so ill that she agreed to go for treatment, but when it was over she went back to an empty flat and there was still nothing to fill her life. She had no close women friends; it was Olof's friends who had come to Medmenham. Very occasionally she saw one of the men she knew before she married my father. There was my godfather, a thoughtful American who somehow found her when he came to London and worried about her, but was baffled by her reticence. She scarcely saw her brother or sister any more, and she hated the Sundays that I took her to have lunch with her mother. The old woman, a widow now, would be waiting at a window of her flat and smiled like a child at Christmas when she saw us coming. The smile was chiefly for me, whom she spoilt. She treated her daughter like a schoolgirl she could not understand but hoped was only going through a difficult stage. She did not know how to comfort her; my mother did not expect it from her, and perhaps never had. She would be bright, as though nothing was wrong, but snapped at the old woman if she pressed her too hard.

At the time I thought those Sunday lunches might be good for her. Now I imagine the first thing she did when I returned her to her flat was to look for one of the hidden bottles. She no longer belonged in ordinary life and her brief re-entries into it were painful, forcing her to look at the world she had left long ago. I was working in Moscow when my brother married and was so wrapped up in my new life that, foolishly, I did not go back to London for the wedding. He sent me the photographs. The one that caught my eye showed the bride and groom with her mother and sister on their left, and my mother and father, taut as soldiers on parade, on their right. I thought how strange to see them together – they had not met for almost fifteen years – and put the photograph away. I shudder when I look at it now. My father, elegant as ever in a tailcoat, is almost scowling. My mother manages a smile, though it takes only a little imagination to see it as a wince of pain. She has aged less than my father, and is still slim and very pretty, but her clothes give her away, for she might have worn the elbow-length gloves and the silk dress that shows off her neat waist at any wedding in the 1930s. Someone was sent to make sure she got to the church, but there was no one to go home with her after the reception, and when my aunt went to see her the next day she did not want to let her in because she was already drunk.

Olof was not rich and her alimony was small. My brother and I helped a little, but she had barely enough money to live on and needed more whenever she was drinking. She moved to a cheaper flat, sold what pictures and furniture she could to local antique dealers, and looked for a job. She worked in a tobacconist's shop and for a time in Harrods' telephone order department, where her show of cheerful politeness must have pleased the customers. I cannot remember ever eating with her in her flat. I took her out to restaurants, where she drank tonic water and asked me the sort of questions mothers ask their children about their newly independent lives, and to which the children give canny answers. But the questions came from far away, like someone asking about a country they lived in once and perhaps loved but will never return to. They were painfully formal, those meals we ate together, and if she did sometimes talk about her past it was with the gaiety of a bad actress. She never talked to me about my father, nor criticised Olof for leaving her. We had our rows in her flat, pointless battles about her drinking in which we shouted at each other and said things we did not know if we meant or not. Once I told her she was spoilt. 'Have you ever done anything in your life that you didn't want to?' 'Have you?' she shouted back. I felt sorry for her, sometimes hated her; and never knew what to do for her.

One day she told me she had a boyfriend. She had met him in a pub near Knightsbridge Barracks, where he was stationed with the Household Cavalry. She said she wanted me to meet him. Perhaps it was a last attempt to break out of the loneliness, for what else can have given her the determination to go into a pub and talk to a younger man she had not seen before, but I did not meet him and she never mentioned him again.

At the end of a long spell of drinking she was sent to a convent just outside London, where the nuns specialised in the treatment of addiction. The Mother Superior was as powerful a woman as Olof's specialist. She called my mother Elizabeth and in her presence my mother became a schoolgirl eager to please a teacher she held in awe. For a while she seemed to find something like happiness in the convent, but when she left she could not hold on to it for long. She had to return there, and this time found herself with a new sort of patient, drug addicts, many of them rough young women of a kind she had not met before, and she hated the idea that people might think she was like them.

My brother took her back to the nuns at the beginning of 1968. The night she arrived she fell into a coma, and died the next day.

At the cremation what was left of her family sang the twenty-third psalm and 'For all the saints who from their labours rest'. The hymn suited better than the psalm. No shepherd had come to bring her lasting comfort but, as an innocent victim of her times, there was surely something worthy of the saints in such helplessness and solitary suffering. Her former husbands sent flowers and so did just one of the friends she knew before the war. My brother and his eldest son attended a requiem mass for her in the convent, the only place in her last years where she had known peace, and her nine-year-old grandson carried her ashes to be buried among the rose bushes of the nuns' Garden of Calvary.

A few years ago my brother and I went back to look at the place, but the nuns were gone and the corridors and grounds were busy with the healthy American-looking students of an international school. We found no trace of the Garden of Calvary nor of the ashes of my mother and the other women buried there. Her name is engraved, though, on the side of her father and mother's tomb in Putney cemetery. She is remembered there as Elizabeth Wijk. Eve Frankland had vanished many years before.

Chapter VII

America! America!

This country agrees with me very much.
Lieutenant-Colonel Cecil Bisshopp, Lake Ontario, 1813

Washington, 1975

As the plane landed at Dulles Airport on a fine autumn afternoon I thought it would be better to be anywhere than back in America. The *Observer* had asked me to go to Washington for them after the fall of Saigon. It was not a job a journalist could refuse, but my uneasiness grew as the moment of departure to America approached, and on the plane it turned into an almost physical sense of nausea. The trouble was Vietnam, not the fact that the Americans fought the war there, but the way they fought it. There were already signs of what the Communists had in store for Indo-China when I left in the summer of 1975: it was plain something terrible was taking shape in Cambodia, and that narrow-minded Marxist-Leninists had taken over South Vietnam, and yet I still could not forget the way the Americans had fought.

It turned the stomach to watch the superbly equipped armed forces of a rich and powerful country wage war against an opponent strong only in the number and determination of its troops and the readiness of its leaders to sacrifice them. When Communist soldiers were caught in a raid by B52 bombers and crawled out of their bunkers with blood streaming from their ears the best they could hope for was that an American would spot them and call in a napalm strike to put them out of their misery. By contrast helicopters lifted wounded GIs from a battlefield almost as quickly as a London ambulance answers an emergency call. General William Westmoreland, the American commander at the time of the Tet Offensive, wore a film-star smile and beautifully ironed battle fatigues and left the impression war was hygienic, almost good for you. Yet when his strategy failed the Americans forced their Vietnamese allies to accept a bogus peace plan and, after that plan collapsed, as it was bound to, abandoned them in a panic to save themselves.

Dulles is as pleasant as an airport can be, but as I waited for my luggage I would have swapped it even for Saigon's slow and sweaty Tan Son Nhut. When I got outside I decided to put off my contact with America for as long as possible and picked a taxi driver who looked obviously un-American. He turned out to be a Turk. He had American and Turkish degrees in forestry, he told me when we got on to the freeway, but the import–export business he had started never got off the ground. I was expecting to hear a tale of trouble, but he turned round and smiled at me. 'It's incredible. This is the only country in the world where you can make a decent living driving a cab.'

And then I remembered. America excited him. He was discovering he could do all sorts of things here that were impossible at home, as I had discovered with the same excitement eighteen years earlier. Several of my friends at Cambridge had applied for scholarships to do a graduate year at American universities and there was one day when I knew beyond doubt that I wanted to go there too. I was walking through Trinity College and saw a picture of a young man pinned up outside the hall. It was torn from a *Life* magazine story on Elvis Presley and though I never found out who put it there, or why, I understood it as a freedom manifesto. I did not know much about Presley and had heard only a few of his songs, but I was sure I understood what the image meant: energy, classlessness, and the chance to make what you wanted from your life.

The desire to go to America became so powerful and so incoherent that on the night before we were to sail on the *Mauritania* I went to Piccadilly Circus with Peter Jenkins, a close Cambridge friend, to soak up the dreariness of late-night London and anticipate the revolutionary world of music, movement and sophisticated bars that afternoons watching B movies in Cambridge cinemas had taught us to expect in New York. Piccadilly did not let us down. The pubs and cafés were shut and there was not a trace of the big city glamour we longed for, just the tired seediness of streetwalkers and a few frustrated seekers after pleasure. A smell of fried onions led us to Great Windmill Street, where a man was selling what he said were hot dogs. We bought a couple and they were foul, which delighted us, for the point was to remember them unfavourably when we ate the genuine article in America.

Cunarders arrived at New York before dawn, perfect timing for those who wanted their first sight of America to be as dramatic as their expectations. We were on deck, of course, watching amazed as thousands had before us as night faded and the red light high above the city we thought was an aeroplane was revealed as the top of the Empire State Building. That first day I bought the Zippo lighter that later brought shouts of approval from Alek and his Moscow friends, and Peter and I went to Harlem, where no one seemed surprised to see two young white men wandering round the streets. We sat in a bar drinking beer and listening to Dinah Washington on the jukebox and the man at the next bar stool grinned and murmured, 'Bless her little black ass.' The next day we ate our first true hot dogs and found a café that sold a 'Hamburger with a College Education'.

We were not so ignorant as to think New York was America. American friends at Cambridge, mostly sophisticated graduates from Harvard, had tried to lower our expectations of a country apparently happy to be governed by the elderly and golf-crazed President Eisenhower. We had heard of *The Lonely Crowd*, the book by the sociologist David Riesman which sought to explain the conformism of 1950s America. I was going to Brown, an Ivy League college in Providence, Rhode Island, where if my Harvard friends were correct undergraduates never deviated from the norm and if I wished to be accepted I would have to wear the same khaki pants and crew-neck sweaters they wore and also get my hair cut. A Brown student, they said, was the epitome of Riesman's 'other-directed man', a creature who reflected his surroundings as accurately as a chameleon, except that in this case the surroundings and the adaptation were constant. And they were right. I enrolled in a political science class and when the professor asked the few dozen students (all in khakis and crew-neck sweaters) how many would vote differently from their parents just two people in the room held up their hands, the professor and myself.

Peter went to the University of Madison in Wisconsin, but stopped off long enough in Chicago to experience another rush of excitement at being in an America that lived up to its B movies.

> I saw Skid Row and went to a real honky-tonk bar . . . Skid Row is horrible. Everything about it is much worse than New York's Bowery. I walked around all by myself looking rather conspicuous in a suit, not a policeman in sight, there were people fighting on the sidewalk, drunks galore, men without legs on home-made trolleys and rows and rows of bums just sitting or standing and waiting. The honky-tonk had a revolving platform behind the bar with a jazz group playing (and this was in the afternoon) and you can sit there with a 15 cent beer. I met a cattle man from Texas in a *ten* gallon hat who told me he was a cattle man from Texas. His pockets were full of 100 dollar bills and so probably was his hat.

At Madison he also came across the autobiography of the turn-of-the-century muck-raking journalist Lincoln Steffens, who exposed some of the greatest scandals of his day and exactly fitted Peter's idea of what a radical reporter should be. 'If this book doesn't make you want to be a journalist,' he wrote to me, 'nothing will.' He already knew that was what he wanted to be, but the Middle West in the conservative 1950s was not a comfortable place for a would-be Lincoln Steffens and he soon ran into trouble. He discovered Madison had a Professor Perlman who was the doyen of American labour studies. It seemed to be just what he was looking for and he decided, he told me, to 'sit at Perlman's feet'. After less than a month in this uncharacteristic position he announced he had 'rumbled' his professor as 'the prize scab of the American labour movement'. This venerable Russian-Jewish émigré had begun life as a Menshevik in pre-Revolutionary Russia but was so changed by coming to America that he gave up Marxism for a theory of his own. In Peter's scornful summary this amounted to the proposition that 'it was not sad but good that labour should turn from socialism and sign a pact with capitalism against the cataclysmic revolutionary tendencies of theoreticians'. Perlman, in other words, had given up hope of revolution and even dramatic change in favour of democratic gradualism.

Many years later, when Peter had become Britain's best political columnist and re-thought his own socialism, he would have been kinder to his old Wisconsin professor. At the time, though, he felt he had discovered a terrible truth:

> I tell you all this about Perlman because I have found it very revealing about America. After all, take such unpromising material as a Russian-Jewish-Menshevik with a good Marxian education and compare it with the finished product and you see something of the power of America in forming American minds. For a man of European origin, speaking four or five languages and considerably travelled during his time in America his extraordinary misunderstanding of the wide world again suggests how America triumphs over mind.

America shocked me, too, but in a different way. Brown had a reputation as a last resort for students who failed to get into Harvard, Yale and Princeton. When I told a Harvard friend I was going there he laughed and said I should not expect too much from 'the Selwyn College of the Ivy League' (Selwyn was unkindly thought to be the dimmest place in Cambridge, perhaps because so many of its undergraduates disappeared into the Church of England), but Brown was not like that at all and I very quickly had to swallow my Cambridge pride. Undergraduates might look as though they had come off a production line and the graduate students, making their ascent from master's degree to final doctorate, certainly led dour lives. Brown's historians, though, were often livelier and more original than my British teachers, and well ahead of them in new areas such as the history of science and in their use of sociology and political science, which Cambridge still did not accept as proper academic disciplines.

Two men in particular caught my attention, not because they were the most brilliant, but because they conveyed the contradictions of a country that was beginning to fascinate me. I became interested in the professor of Russian and Soviet history because of his subject, which scarcely featured in the Cambridge history tripos, but later it was his manner that intrigued me, for he was as nervous as an animal that has been badly frightened or mistreated. One day he took me to his room in the faculty building and talked about what it was like being a teacher of Soviet history during Senator Joseph McCarthy's witch hunt after Communists. One Communist in the faculty of just one American university, McCarthy used to say, was one Communist too many. The Senator had destroyed himself by his own excesses before I got to America, but my professor was still too scared to more than hint at what he had been through at his followers' hands. After that allusive conversation I did not smile so much at the identical appearance of the students; it was perhaps a sensible insurance in a country that took such fright at nonconformity.

There was another teacher of a very different kind, an elderly but still forceful pupil of Frederick Jackson Turner, the historian of the frontier and its impact on American life and character. He gave a course on American economic history from colonial times to the twentieth century, insisting austerely on the facts but with an epic sweep that made it easy to understand how Peter's Professor Perlman lost his Marxist footing in America and learned to live with capitalism. While Europeans devised political theories that imprisoned their adepts, frontier America gave people the chance to breakout to somewhere that might be better, happier and more free. The frontier dissolved ideologies, and even when it reached its western limits left a tradition of mobility you could feel every time you got on a silver Greyhound bus and you knew you could drive for days and nights and get off in a small town or big city and start your life over.

Peter, immune to the romance of Frederick Jackson Turner, suggested we make a trip to Detroit, where there was heavy unemployment and he hoped to find proof that the heart of America's Left was still beating. He worked out an educative and economical programme. We would stay for free with members of the United Automobile Workers Union, visit the Chrysler plant and, 'more important', meet labour leaders. In the end he went to Detroit on his own, was appalled by the breadlines on the streets and saw the Ford assembly line that produced a new car every fifty seconds. He also found, he reported happily, some tough union members, but I suspected they were not the least like European workers trapped in communities they never dreamed of leaving. If the hardships of life made Detroit a prison for some American workers it was a prison with the door wide open, and in years to come many would leave it, to be replaced by others who had their own reasons for seeing it as a place of opportunity.

When Peter first got to Madison he told himself the university's isolation made him 'feel like the Bolsheviks must have felt in Siberia – a good opportunity to brush up one's Marx,' but he soon began to complain that 'nothing much actually *happens* here'. Even a long motor trip with friends proved disappointing. 'After the tiring business of looking at rolling plains, rock formations and the Mississippi we had visions of some lively drinking,' but they ended up in Dubuque, where they were so bored they went to see *I was a Teenage Werewolf* ('excellent, but needs to be seen in the afternoon'). Back in Madison the next day he felt he had been on a three-week trek. Like many left-wing Europeans he was finding it hard to accept that a country so poor in social democratic spirit should claim to lead the Western world. What right had Eisenhower and his hated Secretary of State John Foster Dulles to lecture the rest of the world? 'I don't mind the violence, the sordidness, the philistinism, the fetishism, the materialism and the ugliness of the American way of life (especially in the cinema), it's the idealism which is so revolting.'

A friend who was back in Harvard after a year in England saw things from the American point of view. Like many of his fellow country people he treated technology as a modern equivalent of the frontier, opening new territory into which one could advance endlessly, and he was delighted by the changes that had taken place while he was away. 'Aren't Super Markets [*sic*] splendid? Cellophane means far more to us all than even Mr Dulles.' I was also starting to see America differently, but for reasons I never anticipated. One of my father's closest friends was an American called Sammy whom he met at Cambridge. I had never seen him, but I knew his name well because during the war he and his wife sent us food parcels with whole tinned hams and canned butter that tasted of salt cheese. I had only been at Brown a month when Sammy invited me to Thanksgiving lunch with his mother, who lived conveniently close to Providence in the seaside town of Newport. The large and friendly man who met me at the Newport bus station suggested we go for a drink. His mother, he explained, did not approve of drinking before meals and any guest who wanted liquor then had to down it quickly in an ante-room before entering her presence. He took me to a genteel bar, where we talked to two retired admirals in tweed jackets and Sammy kept looking at his watch, for his mother apparently disliked unpunctuality as much as cocktails. We drove up to what looked like a copy of a grand Elizabethan country house. A butler opened the front door and gestured to a table of drinks set in an alcove, but we hurried virtuously on into a large room, where some twenty people were standing and talking and there was not a single glass in anyone's hand.

Mama was small and straight-backed and had a tiny waist and perfectly arranged blue-grey hair. She was very pleasant to me, but it was plain why her son did not care to break her rules. I cannot remember if we ate off silver but I know she was proud that she could have thirty people to dinner and not use the same plate twice. I do remember the huge roast turkeys which were carved and re-assembled before they were offered to the guests as apparently whole birds by brawny footmen. The house was built by Sammy's grandfather and furnished by him with European treasures. The handsome room we ate our turkey in came from an old house in Bruges. There was a Robert Adam room, the first to be taken entire to America, and the den was made from the dining-room of the Prince Regent's wife, Maria Fitzherbert. Sammy was an uncommonly kind man, and perhaps he did not warn me about his mother for fear of scaring me. The *New York Times* called her 'the dowager empress of American society' and certainly only the brave, the stupid, or someone equally grand like Mrs Cornelius Vanderbilt dared challenge her to her face. Mrs Vanderbilt, a Newport neighbour, was chronically unpunctual. Mama's dinners always started on time and she had the front door locked when her guests sat down to eat. Mrs Vanderbilt would have to ring the bell to get in, but to show she did not care then taunted Sammy's mother by processing slowly round the table and chatting with other guests before she took her place.

I saw more of Sammy's world after Thanksgiving. He had a house outside Philadelphia, where every year there was an Assembly Ball, for which the men wore white tie and tails and only the old families, the so-called Main Liners, were invited. Main Liners took discreet pride in excluding Grace Kelly from their ball, for although she was a Hollywood star and married to a European prince, her father was only a self-made Philadelphian millionaire. I would have hated it in Britain, but in America it did not seem to matter. Americans were more amused than angered by the behaviour of the upper-class communities that still flourished in a dozen old American cities which published a *Social Register* listing the local patricians. They were just one more enclave in a country where many groups and regions competed for the national attention, and most of them much more noisily than this tiny clan of some forty thousand families for whom discretion was a cardinal virtue. When Sammy was a child before the First World War, his family lived in New York and each year had a private railroad car to take them from Grand Central Station to Newport for their summer holidays. His mother believed they would pick up germs if they travelled in an ordinary train, but there was something significant in this keenness to live apart from the rest of a nation that had no tradition of deference. Even the sports that Sammy's world enjoyed were obscure to most Americans. When he was younger he went fox-hunting, played polo and occasionally cricket, but his passion was real tennis, a game scarcely known any more even in Britain and France, whose kings once played it. There were only a handful of American real tennis courts (they were expensive to build, and mostly privately owned), the game's rules were complex and hard for an outsider to grasp, and it was unexciting to watch. It was hard to think of a better metaphor for the community that played it.

Sammy enjoyed his life and was generous in sharing it with others, but he did not expect undue respect and knew his birth did not guarantee him a place in the national hierarchy of fame. America's history and founding principles made sure of that, and so did its populism and fascination with passing celebrities who were the people's temporarily appointed aristocrats. And that was the chief reason why America delighted me. It freed me from the British background I wanted to disown. I had understood the restrictions of the British class system long before I met the radicalism of Harry Iredale. Once when I was six or seven my mother dressed me up for some occasion and I passed some village children on the street and we stopped and looked at each other. I could not guess what they thought, but I knew there was a wall between us, and could see no way to pass through it. There was no wall in America, or if there was it had plenty of gaps and doors to pass through, and I was so enchanted by my sense of liberation that I began to think of staying there for good.

Peter was horrified. His Middle Western boredom was turning into disillusion with all America and he decided even New York was phony because it was so un-American. He was already imagining the life we would lead back in London, there would be Sundays with beer in the morning and movies in the afternoon but above all there would be all our

> *friends again!* I have an idyllic vision of English life, a little misty after all these months, as one long Fabian weekend. I am sure we will soon be visiting eminent economists at thatched cottages where we shall play croquet with long discussions at each hoop . . . And I shall make lots of friends from Bermondsey Labour Party which will help keep your family away if that's what you want.

I did go home, but not till after the summer when I made a trip with Peter to the South. If we had been rich we would have gone to the West Coast, but money was short and the South was just within range of the old Hillman Minx I had been lent by my godfather, the thoughtful American who unexpectedly called on my mother in her last lonely years. It was a close thing. The car overheated on hills and would have died climbing up the Appalachians if we had not revived it by pouring cold water over its engine, and it was so slow on the flat that motorway police stopped us for not driving fast enough.

Peter's idea was to save money by sleeping in the car, which we sometimes did. He also suggested, apparently seriously, that we might make money by picking cotton which, unsurprisingly, we did not. Of course we knew about segregation, and had seen some of the forms it took in the North. Not long after I arrived at Brown I went with another British student to a concert in Providence given by the black jazz musician Lionel Hampton. It was in a cinema and when we got to our seats at the front of the balcony we were surprised to see nothing but black faces. The people in the neighbouring seats were just as surprised by us, though friendly enough when we told them we were British. It was self-regulating segregation, but still shocking in a state like Rhode Island, whose founder, Roger Williams, was the first colonial American leader to treat Indians as equals.

The South taught a harsher lesson. Peter had made friends with one of Madison's black graduate students. He lived in New Orleans and we rang him as soon as we got there. He said he would see us the next morning, but since he could not come into our boarding house we would have to meet on the street outside. It was only then we realised there might be nowhere in New Orleans where two whites and a black could drink or eat together. Nowhere? Peter's friend admitted he knew a sort of restaurant, but it was outside the city and he wasn't sure we would like it. It was plain he did not want to take us there, but we thought anything was better than spending a day on the hot city streets. The place turned out to be a big wooden shack, two storeys tall, on the edge of a swamp. There were tables and a rough bar and a handful of black men and women who were moving about slowly as though they had just got out of bed, which they probably had, for we were in a brothel. No one looked surprised to see us or objected when we ordered beer and fried chicken. Peter's friend began to cheer up, and laughed when a thin black boy came over to our table, opened his eyes wide and announced hopefully, 'Ah's entertains men.' Encouraged by our success in the whorehouse, we drove back to the city to look for a black bar that might bend the rules and let us in (we did not bother trying the white ones). After several failures we found one whose customers were professional people, mostly lawyers and doctors, and we waited outside while they held a conference. They let us in, but it was scarcely a victory for desegregation. They accepted us, they explained when we had ordered our beers, because Peter and I were foreigners, and in their eyes had nothing to do with white America.

'When you ring up a friend these days', the wife of the retired State Department official complained, 'you always find some Latino answering the phone, and they don't speak a word of English. The blacks think domestic work isn't good enough for them any more, so everyone is bringing in Latinos.'

   Eighteen years after Peter and I were in New Orleans white Washington was in two minds about the improvement in the condition of America's black population. Two of my and Peter's early heroes were Stewart and Joseph Alsop, the columnists whose book *The Reporter's Trade* we read while we were in America. Stewart

Alsop died early, but Joe had become a powerful though sometimes unintentionally comical voice of doom, using his column to warn that feckless American administrations were leading the world towards disaster. He too was worried about the blacks, and it was the first thing he talked about when I went to his house in Georgetown for drinks (giant goblets of Scotch on the rocks) shortly after Jimmy Carter's election as president in 1976. Of course he was against segregation, Alsop said, any decent man would be, but he did not like what was replacing it. Whites were fleeing to the suburbs and leaving the cities to become impoverished black ghettos. Where was the good in that? What bothered him most, though, was Carter's appointment of the black Congressman Andrew Young as America's ambassador to the United Nations. He knew Andrew Young (Alsop knew pretty well everyone in or close to power) and he was one of the best of the black politicians, but that did not make him suitable for a key foreign policy job. Young had just proved that by publicly disagreeing with some of the new administration's policies, and yet Carter's hands were tied. If he sacked Young for insubordination, as he ought to do, he would be accused of being anti-black; if he did nothing he would seem weak. Alsop wore circular horn-rimmed glasses that gave him an owlish look and he leant forward, as though tracking a rodent before the kill. 'If you're going to put a coon in a top job, then you must pick one you understand.'

Joe Alsop lived in a frightening world. He believed two-thirds of Africa had fallen under Soviet influence, and that the Russians were now advancing deeper into the Caribbean as well as controlling the re-united Vietnam. The Chinese had given him this last piece of intelligence when he was in Peking. They also told him he thought like a Chinese. That pleased him, and for a moment the owl became a far-sighted mandarin, though still a worried one, for what use was the wisest mandarin when the emperor ignored his wisdom?

He thought Carter did not understand the rules of the Cold War, which had dominated most of Alsop's adult life and had ensured the continued prominence of his fellow WASPs – White Anglo-Saxon Protestants – in American affairs. The world, and especially Europe, the crux of the Soviet-American rivalry, were passions of the WASPS, who deplored the insularity of their fellow Americans, and over generations they had tried to keep America in touch with the culture from which it sprang. Sammy's grandfather, who built the Elizabethan mansion in Newport where I went for Thanksgiving lunch, was an early example of patrician America's romance with Europe. He owned an estate in Northamptonshire and a house in Cannes, hunted in England and fished in Scotland. A connoisseur, he collected Dutch paintings and English silver, and went cruising in the Mediterranean with the novelist Edith Wharton. Queen Victoria gave him an honorary knighthood for equipping and commanding a field hospital for British soldiers in the Boer War. He would have been American ambassador to Rome if an American newspaper had not pilloried him for being rude to one of its journalists.

It was said that the descendants of the Bostonians who led America's fight for independence still 'knelt in self-abasement' before British standards long into the nineteenth century, but that no longer fitted Americans like Sammy's grandfather. They were rich and clever enough to acquire some of Europe's best art and most desirable women, and to match its aristocrats in elegance and sporting skill. Europe also offered them an escape from American egalitarianism, and Sammy's grandfather moved to Britain for good after Prohibition, which, he said, made America unfit for gentlemen to live in. His funeral was held at St James's, Piccadilly, just opposite the disreputable Cavendish Hotel, where he stayed when he was in London. His family kept his death out of the newspapers until the funeral was over, fearing that if the hotel's owner Rosa Lewis heard about it she and all her ladies would appear at the service.

His son, Sammy's father, was brought up to be an Englishman, though of a decidedly European sort for he spoke perfect German and French as well as English (rather than American). When the First World War began he gave an ambulance to France and after America's late entry into the conflict became interpreter for President Wilson's key adviser Colonel House, a fine example of a

WASP fulfilling the role of Europe's advocate at the old continent's hour of need. My godfather Billy's family was another example of the transformation of East Coast patricians from mimickers of Europe into its patrons and protectors. Well-off American families often set up charitable foundations to support good causes and Billy's had the peculiarly WASPish purpose of encouraging the teaching of international affairs in schools. I wondered if this was expiation for the family's black sheep, Congressman Hamilton Fish, who opposed America's entry into the Second World War and conducted a brutal, lifelong vendetta against President Franklin Roosevelt, with whom he shared the same New York background. The controversial Congressman so upset his sister, Billy's mother, that she broke off all relations and still refused to speak to him when she was dying.

The Cold War concentrated American minds on what was seen as a Soviet threat to Europe, especially that part of it known and admired by WASPS, who for this reason seemed well-qualified for a special role in the conduct of America's foreign affairs. A Washington hostess remembered the early post-war years of the Central Intelligence Agency (which grew out of the wartime and WASPish Office of Strategic Services in which Sammy served) as 'just like a gentlemen's club'. And some of the gentlemen were still around, for example in the Alibi Club, which occupied a small red-brick house next to a cheap hotel and a garage on an undistinguished street not far from the White House. The Alibi was run by an admiral who had served heroically in the Second World War. It had some fifty well-off members, most with connections to power, among them a Supreme Court judge, the director of a White House intelligence committee and a senior official in the State Department.

Inside the club looked like London's Fitzroy Tavern in the days when Bohemians still drank there. Crammed with plain wooden furniture, the walls and ceilings were hung with curious objects, weapons and pots and pans and Toby jugs with the faces of Roosevelt and Churchill and other wartime characters. There were slightly risqué oddities like the piece of pottery inscribed with 'old golfers never die, they only lose their balls' and mechanical paintings made by the admiral. One was of a black man who, when wound up, opened and shut his eyes and grinned, and there were others from which dancing girls emerged. The day I was taken there for lunch the admiral made a punch of dark navy rum, hot water and butter, which we drank out of blue and white china mugs. There was no dining-room table. People helped themselves from dishes of corned beef hash, sausages and beans and after that a griddle was brought in and the admiral made pancakes. Conversation was conducted in the customary drawl of well-born Americans and the mood was courteous and jovial, for it did not do to be too serious on social occasions.

By the time of Jimmy Carter's election, however, the Alibi could no longer be considered a secret bunker of patrician power. The first years of the Cold War had given WASPs a purpose, but Washington was more the capital of a truly global power and needed thousands of new experts and officials, not to speak of a chorus of journalists and academics to comment on their work. The city had become a paradise for anyone from any background with an addiction to power. You did not need to be very important to get a kick from this new Washington. The most junior members of the White House staff might talk of going on their first presidential trip and seeing the White House tags on their luggage for the first time as though it was the night they lost their virginity. Even the assistants needed by senators and congressman to help them with their new world-wide responsibilities felt they were deciding the fate of nations. What could be done to help poor countries threatened by the rise in oil prices? For some of them – nothing, a young senatorial assistant said. India and Bangladesh would have to 'go down the tubes'. 'You mean let them starve?' his wife asked. He nodded, already quite comfortable with the ruthlessness of power.

It was tough to live in this Washington if you did not give off the scent of power. The wife of a lawyer who dabbled in politics grew so fed up at being ignored at dinner parties because she was just a wife that she began introducing herself as the Under-Secretary for Climate Control. People were scared to say they had not heard of her job, and so they talked to her and listened too. In the new Washington an Under-Secretary no one had heard of was quite as attractive as any Mrs Vanderbilt.

Jimmy Carter, though white and a devout Protestant, turned out to be an uncomfortable president for those members of the old elite who still pursued Washington careers. He knew little about the wider world beyond America. Joe Alsop said Carter was *borné*, the choice of a French word and the lift of an eyebrow signalling the chasm that separated the former governor of Georgia from true men of experience. Carter was also a compulsive populist, the word 'people' cropping up as often in his speeches as in Tony Blair's twenty years later. His standard election speech included a passage about America needing a government as good, and kind, and simple as the American people themselves. Carter spoke these words slowly, with the sentimental smile of a schoolteacher wooing his pupils with flattery. He knew many ways to please 'the people', saving money while campaigning by staying at the houses of Democrat supporters and astonishing his hosts by folding and hanging up his towels in the bathroom and making his own bed. He spoke of Washington as though it was an alien growth on the good and kind American people, and promised to conquer the wicked capital and bring 'the people' into government, a pledge that particularly displeased a well-known Washington party giver. What, she asked, did this obscure Southern politician mean by 'bringing the people' into government? She entertained governments, or those members of them who in her eyes counted for something, but she neither could nor would invite 'the people' into her house.

Carter's populism was calculating as well as naïve, and some thought it a useful way to restore people's faith in politics after Watergate and the shaming of Richard Nixon. My godfather Billy and his wife thought so, and cried when Carter stopped his car after his inauguration on Capitol Hill and walked back to the White House down Pennsylvania Avenue with his wife and daughter, something no newly installed president had done before. Herblock's cartoon in the next day's *Washington Post* showed the presidential family disappearing into a White House at whose gate was the sort of post-box every suburban American home has and written on it simply was 'the Carters'. When Carter said he wanted his inaugural gala to be a tribute to Main Street America, the stars of Hollywood obliged: even Bette Davis was sufficiently swept away by the excitement to predict an America 'up to its brawny shoulders in new hopes'.

Much of it was nonsense, the sort of agreeable lightness that comes on people at Christmas and is gone by New Year but which also affects Americans at the start of each new presidency. There was nevertheless something substantial at the core. During the celebrations of America's bicentenary in 1976 I chanced upon a schoolhouse in a town in the Virginia hills where a young actor was reading from the writings of Thomas Jefferson. He had a striking natural resemblance to the author of the Declaration of Independence, but it was not as striking as the relevance of the Jeffersonian words he was reciting. The first time I went to the Lincoln Memorial in Washington a girl was reading aloud to two other teenagers Abraham Lincoln's Gettysburg Address, which is engraved on the monument's walls. When she reached the passage about a nation 'conceived in liberty and dedicated to the proposition that all men are created equal' a boy broke in. 'But how long have we acted as though we believed that, I mean as though we *really* believed that?' The words on which America's identity rested, not just those that inspired but also the cautious sentences of its constitution makers who knew even Americans were not and never would be angels, were another solvent on any powerful group that imagined itself more than a transient plutocracy.

Small wonder there was an air of siege in some of the grand houses of Washington because so much of both new and old in America conspired to spoil the self-esteem of the people who frequented them. At a dinner in Georgetown a woman raged about Rupert Murdoch. She had just been at a weekend house party held to introduce him to *le tout* Washington, but the Australian, she said, had not 'given' socially at all. It took her breath away. She could not understand how anyone offered an entrée into the capital's old elite could not just blow the chance, but show he did not care that he had blown it.

Murdoch was a disrespectful power from a new world whose outlines would become clearer when the Cold War ended, but he was not alien to the American tradition: forces disruptive of the old order were building up in America too. Young blacks who walked down central Washington streets, where they would have rarely ventured ten years earlier, now drew attention to themselves by the cocky, bouncing way they moved. Blacks called it 'dipping' or 'pimping,' and explained it as bravado to disguise the nervousness they could still feel appearing in places that so recently had belonged to whites. Washington's preoccupation with the Cold War had pushed the blacks to the bottom of the national agenda, but amends were now having to be made. Other groups beside the blacks were intent on changing America's values as well as its balance of power, all of them helped by the disillusion with government that followed the war in Vietnam and the Watergate scandal. Vietnam War protesters and black civil rights demonstrators prepared the way for women, gays, the disabled and other special-interest groups who now found the confidence to challenge the established order. They would be joined by new ethnic groups who continued to believe they would find a better life in America, among them the Latinos, who flowed into many jobs, legal and illegal, beside domestic service with Washington WASPs. Soon, too, there would be several hundred thousand Vietnamese like Mr Loc's son Phuoc, who never doubted for a moment that America was the best country in the world in which to rebuild his shattered family.

On the evening I went to see Joe Alsop, he talked for a long time about Walter Lippmann who until his recent death in 1974 was America's most powerful columnist. Lippmann, he said, made his impact by the lucid way he put into words the thoughts and attitudes of people in what Alsop called the 'procession' of American public life, and in this way helped bring about consensus on America's role in the post-war world. Where was Lippmann's procession now? After

Watergate and Vietnam many questioned the idea of an honourable leadership moving the nation towards a common goal. And there was no longer just one procession. Blacks now had theirs and others were taking shape among other ethnic and rights-conscious groups. None of them wanted to form up meekly behind the old one in Washington, in which WASPs and a handful of patricians were still prominent members.

Competition to make yourself heard was more American than taking a place in a Washington procession that had now begun to falter. 'Ambition must be made to counteract ambition,' James Madison wrote two hundred years earlier, believing conflict was liberty's surest safeguard. It explained the sense of possibility that enchanted me when I came to the country as a student, and why Peter, whose left-wing ideas were more precise than mine, was so often shocked by what he saw. It also explained the discretion of the WASPs I unexpectedly found myself among, for however important their services to their country they knew they had no permanent charter of privilege. In the end I had discovered that the American Dream was as tough as the political ideas of America's Founding Fathers. This toughness suited a country where nature was as often foe as friend, and had a savagery little known in Britain. I often spent weekends at a house on a neck of land stretching out into Chesapeake Bay. A British friend who knew it well said it was 'all that's best in America', but it was not a place to be sentimental. Spring with the elegant flowers of the dogwood was sweet, but summer, while abundant with peaches and subtle varieties of corn, brought a draining, humid heat, a plague of mosquitoes and jellyfish that invaded all the little beaches of the bay. You could cut wild chives, which grew among the grass, but you also had to watch out for poison ivy. The oysters caught by the sailing boats that skimmed the shallow reaches of the bay were large and plump but tasted almost of nothing, and over waters where a man could almost walk a storm might whip up in minutes and drown the careless boatman. Raccoons chewed their way into the roofs of houses and the vultures known as turkey buzzards kept a mortuary watch from the sky.

Each spring and autumn an army of migrating Canada geese stopped on water near the house, and for the several days they rested there they cried like a pack of hounds before the hunt. It was an appropriate sound for a restless country. This part of America had been under cultivation for more than three hundred years and the land around the house I stayed in once belonged to Mathew Tilghman, one of the signers of the Declaration of Independence, but it was still nothing like Britain, where nature had been all but tamed for human convenience. America's war with nature was unending, just as Americans' competition among themselves was always taking on new forms. You could do anything you liked here except stand still, or imagine there were no more battles to be fought. That was why it was so hospitable to newcomers, innovators and the young, in short to anyone without a vested interest in the past. Thinking myself still young, and well rid of my own past, I found the country agreed with me very much.

Chapter VIII

The Watch

Happiness will come from materialism, comrade Voshchev, not from meaning.

Andrei Platonov, *The Foundation Pit*

Moscow, 1983

The man who called my name was wearing a long black leather overcoat and had his arms round the waists of two young women. The three of them were familiar characters in the Moscow of the early 1980s, a pimp and the sort of prostitutes and part-time informers, Russians joked, whose KGB shoulder straps showed through their tarty blouses. I could not place the man until he asked if I remembered Alek and then the close-cropped hair and wary eyes dissolved into the face of a teenage member of the gang I had known twenty years before. Alek, their leader, was the magician who had conjured up a make-believe Western world out of the unpromising streets of Moscow. The man in the leather coat was already pushing the two girls into a lift when I asked where Alek was. He stopped and looked at me. 'Dead,' he said, and flicked a finger against his throat.

Alek had drunk himself to death. Russians were not surprised by such stories, and often had similar ones to tell about their own family and friends. I was already wondering if it had been Yegor's fate. I telephoned him when I returned to the city at the beginning of 1983, but the line to the communal apartment where he had taught me how to drink vodka was out of order. When I went to look for him the crooked wooden house was no longer there, probably pulled down when they made the new wide road that ran through the edge of the Arbat towards the Kremlin. I knew no way to track him down and was not sure I wanted to. Moscow and the life we had known had vanished as surely as his house; if Yegor was alive he would certainly be drunk and we might have nothing to say to each other.

The best way I know to convey the atmosphere of the city I returned to is to tell the story of how a watch came into my possession. There was nothing special about it from a horological point of view. It was the sort of old-fashioned timepiece men once kept in a waistcoat pocket, the chain linked through a buttonhole, with ordinary numerals and a small second hand at the bottom of the face. Nothing could have been more masculine and plain, until you turned it over and saw the back where someone had engraved in sinuous loops the letters R and A.

R was Robert, the watch's owner. He came to Moscow with his wife and children shortly after I arrived there in 1962. We got to know each other, but it was not easy. He was a British Communist journalist, and in those days Moscow's foreign Communists kept their distance from 'bourgeois' correspondents like myself. Robert was polite, but made it plain he did not intend to mix much with his unenlightened British colleagues. He had a long face and a strong nose which, with his habit of brushing his hair in a fringe over his forehead, made him look like one of those pious knights who lie stretched out on old tombs in English churches. To me he seemed shy, but some of the British journalists thought him more aloof than ideological differences justified; it was true that even when he smiled it could seem like a signal from a superior planet.

He intrigued me and I grew to like him, and I think he came to trust me. We did not talk about politics; they apparently did not interest him. I supposed his Communism was about morality, and that he knew politics could only get in the way of that. He did, though, manage to see traces of his ideal in Khrushchev's Russia. One winter day we were driving through Pushkin Square when he pointed at the people on the pavement and asked if I could see how different they were from a London crowd, how dignified and conscious of their own worth. That was what he saw and it was pointless to say I disagreed. The only time I saw him angry was when we were at some meeting and two Soviet officials sitting in front of us began swapping anti-Semitic jokes. Robert lost his temper with them, and his tenor voice took on an edge I had not heard before.

He lived with his family in a flat off the Arbat, scarcely five minutes' walk from Yegor's place. The Soviet elite took over this pleasant part of Moscow from the old aristocracy and living there was a sign of Robert's privileged status. I sometimes went to the flat when I was visiting the city in the 1970s. The hope inspired by Khrushchev's changes had faded and Muscovites' attitude towards their leaders zigzagged between despair and contempt, but I never heard a word of this from Robert. When other people were talking about such things he just sat quietly, giving his distant smile as though none of it concerned him. And then he changed. I noticed it when I was in Moscow one summer at the end of the 1970s. He and his wife asked me round and as I was walking up the stairs to their landing he came down from higher up and we met outside their door. He had been sunbathing on the roof of the apartment block, which astonished me for he was such an unlikely sun-worshipper. He looked stronger and healthier than I had ever seen him. Some time after that he got rid of the fringe and started to brush his hair back from his forehead. The austere knight became a handsome, sensual man.

Robert was in love. Anna, the loved one whose initial was joined with his on the back of the watch, was several years younger. She had a husband, but by the time I went back to live in Moscow their respective divorces had gone through and they were married. I never saw two middle-aged people so obviously devoted. One evening they invited me to a concert. Anna's teenage daughter was with us and it seemed right that I take the seat next to Anna. As I was about to sit down Robert coughed and said he liked to be beside her, and almost as soon as we were seated they were holding hands. That was their habit. Even when they had people round to their flat they sat together holding hands, like youngsters in love for the very first time.

I did not understand why they needed to be so demonstratively protective of each other. It was only later I learned that Anna's friends had warned her against the romance with Robert, predicting it would never be allowed to end in marriage. 'This shouldn't be happening,' one of them kept saying, and though she stuck by Anna loyally she cried tears of anguish, not happiness, when the wedding took place. Another prophet of doom was an older woman who married a French airman during the war and was sent to the Gulag when it was over. The Soviet regime did not like love across Cold War lines and, though a Russian was no longer likely to go to prison for it, a love affair of this sort was seldom trouble-free. One might have thought there could be no objection if the Western partner was, like Robert, a British Communist well known to the all-powerful Soviet Central Committee, but that was not the case. The old men who sat in the Politburo did not care for divorce. Mistresses and Party prostitutes were one thing, but swapping an old wife for a new one caused unwelcome problems. Which wife, the old or the new, should get the special rations and medical treatment and holiday dachas that went with the husband's rank? Stability of marriage was one virtue the Soviet leaders could claim, and even a member of the Politburo might damage his career if he ignored the taboo and took a new wife.

Robert's difficulties with his Soviet comrades were evidently of an even more serious kind, for not long after he decided to start his new life with Anna it became plain someone powerful was harassing them. Anna was sacked from the institute where she worked as an ethnologist. Her ex-husband reported – most likely was encouraged to report – both her and her mother to the KGB as 'anti-Soviet' and also threw in the accusation that Anna speculated in gold and diamonds. Anna and Robert themselves now feared an attempt would be made to stop the wedding, and it may only have been saved by

Robert's heart, which under the strain of events began to give him trouble and needed attention in hospital. Convinced something bad would happen to Anna if he went into hospital before they were married, he persuaded the registry office to advance the date of the wedding on urgent medical grounds. Robert sounded proud when he told me the story. I never imagined him as a conspirator, but that was what he had become.

There were limits to his transformation. Another man in his position would surely have become a dissident. There were many sorts of dissident in Moscow by that time; it was a sign, though few then recognised it, of the regime's terminal decay. Anna herself was what might be called a passive dissident. Like many of her friends she was entirely cynical about the Soviet system, but since she expected it to survive she made the best she could of it. Many Russians lived lives like that, a pungent blend of the sweet and the bitter. Anna grew up in the post-war Arbat and went to school in a cut-down dress of her grandmother's. When ice cream re-appeared on the city's streets after the war she and three friends had to club together to buy a single cone and split it into four. Fifty kopeks earned by selling a kilogram of old gramophone records for scrap paid for a ticket to one of the Deanna Durbin movies that for obscure reasons were thought suitable for Soviet audiences. Her family was cautiously free-thinking. Her father hid himself under an overcoat lined with kangaroo skin to listen to forbidden foreign broadcasts. On Stalin's seventieth birthday they went to see the model of the Palace of Soviets that was to be built near the Moscow river, but Anna was more impressed by a giant picture of Stalin suspended above the crowds from an airship. It floated over their heads just as the man whom even in the secrecy of their home they dared only call 'the cat with whiskers' hung over every moment of their lives.

'Each day is a holiday in the Soviet Union,' said Valya, the friend of Anna's who cried at the wedding, and I was struck by this mixture of amusement and despair with which her circle talked about their lives in what Anna herself called this 'land of wonders and disgrace'. Still none of it seemed to affect Robert. He would listen as usual to the jokes and gossip about the vulgarities and misbehaviour of the powerful and smile his distant smile as though it was no concern of his, but I do not believe anything Anna might have said could shake his love for her. She was certainly good-looking, but she also had a vibrancy and directness that were set off perfectly by his detachment. They were a natural pair, and I think he loved everything about her.

Nevertheless it was odd that a British Communist was so uninterested in the problems of the country he had chosen to make his home in. He never once hinted to me that he knew anything of the anxious discussions about the Soviet future that were then taking place in Communist Parties abroad. The former Foreign Office spy Donald Maclean, a top-to-toe Communist if ever there was one and now a Soviet citizen who insisted on being addressed as Donald Donaldovich, regularly wrote letters for circulation among British Party members, in which he analysed the Soviet decline. He even wrote articles under a pseudonym for *Marxism Today* in which he criticised Moscow's policies.

I had heard that Robert fell out with Maclean in 1968 over the Warsaw Pact invasion of Czechoslovakia. Robert would not protest against it. Maclean did, and only stayed out of trouble because the foreign affairs institute where he worked allowed him to be absent on the day when its members were made to declare support for the Soviet action. In later years Maclean wrote letters to the KGB protesting against their treatment of well-known dissidents such as Zhores Medvedev and Vladimir Bukovsky. And he was so angry when the security service put a woman he knew into a psychiatric hospital that he spoilt his ballot paper in a Supreme Soviet election by writing on it that he would not vote again until she was released. He was as methodical a dissident as he once had been spy, tracking down the unofficial historian Roy Medvedev (the brother of Zhores) to obtain a samizdat copy of his *Let History Judge*, the first Russian account of Stalin's crimes. Later he took part in dissident seminars, and when a man Maclean knew as a Soviet agent in London in the 1930s tried to join them warned that he was probably still working for the KGB.

Robert could have become a dissident without abandoning his ideals. Russian Communists managed it. There were many Party members among the intelligentsia who knew there had to be change, and some of them were ready to risk punishment by debating how to bring it about. Robert inhabited a different world. I thought of him as a transcendental Communist, whose chief care was to keep alive the image of his ideal. Or you could say he was a dreamer who disliked being bothered by the chores of politics, and perhaps the chores of life, too: whatever the drawbacks of living in Moscow, you did not have to bother about pensions and mortgages and all the other tiresome matters that were part of life in the West. Robert gathered his dream around him like a cloak that had to be kept out of the dust. Small wonder he showed no interest in the details of politics, and disliked journalism so much that after a few years he gave up the job he came to Moscow to do and took work as a translator instead.

Nevertheless, living with Anna changed more about him than his appearance. He was more mellow and, when I was with them, much readier to laugh at himself and the world around him. He did not mind when Anna teased him that nothing made him so nervous as encounters with the working class. Confronting the mechanics at the garage was a particular trial for him and a frequent one, for Moscow roads and weather had made an invalid of his old Toyota. The car's advantage was that it still had number plates identifying it as a British correspondent's, and when he drove us one evening to a concert he parked the car on the pavement in front of the Conservatoire's statue of Tchaikovsky. It was illegal, but policemen let foreigners get away with such things. Robert noticed my surprise. 'That's an example of what's called negative behaviour,' he said, and grinned like a man on a diet who has been caught taking a piece of chocolate cake. I think food had something to do with his mellowing. Anna was a good cook and, in the Russian way, a generous one and I learned to brace myself when they asked me to a meal. It was always a feast, starting perhaps with soup accompanied by little pies stuffed with egg and cabbage, and followed by meat pancakes, ice cream and a blackcurrant jelly, a meringue-covered fruit tart and to end with chocolates and Turkish coffee. Guests who stayed late were rewarded with glasses of tea and freshly made cheesecake.

It was hard to grudge them any comfort they could find, for though they proved the doomsayers wrong by managing to get married they soon discovered how vulnerable they still were. Their invisible enemy shifted the battle to the flat in the Arbat where, after his first wife went back to England, Robert planned to start his new life with Anna. The first danger signal came when they moved out of the flat while it was being redecorated only to find someone had sealed the door so they could not get in again. Robert protested and the seals were removed, but once back in the flat they began to get telephone calls from anonymous Central Committee officials advising them to leave. They said that Robert was a foreigner with access to hard currency and should therefore join one of the exclusive new co-operatives where flats could be bought legally for hard currency. Robert had no hope of putting together even a few thousand pounds because the publishing house paid most of his salary in non-convertible roubles and what British assets he possessed had gone under the divorce settlement to his former wife.

There was a weak spot in his defences. He was given the Arbat flat because he was a Communist correspondent. It was a Soviet version of a tied cottage: the building belonged to the Central Committee, which took Party journalists like Robert under its wing. In theory he might have been expected to surrender the flat when he switched jobs and became a translator, a less important occupation that did not call for such a prestigious address. He side-stepped the difficulty by getting a letter from the Central Committee, signed by the Party leader Leonid Brezhnev himself, authorising him to stay in the Arbat in spite of his change of work. It was a useful defence, but not impregnable, for if an authorisation could be given it could also be revoked, and the way in which the warnings were conveyed certainly promised no good. Nothing was put down on paper. Everything was conveyed during telephone conversations in which the nameless voice never said on whose authority it was speaking. This was how the Soviet system dealt with tricky problems. Most organisations had one or two people whose job was to receive and pass on telephone commands from unidentified higher authority, and it was not a good sign that some powerful person had apparently decided to deal with Robert and Anna in this unaccountable way.

They got a warning of a different kind when Robert decided to take Anna on her first visit to Britain. She applied for the exit visa without which a Soviet citizen could not leave the country, and after two months' silence was told by an official at the visa office that it was not 'expedient' to give her one. Why it was not expedient he would not say. And then there was another shock. Though Robert was no longer earning his living as a journalist he had still qualified for correspondent's status by writing occasional pieces for a London monthly. Even when this magazine closed down he was allowed to keep his accreditation and the privileges it brought, a bending of the rules but quite common for someone who was in Moscow's favour. Among the privileges was the right to ask the Soviet Foreign Ministry to help get entry visas for any guests he invited to Moscow. Robert was expecting a British friend, but when he rang his contact in the Foreign Ministry press department in the usual way the man said he could not help. The Central Committee, he explained to Robert, had instructed the Ministry that he was no longer an accredited correspondent and therefore nothing could be done for him.

Robert's misfortune was to have made an enemy of a man well placed to ruin his life. Valentin was not a policeman or a particularly sadistic functionary in the KGB. He was something much more dangerous, an inhabitant of Old Square, headquarters of the Communist Party Central Committee, which squatted like a spider at the centre of the meticulously woven web of Soviet power. A member of the Committee's International Department, Valentin looked after the party's interests in Anglo-Soviet relations, his job, among other things, being to keep a check on Soviet citizens travelling to Britain and every Briton who had business in Moscow. A word from Valentin – by telephone, naturally, without leaving any evidence on paper – was certainly enough to stop Anna leaving the country and the Foreign Ministry helping with Robert's friend's visa. It might also one day persuade Robert's publishing house to end his contract, or even the Moscow authorities to cancel his permission to live in the city. Valentin's duties demanded co-operation with the KGB and people said he had worked for the security service before moving to the Central Committee. This could only extend his powers of harassment, for it would be easy for him to get a friend in the KGB to make threatening telephone calls to Robert's flat, or slash the tyres on his car, or perform any of the many other unpleasant tricks used against those who annoyed the authorities.

Valentin's threat was worse for being imprecise. Robert and Anna suspected he had a private reason for harassing them, but they could not be sure. What if he was acting on orders from above? And if so, whose? Even a loyal Communist like Robert had no way of finding out. That was typical of any affair in which the Central Committee was involved, and the reason why Anna and her friends did their best to have nothing to do with it. 'Everyone keeps as far away from that place as they can,' Anna would say. 'They know it only means trouble.' Robert was now paying the price for living imprudently close to this mean and unpredictable spider.

Valentin was not popular with British left-wingers who knew Moscow well. It was the Soviet custom to invite sympathetic foreigners to their Party congresses and to reward each guest with a little brown envelope containing vouchers that could be spent in special shops usually reserved for senior Soviet officials. A visiting British Communist was taken to spend his vouchers in the special shop attached to GUM, Moscow's main department store. He was watching the leader of a Latin American Communist party trying on a pair of trousers and thinking how undignified it was when he caught sight of Valentin, whom he had known for many years. Valentin was also out shopping and had loaded his supermarket trolley with foreign-made clothes unobtainable in ordinary Soviet stores. 'The look in his eyes', said the Briton, 'was pure greed. That man is a shit.'

Robert had come across evidence to prove it. There was no hiding the corruption of Moscow in the 1980s. The husband of Anna's pessimistic friend Valya died after a long illness and she had countless stories of the bribes she paid to get him decent treatment, her conclusion being that 'there's nothing so expensive as a free health service'. It was plain that a system in which power was accountable only to itself invited corruption, and that some of the country's most senior officials had happily accepted that invitation. People were no longer shocked by scandalous rumours, and if the story went round that a gold samovar had been found in the safe of a dead Politburo member they just laughed. An official like Valentin who dealt with the Western world had many opportunities to make money. The deal Robert learned about involved stamps. Learning from inside information that an issue of Soviet stamps was about to be cancelled, Valentin went out and bought a large quantity. When the stamps were withdrawn from sale he gave his sheets to a friend who was going to London to sell to dealers there for a good hard currency profit. Another incident concerned a foreigner who was leaving Moscow and wanted to take a collection of ikons abroad. This was strictly forbidden, but a word from Valentin was enough to make Soviet customs look the other way and the precious paintings left Russia for good.

As the pressure to leave the flat grew, Robert put down everything he knew about Valentin in a formal affidavit, had it witnessed at the British consulate, and sent it to the Central Committee. I am not sure what good he thought it would do, but I imagine he felt he had to do something. He told me there were moments when he felt ashamed that after asking Anna to marry him he could not guarantee her a place to make their home. At the same time it was not in his nature to abandon dreams. It seemed to me he turned to Communism because he thought it the opposite of everything he disliked in Britain, and however much the Soviet Union disillusioned him he kept those old dislikes. Even now, when he was battling against Valentin, any criticism he made of the life around him was still little more than gentle mocking. His delight was translating poetry, but to earn

enough money he also had to edit routine Soviet propaganda. He
hated it but dismissed it as just 'dogs barking' and said nothing
could be done to change it. I was in their flat one day when there
was talk of how the children of powerful officials got easy entry into
the most popular institutes and universities. Robert sighed and said
he wished there was a Soviet equivalent of Swiss finishing schools,
where the privileged could send their daughters so they did not get
in the way of serious students. He made me think of those pious old
Jews who believed the world was irreparably unclean, and that only
God was important. Robert had given up worrying about the flaws
of a society that supposedly aspired to Communism; what mattered
was keeping his vision pure and intact. The horror would have been
to give that vision up, and though there must have been moments
when it faded I do not believe he ever let go of it.

I never met Valentin, but I could imagine how Robert irritated
him. What I saw as the Englishman's innocence must have seemed
dangerous stupidity to the Russian, dangerous because it meant
Robert could not be counted on to play according to the rules of
the Moscow game. And the more I learned about Robert the odder
it seemed that he, of all people, should have ended up in the Soviet
Union. His father was a successful businessman and a Christian who
late in life was carried towards Communism by his religious beliefs.
Robert had a tape on which his father described how this conversion
came about and there seemed to be a good deal of the father in the
son. Not long after Robert and Anna married he bought a record of
Handel's *Messiah*. He was so taken with it that he taped Kathleen
Ferrier singing the aria 'He was a man of sorrows, and acquainted
with grief' so he could listen to it over and over again. One day Anna
noticed there were tears in his eyes as he listened, and he said to her,
'Think how he suffered. Think how Christ suffered.'

I hope Valentin did not find out about that, for it was not the
behaviour of a man ready to deal as ruthlessly with the Soviet
system as it dealt with him. Roy Medvedev, the historian who
guided Donald Maclean through the underworld of Soviet dissent,
used to say the system would never crush him because he knew

it too well and could not be frightened by it. In early 1984 when Robert was listening to Kathleen Ferrier a uniformed policeman was posted outside Medvedev's front door in an attempt to isolate him by scaring away visitors and friends. He took it like a shot of vodka, and doubled his efforts to outwit the people he believed were behind the harassment. Resistance of this kind did not come so naturally to Robert. How could it, for he was not a natural inhabitant of this harsh Russian world. His logical mind could work out his future moves, but his body was not able to take the strain. One morning he came to see me in the flat I had just moved into. I remember it clearly because the furniture had not yet been delivered and we sat on the office car's spare tyres. He needed to get some papers to London in time for a court hearing on some matter related to his divorce, and he asked me to persuade the British consul to send them through the diplomatic bag. He was nervous and did not look well and I was not surprised when I heard he had again gone into hospital with symptoms of a heart attack.

The doctors discovered a weakness in the heart but said he would live another twenty years if he looked after himself, and when he came out of hospital in April Anna took him away for a holiday in the Crimea. They stayed in Yalta on the Black Sea coast, where it was already spring, and went for walks and read books, but I do not think they had to do anything to be happy. They had escaped the chores and worries of Moscow and had only themselves to think about. It was all the happiness they wanted. Anna watched over him, made him rest each afternoon, and thought she saw him growing stronger. When she noticed he was waking up in the middle of the night she made him turn on the light and read *Eugene Onegin*. That was better, she thought, than lying awake worrying in the vulnerable early hours. Robert did as he was told. If they stayed in Yalta long enough, he said, he might for the first time in his life reach the end of Pushkin's long poem.

I went to the flat in the Arbat as soon as I learned of Robert's death. Masha, Anna's daughter, opened the door. She looked older and her

face was swollen for she had been crying, but only in the bathroom by
herself for fear of upsetting her mother. There were several people in
the dark sitting-room and Anna, quite grey, sat like a ghost among
them. She told us what had happened, how she had woken early on
the morning of 1 May, Robert's birthday, and sensed something was
wrong, for he was lying with his back towards her and he usually
faced her when he slept. By the time she got up and went round
to his side of the bed he was dead. There had been no struggle. His
heart had just given out.

In another country death would have brought the story to its end;
in Russia there had to be one more chapter in which revenge could be
taken on the survivors. I do not know if Anna knew what was in store
for her, perhaps not at first, for she had so many other things to worry
about. The first of May was a holiday in the Soviet Union and Yalta's
streets were closed for the usual May Day parade. She had to stay in
their room with the body until the afternoon, when the hotel at last
sent round the van they used for carrying suitcases. There was no
stretcher, so the porters carried the body in a sheet and when they
had put it in the back of the van made Anna climb in beside it. At the
morgue the man in charge refused to accept the corpse, claiming the
doctor had put the wrong sort of stamp on the death certificate. He
only relented when Anna told them her husband was British. 'Oh,
he's a foreigner. We'll take him then.'

Soviet Communists kept foreigners at arm's length by giving
them the title *gospodin*, an antiquated and rather grand form of
the English 'Mister'. And though Robert, as a Communist, had
been been embraced as *tovarishch*, comrade, it seemed he could
only be admitted into the official process of death because he was
not, after all, a comrade through and through. Anna ran into other
problems caused by the Soviet compulsion to distrust foreigners
and at the same time give them special treatment. The morning
Robert died she cabled her friend Valya in Moscow, asking her
to come to Yalta. When Valya arrived the doorman would not let
her in to the hotel saying it was reserved for foreign tourists. Anna
sought out the manager and made a scene. How dare he keep out

the friend of a woman whose husband had just died when she knew
he let in any Odessa black marketeer or slippery trader from Baku?
The manager accused her of holding a political meeting. She said
she hoped he too would one day die in a hotel leaving his wife to
cope on her own. 'He was more reasonable after that,' she told us.
'It made him think of his own mortality.'

There was another incident of a more threatening kind. While
Anna was still in Yalta her daughter began preparing for the *pominki*,
the wake that is held after a Russian funeral. Masha came back to
the flat from one of her errands to find it had been burgled. It
was plainly no ordinary robbery. The thief had gone straight to
Robert's study, where he took only a box containing the family's
most important papers. Almost everything they had of value was
in it: Robert's passport, the travellers' cheques he had ordered for
a trip to Britain that was postponed because of his heart, their
savings bank books and marriage licence, and copies of the affidavit
against Valentin that Robert had sent to the Central Committee.
Masha was certain she had seen the thief. When she went out
to the shops she noticed a man hanging around the apartment
block's inner courtyard where the residents kept their cars. She
thought he was one of the chauffeurs who drove important officials
in big black limousines, but after the flat was broken into she
remembered his florid face and insolent manner and was sure he
was the thief.

The KGB did not trust dead foreign Communists, for who could
tell what evidence they might leave behind of disaffection with the
Soviet Union. Security men were the first into Guy Burgess's flat
when he died, and were just as quick to investigate the papers left
by Donald Maclean. It would have been normal for Valentin to have
them pay a visit to the flat in the Arbat to retrieve any evidence of
Robert's 'slanders' against Party officials, in other words himself.
He might even have got a friend in the KGB to do it for him as an
unofficial favour. There was no other explanation for the break-in.
No one used the savings bank books to withdraw money, though it
would have been easy enough to do. The travellers' cheques were

never cashed. Neither their marriage licence nor Robert's passport were seen again.

Robert was cremated at Moscow's main crematorium. It was just outside the walls of an old monastery, but the architects had done their best to make the building look as unlike a church as possible. The plain exterior was a municipal grey and the inside might have been a hall in any provincial Palace of Culture. A worn-out bus identical to those that struggled every day across ill-kept country roads brought the coffin from the morgue, with an exhausted Anna clinging to a bare metal seat beside it. The coffin was carried inside and people laid flowers on the lid, which Anna, ignoring Russian custom, had ordered closed because that was the English way. Friends from Robert's publishing house made brief speeches of farewell, one man pressing his knuckles to his eyes as though to stop a flood of tears. Anna, supported by Masha and a friend, was hardly standing. A plump young crematorium official pressed a button. There was the sound of machinery; the coffin, shivering, disappeared into the floor.

It was a brutal ceremony, but what else could Anna do? She might believe her husband to have been at least as much Christian as Communist, but in spite of all that had happened to him he could not quite give up the faith on which he had built his life, and Anna loved him too well to deny that. And the crematorium's chill mechanics were soon forgotten when the mourners came back to the flat in the Arbat for the *pominki*. Mother and daughter had set out a long table in the sitting-room and a smaller one in Masha's room. There were bottles of mineral water and two kinds of vodka and the food, as abundant as at any meal I ate with Robert and Anna, came in waves. Hot chicken was followed by salads and then marinated fish and pies of different kinds and sizes. Anna sat in the middle of the long table as one after the other people stood up to propose toasts to Robert's memory and then to speak about him. In this atmosphere Anna recovered some of the natural resilience that had left her in the crematorium. She took particular comfort from a man who sat across the table from me. He was middle-aged and unremarkable to look at and though he ate and drank a great deal he made no toast to Robert's memory. Anna could easily see him from where she sat and when their eyes met she thought she saw in his a message of shared mourning, as though he, too, had known great sadness. She became convinced that he, like her, had lost someone precious, and it helped her. The man got up to go when I did. I was giving lifts to two of Anna's friends and offered to take him too, but he refused, saying he lived in the next street. Anna supposed he worked with Robert but when she asked other guests who he was it turned out no one knew him. The more they talked about this man with the expressive eyes, the more convinced Anna became that he had been sent to spy on her by Valentin.

Two days later she got a telephone call from the Central Committee. An official in the housing section ordered her to get out of the flat at once. If she was still there in three days' time she would be fined fifty roubles. If they had to give her another warning the fine would be five hundred roubles. A third warning would bring an order banning Anna from living within the Moscow city limits. The official threw in a further demand that she pay two thousand roubles (ten times a good monthly wage) for the furniture that was in the flat when Robert moved there with his family twenty years before. A little later the doorbell rang. It was the manager of the apartment block and he gave her the same warning, but he was trembling as he repeated the words and seemed on the point of weeping. He asked Anna to understand him: he was a human being too, but he had to speak to her as 'they' instructed him.

She had always known she would not be allowed to stay on without Robert in a flat that belonged to the Central Committee and was already planning to move back to a pleasant, though tiny, flat of her own on the other side of the river. But she needed a month or two to clear up Robert's affairs and the cruelty of the order to get out within three days enraged her. Advised by a friend who had fought her own battles with the authorities, Anna struck back. She wrote to the KGB, telling them that Robert's passport and travellers' cheques had been stolen and asking them to do something about it. She sent a second letter to Konstantin Chernenko, the new Communist Party general secretary. She addressed him as 'dear Konstantin Ustinovich' (a fawning style proposed by Anna's friend on the principle that 'demagogues should be treated demagogically') and asked for just one 'favour': that she be allowed one month before moving out of the flat. She also consulted a lawyer, who told her that the law allowed a widow two months' grace before she had to leave her dead husband's flat if someone else had a stronger claim to it. If police were sent to throw her out, as the man from the Central Committee threatened, he told her to ring the office of the procurator general, the highest Soviet legal official. It was sensible advice for, lawless though the regime was, it hated being caught out in infringements of its own routine regulations.

A short while later the doorbell rang again and a man in a dark suit introduced himself to Anna as the Central Committee official who had spoken so roughly to her on the telephone. He was amazed, he said, managing to suggest he was even hurt, that she had so misunderstood his words to think she was being ordered to get out of the flat at once. How could anyone expect such a thing? Of course he understood she needed time to clear up her husband's affairs. He seemed to have forgotten his earlier demand that she pay two thousand roubles for the old furniture for he made no mention of it. The encounter left Anna shaken. She might have won the battle, but she felt tainted by the presence in what had been Robert's and her home of this representative of the great spider. She had been drawn into the Central Committee's web, and now one of its apparatchiks had sat in a chair in her sitting-room and talked to her and smiled as though he knew everything about her. She could not get over his eyes. They were, I heard her say several times, a 'fascist's eyes, the sort of eyes that look straight at you but do not see you.'

The fascist kept his word. No one bothered Anna again and she moved in her own time to her flat across the river. Not long after that she gave me Robert's watch, as though she felt it had done its time in Russia, had its memories of Moscow and herself engraved for ever on its back, and could now go home to England. I had no more reason to think about Valentin until the autumn of the following year when I learned I was one of the British diplomats and journalists who were to be expelled from Moscow and I wondered if Valentin had a hand in it. There were, of course, other possible reasons for selecting me, but Valentin would have seen the list of those who were to be expelled, and could have made sure my name was among them. It was a chance for him to get rid of a foreign journalist who not only knew damaging stories about him but who, as Robert's friend, had become his enemy by proxy.

I no longer had the watch by then. For months I kept it in the drawer in my desk, and sometimes took it out to look at the sinuous initials engraved on the back and to weigh it in my hand as though it had something to tell me. Then I gave it to Masha, to remind her of the English stepfather who had treated her like his daughter. It was difficult to say what lay in store for her. Anna was afraid she might be punished as the daughter of someone who had challenged the Central Committee – a common enough sort of petty revenge-taking – or that she would find it hard to get a place in a university or a decent job. The watch engraved with her mother's and stepfather's initials would scarcely help her, but it was part of her life and I did not want her to forget Robert.

I did not need anything to keep him in my mind. On the Soviet scale of horror his story was insignificant. No one was shot or imprisoned. No one was even arrested, let alone interrogated. It was never even plain to me whether his persecution was just the work of Valentin, a moderately powerful man abusing his position, or whether he was tormented strictly according to the rules of Communist bureaucracy. It made no difference; the poignancy of Robert's story lay elsewhere. A system for which many people had willingly laid down their lives, and to which millions more were sacrificed, had in its last moments chosen, quite blindly, to persecute a man who wanted with all his heart to believe in it.

His was a singular footnote to the saga of twentieth-century Communism, itself an ill-fated story in which the human dream of justice settled, like a butterfly upon a poisonous plant, on a country that could only destroy it. For decades the dream remained dazzling, shining with particular brightness for many men and women who lived beyond the borders of the Soviet Union whose own citizens were discovering that the vision scorched as often as it illuminated. Shortly before I left Moscow Roy Medvedev gave me, as a farewell present, a copy of the programme and rules of the Communist International, the organisation that united the world's Communist parties into a revolutionary movement controlled by Moscow. It was an ironic gesture, a wry apology for what Russia had done to the dream of so many millions. We Russians can take the unpleasant truth, Medvedev might have said, for over centuries we have been toughened by our history. But you foreigners are a vulnerable lot, and I'm afraid our great experiment has left behind a lot of cripples in this world.

The book was published in 1933, the year before the murder of Kirov, the signal for Stalin's blood purge of his closest colleagues. Bound in red, it is just four inches by three, perfect for slipping into the pocket of revolutionary or dreamer. On almost every page there is an evocation of the dream that Robert could never quite abandon, but also words that spell out clearly how Russia's Bolsheviks subverted and betrayed it. There were foreign Communists much more sophisticated than Robert, and some who knew far better than he what had gone wrong, and yet they too could not let go of the dream. Guy Burgess was as ruthless as any revolutionary, but he was at least trying to be honest when he wrote that 'socialism' in Russia had produced 'a beginning of an approximation' of the world he once dreamed of with his friends at Cambridge. Donald Maclean revived his flagging spirits by turning to the column in *The Times* that records. the wills of people who have recently died. He would go down the list of old women who had left fortunes of hundreds of thousands of pounds and comfort himself that at least the Soviet Union had got rid of that sort of inequality. It was dreaming in reverse, but still a sort of dreaming. Foreign Communists were slow to grasp that few Russians went through such contortions any more. The mocking indifference of Anna's friends towards the official world that cramped their lives was shared by much of the intelligentsia: how else could the system have collapsed so quickly after Mikhail Gorbachev began his blind attempt to reform it? Yet Russians could be tolerant, almost protective, of foreigners still dazzled by visions of a Communist future that few in Moscow believed in any more. I was talking one day with Anna and Masha and Anna had again remembered how hard it was for Robert to surrender his belief, and how, as he fought against the invisible Valentin, he would sometimes murmur, as though surprised, 'The bastards, oh the bastards.' We were silent for a moment and then Masha said, 'He lived here for almost twenty-five years and he still didn't understand anything.'

I thought Anna would protest, but she nodded. 'Thank God he didn't,' she said calmly. 'Thank God he didn't.'

Epilogue

Citizen of Babel

Most evenings that week after supper in the camp we took the car and drove through the empty countryside to a pub, where we drank beer, but not much, for mostly we talked and on the way home stopped at the side of any quiet road and made love. It was a crude sort of love-making; the seats of the pre-war Austin and my lack of experience made sure of that. But when we got back and had left the car in its shed by a disused drill square and said goodnight I lay on my bed in the barrack room and smoked a cigarette, and when it had burned so low it hurt my fingers I stubbed it out on the inside of my locker door. By the end of the week there were five dark round marks in the wood. It was the only way I could think of to record such prodigious events.

It was – I suppose many first loves are – an affair of great selfishness. He was a mirror in which I thought I could admire myself, for the first time in my life, as I believed myself to be. I recited to him, though after some hesitation, poems I had written. I talked of ideas and feelings that, till then, I thought no one would ever listen to. After a while I realised that when he was not with me I could not remember his face. It dissolved like watercolour under rain. I told him this in a letter and he answered, curtly, that he never had any problem remembering what I looked like. He was several years older, had been to Cambridge before starting national service, and naturally I was not his first love. I suspect he quite soon grew tired of the self-obsessed dream into which I drew him. And I quite soon began to doubt he was the perfect lover I had supposed. During one leave he took me to Cambridge to show me the world that was waiting for me when I left the Navy and also, he said, to introduce me to the delights of the flesh. Those were his words, 'the delights of the flesh'. It was not the sort of promise you forget, but though we shared a room for two days I cannot remember much more excitement than was generated in the cramped seats of the old Austin.

Later, when I was posted to a minesweeper as a superfluous midshipman whose only skill was speaking Russian, I wrote him lovelorn letters, for I missed the pleasure of inspecting myself in the mirror he held out to me. I got a sharp reply in which he summarised Proust's warning about the hopelessness of homosexual love. He was writing from Italy, where he had gone to study music and suggested I follow what he said was the Italian example and go to a brothel when I needed sex. What irritated me was the obvious impracticality of the advice. I did not know if there were homosexual brothels in Italy, though I doubted it, but I was sure there was no such thing in London. My inability to imagine him in his absence made the affair easier to end, and to this day I have only the vaguest idea how he looked.

I do not know if anyone at the camp knew about us, but if they did they were unlikely to care. We were a strange lot, Russian language students from the three services, picked for the job because we were supposedly bright boys who had won places at university. We had to wear uniforms but there was little other military discipline. Life was dominated by our Russian teachers, clever, slightly crazy émigrés who fought off the boredom of life in Nissen huts on the edge of Bodmin moor by talking to us about their passions and drilling us in complex Russian swearwords. Of course there were other homosexuals among the students, some as virginal and unrecognisable as I was, but a few quite open, notably Jeremy Wolfenden, the brilliant Eton boy commemorated by Sebastian Faulks in *The Fatal Englishman*. When we were in London for the main part of our language training there was talk that Jeremy and another old Etonian went to homosexual clubs. Neither made a secret of what they were and I cannot remember anyone expressing outrage. Among young people like us it scarcely mattered that homosexual acts were still a crime.

I had suspected I was homosexual from the time I was at public school, though contrary to popular belief about such places there seemed to be little sex at Charterhouse, just platonic, calf-like crushes on pretty, younger boys. Naturally it was out of the question to talk to an adult about such things. I would no more have dreamed of discussing sex of any kind with my parents than they would have with theirs. It was not parents' business, and parents seemed to agree. When my aunt asked my grandmother on the eve of her wedding for a hint about what was in store for her, she would not say a word. Schools still thought it their duty to block out sexual knowledge. The final interview with the headmaster of my first boarding school was an interrogation designed to discover how much each thirteen-year-old knew about sex, and to stop it there. He had on his desk a metal contraption with which I thought he was going to illustrate the mechanics of the penis and when he asked me if I knew what an erection was I gave the most innocent answer I could think of. He assumed I was in a decent state of ignorance, and I never got to see him demonstrate the fascinating device.

Later I came across enough references in books to men loving men to understand that, though it might be unnatural, it was certainly not unusual. And even before the first clumsy experience at the side of a dark Cornish lane it seemed natural enough to me, whatever others might think and say. If my background had an advantage it was that I was easily indifferent to the opinion of others, and even enjoyed finding myself on my own. I had never liked being fitted into groups. Boys at my first school were divided into sets named, since it was wartime, Spitfire, Blenheim and Lancaster. When peace came the sets, out of respect for tradition, went back to their old First World War names of Haig, Jellicoe and Kitchener. Both old and new were meaningless to me. At public school it was as though I lacked some gene that others had, for I could not feel the pride in my house that was expected of us, and at Cambridge I developed no particular affection for my college. It was a sort of arrogance, but a useful defence when I grew older and understood that there was one group I could never properly belong to even if I wanted to.

Of course my parents groomed me for membership in the heterosexual world. However wretched my mother felt, she always did her duty in that respect. She sent me and my brother to dancing classes, where we learned the quickstep, foxtrot, waltz and samba, and also Scottish reels and English country dances such as Strip the Willow and Sir Roger de Coverley that my ancestors had performed for generations. The other boys in the class were as unenthusiastic as I until they realised that dancing was the price to be paid for a chance to kiss girls on the lips and feel under their dresses. The country gentry who had survived war and post-war austerity were returning to their old customs, among them the dances in private houses at which adolescent sons and daughters began the mating ritual. These parties were all much the same. A band played music little changed from the 1930s; there might be some gentrified swing but definitely no jitterbug or jive. Food was important, for most of the guests were still really children. Knobbly pieces of fruit floated in bowls of non-alcoholic punch. Girls wore long dresses, boys dinner jackets, unless they were baby brothers in which case they made do with dark blue suits.

My dutiful mother took me to a tailor in Eton to have my first dinner jacket made and she supervised each fitting. It was the uniform of orthodox adulthood and had to be just right. My stepfather taught me how to tie a bow tie, the hardest kind with a single end, for it was out of the question to allow even a boy to wear a tie that was already made up. I was fifteen when I first wore this uniform to a dance. It was in a large house belonging to a friend of my father's. My brother, who was two and a half years older, looked forward to it and, not knowing what to expect, so did I, although I was terrified my bow tie would collapse and I would not be able to re-do it. And I did enjoy it at first, walking round the tables of food trying whatever looked good and learning to avoid the pieces of fruit when I took a glass of punch. The band played tunes I recognised from dancing class. I understood that I was expected to ask a girl to dance with me but I did not much want to do that. I was standing in a corner of the room watching the dancers and wondering where I might escape to, when a man and woman spun off the floor and stopped in front of me. There were usually older people at these dances to supervise and encourage the young, but this couple looked more ancient than my parents. The man placed the woman's right hand in mine and laughed and cried, 'Dance on, young man, dance on.'

It was an old-fashioned waltz, a nightmarishly rapid step that our dancing mistress had scarcely tried to teach us, but my partner took care of that. Tightly gripping my right hand and clamping my left arm to the back of her brown velvet dress so hard I could feel the bones of her corset, she carried me round the floor. She was as good-humoured as the man I supposed to be her husband and laughed when the music stopped and thanked me for a splendid dance. As I grew older there were girls with whom I danced with more pleasure, but I never forgot 'Dance on, young man, dance on' and the sense of having in my hands a substance as alien as the plump lady's corseted body. I was an impostor at these affairs, and kept on getting into trouble because I could not recognise the symptoms of a teenage girl's crush. I was not interested in them, and supposed they had no interest in me, and so I blundered about this adolescent world as clumsily as in the waltz that was my first real dance.

It took time to understand the subversive consequences of my sexual nature. I could not imagine there was a separate homosexual world into which I might retreat, and supposed I would live my life among people with whom I did not share one vital interest. It did not worry me because it seemed inevitable and at times comical, this looking at the world askew because 'thou read'st black where I read white'. I watched dispassionately as boys and girls I knew began their first affairs. And as though I was made of some strange material not subject to the ordinary rules of physics I was never quite moved, or not as I supposed others were, by stories of romance in books and films and plays. At Cambridge, though, I found a world in which homosexuals and heterosexuals lived openly and amiably together.

There were queer dons, some little older than the undergraduates, and even openly queer clergymen. It was a clever world, often eccentric and sometimes flash. Its mascot was a young man who might have been a good classical scholar if his louche beauty (the eyes of a young animal but a poor skin) had not made him so tempting to both sexes. He had a smart mistress in London, but at parties given by a rich local homosexual made his entrance down the stairs dressed only in the host's mother's jewellery.

Much of this was playing games; what mattered to me was that, for the first time in my life, I could visit both worlds, and have friends in both, and yet commit myself to neither. It was harder for those who lost themselves in the sexual maze ('sex ruined my life,' said a friend, explaining why he never became the philosopher he wanted to be), or through logic concluded there was no hope for lovers of men. The rooms opposite mine across a courtyard of the college were occupied by a brilliant undergraduate who was obviously homosexual. Sometimes after dark I saw him conducting ceremonies involving candles and something like an altar because from time to time he bowed to it as though in worship. One day he committed suicide. He had fallen in love with another undergraduate in the college, a good-looking and quite normal athlete and apparently the object of the night-time prayers. My neighbour across the courtyard declared his love, was rejected (politely, and even with gentleness) and decided it was better to die than live a life of foreordained unrequited love.

There was another friend, an unremarkable-seeming public school-boy who wore a grey tweed jacket and grey flannel trousers and was one of a group of students inspired by the college Dean to follow a bracing Anglicanism. He even began to talk like the Dean, in a loud, pedantic Oxbridge voice as though he was delivering a sermon to the college boat crew. His nemesis was a poet, a black graduate student from Harvard. At the end of a year the poet went back to America and the Englishman was shattered. Like me he could not remember his lover's face, and tried to force his memory by painting portraits of him. He saw clearly the poet's teeth and ears and nose;

he even remembered in detail the shoes he usually wore. But these pieces would not join up. He turned to photographs of the poet, but found he did not recognise the young man represented there. In spite of that he kept on painting, always a brown face against a blue or yellow background. None of the portraits looked like the poet and their twisted angularity was probably a better representation of the artist's state of mind. I was not surprised when I heard that he married not long after graduating. Perhaps he also understood more quickly than I that our passions would cease to be unexceptional when we left Cambridge.

There was, of course, a more or less public homosexual world in London. Almost invisible compared to the commercial gay scene of the 1990s, it amounted to a few dodgy pubs and a handful of members-only bars. The most pretentious of these, the Rockingham, presumed unconvincingly to be a distant relative of the grand clubs of St James's; the others were more cosy than erotic, a refuge from the straight world's disapproving eyes. And there was an even less visible world, which was almost as grand as the Rockingham dreamed of being. Its inhabitants were successful doctors, lawyers, and businessmen, and there were also interior decorators who if they did not themselves come from old families were the courtier-servants of the rich. These men lived in handsome houses in Knightsbridge and Chelsea, wore suits that were rather too well cut and, though they gave parties that would then have been called 'raffish', never dangerously muddied class lines.

I did not care for a little world that was too much like a club. It did not occur to me that joining a club was exactly what I was doing when I went to work in Broadway Buildings nor, hard though I find it to believe today, did I worry that, as a homosexual, I might one day be blackballed from it. Or did I? I had been positively vetted, and an enquiry among my Cambridge friends would surely have raised questions about my sexual preference. Perhaps no one asked the right people the right questions, just as no one found out about the mildly seditious pamphlet I wrote with Peter Jenkins and other friends at Cambridge during the Suez crisis. Yet by the late 1950s the British security services were supposed to be learning the lessons of the defection of Burgess and Maclean and one of these was that you could never trust homosexuals. Oddly there still seemed to be homosexuals inside SIS. A senior figure in my department was unmarried and had some of the effeminate mannerisms supposed to indicate homosexuality. And there was Maurice Oldfield, shortly to be appointed to the important job of SIS liaison with the CIA in Washington. He too was unmarried, but he handled rumours about his sex life with the skill one would expect of an accomplished spymaster, conceding that bachelors were bound to come under suspicion. And when he got to Washington he took and passed a lie detector test designed to find out if he was queer, a performance that cleared the way for his later appointment as C.

Did it matter that he fooled the system? No. Oldfield apparently did a good job. Listening to my boss P15 talking about sex and spying I got the impression that he and other spymasters who were as dispassionate had nothing against homosexuals if they did the work required of them. According to the public orthodoxy of the time, though, there were several reasons why homosexuals were chronically untrustworthy. The MI5 mole-hunter Peter Wright argued that for homosexuals 'loyalty to their kind overrode all other obligation'. They were also thought more likely to be blackmailed than heterosexuals; and there was the unspoken argument that because they were, well, queer they were undesirable members in any of the 'clubs' that made up the British establishment. This prejudice was typified by Sir Dick White, chief in turn of MI5 and SIS, who admitted underestimating Guy Burgess because he could not believe such a disreputable queer might be an effective spy. On the other hand, White accepted Maurice Oldfield's word that he was not homosexual because Oldfield was such a dutiful churchgoer. His only wish was that Maurice would find a wife who could help him unwind after a long day poring over the nation's secrets.

The belief that homosexuals presented a peculiar threat to the security of the British state pervaded the post-war years and was an expression in Cold War language of the distaste of the majority for sexual acts between men. It was scarcely affected by the 1967 decriminalisation of homosexuality, though that removed both the special risk of blackmail and the need of homosexuals to live clandestine lives that was supposed to give them a knack for secrecy that made them particularly suitable as spies – though only, it seemed, for the other side. Nor was it affected by evidence suggesting sexual preference was a poor indicator of reliability in security affairs. The case against queers was only superficially supported by the fact that two of the Soviet ring of five Cambridge spies were homosexual. The truth was different, and not very hard to grasp. The homosexual Guy Burgess and Anthony Blunt became spies because they believed in world revolution and the Soviet Union as that revolution's (temporary) leader. Their Soviet spymasters correctly judged that the two men's sexual tastes, about which they reported clinically and without judgement, would not affect their work for Moscow. The general wildness of Burgess's life did eventually worry his handlers, but that wildness made a mockery of the theory that queers were particularly dangerous spies because they had to be so secretive in their sex lives. There was never anything secretive about Burgess's sex life, and not very much about Blunt's.

Facts were as scarce when it came to showing that homosexuals were a special risk because more likely to be blackmailed when abroad. There was the case of my Moscow colleague Jeremy Wolfenden who was tempted into the bed of a young Polish provocateur and picked up by the KGB, though with what benefit to them is unclear. And there was the foolish Admiralty clerk William John Vassall, whom the KGB enticed into a homosexual 'honey pot' when he was working in the British embassy in Moscow. But straight sex could lead to just as much trouble. A talented young British journalist, a friend of Wolfenden's but a great lover of women, was blackmailed by secret police in Poland when the Polish girl he was having an affair with produced a fiancé who threatened to take him to court. The journalist went to MI5 when he got back to London. He also told his editor, who sacked him, which can only have delighted the Poles who laid the trap for him.

In Moscow the KGB never stopped trying to get hooks into foreign residents of any sexual persuasion, and they succeeded often enough for no one to be surprised when a diplomat or military attaché left the country in a mysterious hurry. The KGB's luckiest coup against Britain came when a British ambassador tumbled one of his Russian servants while his wife was away in London. No one was more astonished than the wife of an earlier British ambassador, who remembered the maid well: 'Katya, that square, dumpy thing!' Her shock was more aesthetic than moral, but these tragi-comedies of the flesh were performed by many unlikely actors, and an ambassador as dry as his own despatches and a potato-shaped Russian girl were as likely a coupling as any. And as the world changed it was not just sexual indiscretion that ruined the careers of the straightest officials. In 1973 the head of SIS resigned after his son and daughter-in-law appeared at the Old Bailey on drugs charges. He was succeeded by Maurice Oldfield, whose period of leadership was blameless and scandal-free. Yet the belief that homosexuals were a particular security risk endured. Early in the 1980s a friend who was always open about his homosexuality was rising to the top of a non-secret Whitehall department. To qualify for the senior rank of under-secretary he needed security clearance and was grilled for hours by a Colonel X about journeys he made abroad as a businessman before joining the civil service. He was asked to list all the countries in Africa and Asia he had visited and when, and the names of any sexual partners. He was not surprised that his clearance was refused, and that the head of his department, a careful Whitehall operator, failed to express any sympathy. I can imagine P15 rolling his eyes in despair at such things, but then a good spymaster sees the world as it is and does not bother with the taboos even of the society he is charged with protecting.

While I was still at university in America, Corinna Adam, a friend from Cambridge, got a job in the Paris office of the *Observer*. Most of the people I knew at university read the *Observer*, not least because of its opposition to the Suez invasion, and she was amazed at her good luck. She was learning, she wrote in a letter to me, as much in an afternoon talking to the paper's Paris correspondent Nora Beloff as she had from the longest supervision at Girton, for Nora was 'mentally every bit as tough as the dons'. Corinna made other *Observer* staff writers who passed through Paris sound equally intriguing. There was John Gale, just back from the foul French war in Algeria, 'an absolute dear and marvellously right-minded, but unfortunately quite mad'. (Gale, who was on the brink of a nervous breakdown, had told the British embassy that Corinna was putting poison in his coffee.) She also met the diplomatic correspondent Robert Stephens, 'brilliant in that appealing diffident way' and, she thought, typical of *Observer* journalists who were 'good and honest and *never* write *anything* they know or even feel may not be strictly true'.

It was not surprising that friends who became journalists were keen to work for the *Observer* and I felt myself very lucky when, after abandoning Broadway Buildings and a year on a struggling political weekly called *Time & Tide*, I was asked to be the paper's Moscow correspondent. It was typical of the *Observer* to hire a twenty-seven-year-old with little experience of journalism and none at all as a foreign correspondent. When David Astor became editor of the paper after the war he recruited some people who had never written a word of journalism and even students straight from university. My strong card, I supposed, was my knowledge of Russian and I never thought that being homosexual might disqualify me. Of course I knew that journalists were as likely to be prejudiced as anyone else and as more of my friends got married people gossiped, and not always in a friendly way, about my still being single. The wife of a colleague on *Time & Tide* who liked to grill me about girlfriends one day told me how shocked she had been at a dinner party where the host, a young writer, sat at one end of the table and his boyfriend at the other. 'They were acting as though they were a normal married couple,' she said. 'I don't think that's quite right, do you?' and she paused to watch my reaction.

I knew the steadfastly liberal *Observer* was not like that. What I did not know was that *The Times* had ruled out sending Jeremy Wolfenden to Moscow because he was homosexual, and that the proprietor of the *Daily Telegraph*, which *did* send him there, was apparently not aware of the fact. Nor did I know that while I was waiting for my Soviet visa the *Observer*'s deputy editor John Pringle heard a rumour that I was homosexual. Unlike most of the *Observer* staff Pringle was an experienced journalist who had worked on the (then) *Manchester Guardian* and later would edit the *Sydney Morning Herald*. A gentle, shrewd man he chose not to confront me, but summoned George Seddon, with whom I was temporarily working on the paper's world affairs survey 'The Week'. Was is it true that Frankland was queer? 'No,' said George, who knew I was, 'but I am.' George, also a newspaper pro from Manchester, was married with two teenage children. He had long grey hair brushed back from his forehead and heavy spectacles that gave him a professorial look in keeping with the *Observer*'s intellectual reputation. It was difficult to imagine anyone less like the popular idea of a homosexual, and impossible to contrive a diversion better calculated to stop Pringle's enquiry in its tracks.

George certainly was gay, and so happy with his belated discovery that, when he told me some years later about his confession to John Pringle, he still seemed delighted to have had this chance to reveal his new self. It made no difference to his career, and his unusual skills as talent spotter, ideas man and creative editor helped guide the *Observer* into what for it were the daunting new worlds of women's and consumer journalism. He was not the only member of the staff known to be homosexual. There was also William Clark, one of the paper's stars since 1947, who knew everyone who was anyone in British public life. In London he lived in Albany, the snobbish block of gentlemen's flats off Piccadilly, and he managed to be both open and discreet about his private life, He dealt with the intolerant by a mixture of self-deprecating humour and massive self-confidence, which came easily to a man for whom 'never say you don't know' was a rule of life.

But would even the *Observer* have sent a journalist they knew to be homosexual to Moscow? And would I have admitted I was homosexual if John Pringle had asked me directly? I do not know; it was a question I did not expect to be asked. As for the *Observer*, there would surely have been much discussion and a determination to do what was both morally right and right for the paper. I like to think that in the end they would have decided to trust me, but given the general belief that homosexuals were a high security risk, anyone they asked for advice, the Foreign Office for example, would certainly have warned against it. I could not have proved in advance that I was capable of leading a celibate life, although I knew from what I had learned in Broadway Buildings that it was the only sensible thing to do. Nor could I explain, for I did not know it yet myself, that the Moscow of those days, KGB 'honey pots' apart, was unpromising from any erotic point of view. It was not just that most Soviet citizens were scared of contacts with foreigners. After the Revolution and the explosion of new ideas that accompanied it, the Bolsheviks had tired of free love as rapidly as they had of modern art. The Soviet government seemed determined to make sex as uncomfortable and sordid an activity as possible. Abortion was the chief means of birth control because the only contraceptives Soviet planners thought fit to produce were thick rubber condoms known as 'galoshes', and even they were hard to find. An acute housing shortage meant most young Moscow lovers had nowhere to go, except during the brief summer, when they could hide in the city's parks. The closest thing to erotic displays in public were those moments during Communist Party ceremonies when Lenin's Lolitas, pubescent girls in the red scarves and tiny skirts of the Pioneers (the Soviet Brownies), rushed forward with bunches of flowers for the leaders and were rewarded with pats and rough kisses. In the nearly three years I lived in Khrushchev's Moscow the closest I came to homosexual activity was a whispered dirty joke, which he thought I could not hear, made by my friend Yegor to an acquaintance we bumped into on the street.

I cannot remember worrying much about any of this when I set off for Moscow, for my mind was occupied with more immediate, and seemingly insoluble, problems. The *Observer* had equipped me with an identity card the size and thickness of an invitation to an expensive wedding. Embossed at the top with the paper's name and a gold royal crest like the one on the *Observer* mast-head, it requested in finest copperplate writing that I be given all possible assistance. I soon abandoned it, for it was too big to fit into any pocket and quickly got creased and even I knew there was no point in showing it to any Soviet official. More useful would have been a manual on how to get hold of this commodity called news that I was now supposed to be dealing in and, when I had it, what I ought to do with it. I invited the bureau chief of Reuters to lunch at the restaurant of the National Hotel and in my innocence asked how a journalist got news in Moscow. We all have our sources, he said, but we do not share them with anyone else. He was kind about it, but the mysteries of my new trade remained as impenetrable as the Kremlin walls we looked down on from our table by the restaurant window.

With time I realised that there were few reliable sources of news in Moscow, apart from official ones available to anyone who read Soviet newspapers and the despatches of the Tass news agency. But I still envied the skill with which my Moscow colleagues, turned out perfectly shaped stories while I was struggling over the first paragraph. Jeremy Wolfenden could do it impromptu on the telephone to the copy-takers of the *Telegraph*, and on several occasions I heard him extemporising impeccable despatches while drunk. Part of my trouble was that a story for a weekly paper like the *Observer* could not usually be written according to the Fleet Street template 'Who, Where, What, When and Why'. Nevertheless even an *Observer* story required a measure of simplicity and directness that was beyond me. Any other paper would have sacked me; the response of the *Observer* was to have its expert on Soviet affairs Edward Crankshaw give me a correspondence course in newspaper writing. Crankshaw diagnosed my problem as lack of 'focus'. My stories rambled, had no 'vertical compression, only a horizontal line'. I was missing the point that 'a newspaper article, if it is to come alive, must appear to be confined to one clear-cut point or subject – with other interests woven into it'. 'Newspaper reporting', he concluded one lesson, 'is the hardest thing in the world until you have got the trick: then it is the easiest.' And he was right. Like a child that after many spills suddenly finds it can ride a bicycle I began writing passable stories, though for many years there were still occasions when I wobbled.

What to write was as big a problem as how to write. One spring afternoon three months after my arrival in Moscow I was walking back to my hotel, after lunch with a diplomat who lived above the old stables of the British embassy. At Pushkin Square I saw a crowd in front of the statue of Russia's favourite poet, and heard a youthful voice that seemed to be making a speech to people standing round the statue's base. That struck me as odd: spontaneous public meetings were not a feature of Soviet life. When I got closer I saw the speaker was a teenage boy and he was reciting a Pushkin poem. It was the anniversary of the poet's birth, and when the boy finished friends and relatives pushed other girls and boys forward and, as proud as they were nervous, they too recited verses so familiar that many of those listening mouthed the words silently with them.

It was a Saturday, the day the *Observer* went to print, and I thought 'this is what I should be writing about'. Here, surely, was a clue to this strange country, a clue of a kind not to be found in articles in *Pravda* or a Khrushchev speech. And it was then that the excitement, the almost sensuous delight, of living as a foreign correspondent in another country began to infect me. Anything that I saw and smelled, touched and heard, might hold a clue to be recorded. There was reason to note the sweetness of the bakery where I bought flat buns with a cheese-curd filling, a sweetness so overpowering that if I had been kidnapped and driven away blindfold I would have known at once when we passed it, or any other Moscow bakery for that matter. The gorgeous decoration of the Moscow metro stations; the undisguised boredom of beautiful Galya, the hotel maid who brought me the same breakfast each morning; the Soviet soldier's long winter greatcoat that could have been taken straight from the shoulders of a tsarist infantryman – all were clues, big or small, to the Russian puzzle over which I pored. From that time a pattern was set. There

had to be an initial spark of sympathy for a country, but then it
became an affair of the heart, a passion always to know more, and
also something of the lover's protectiveness, not towards regimes in
power but the land and people that endured them.

Out of this grew the desire to convey in what I wrote a feeling
of what it was like to be in Russia or Vietnam or America, so that
anyone who read my despatches could share in the excitement, the
horror, and occasionally the happiness of the events I witnessed. It
was some time before I realised that this was what the *Observer*
wanted too. It had the right, if any paper did, to adopt as its own
Conrad's definition of his purpose as a writer: 'By the power of the
written word to make you hear, to make you feel – it is before
all, to make you see.' The best *Observer* writers such as Patrick
O'Donovan and Gavin Young could pull this off and it was up to
each new member of the staff to learn the lesson for himself; for me
a bitter process with many moments of despair and the occasional
sense of triumph.

Attention to language and appreciation of good writing permeated
the paper. A sub-editor might consult a journalist before changing a
word in his copy. The matter-of-fact Yorkshireman who edited the
service that syndicated *Observer* writers to newspapers round the
world could recite not just the first sentences, but entire opening
paragraphs, of the pieces he most admired. Fleet Street copy-takers,
to whom correspondents dictated their stories over the telephone,
were notoriously indifferent to the words they took down, but those
who worked regularly for the *Observer* sometimes made appreciative
noises when they heard something of quality. A greater compliment
could not be imagined.

One day while I was still in the *Observer* office waiting for my
Soviet visa, a young man called Michael Davie in shirt sleeves and
bright red braces stopped me in the corridor. I scarcely knew him but
he looked at me cheerfully and said, 'You're off to Moscow, aren't
you. You know, there'll be times when you think we've forgotten
you. But we won't have.' As though to double his reassurance he
repeated, 'We won't have,' and then hurried off. It was the best

piece of advice anyone gave me. As a weekly paper the *Observer* did not need to be in daily contact with its correspondents abroad, and was anyhow ill equipped to keep a close watch on them since there was only one news editor for both home and foreign affairs. Contact was limited further by the difficulty and expense of communication. These were extreme in the Soviet Union of 1962, where only foreign news agencies were allowed to have the telex machines that were then the speediest and cheapest way of sending messages and copy. Correspondents of newspapers made do with the telephone, which was costly and, because calls had to be booked in advance, slow.

The result was I seldom talked to London more than once a week, and there were often moments when I had to repeat Michael Davie's cheerful reassurance that whatever happened I would not be abandoned. This self-pity vanished as soon as I understood that the *Observer*'s apparent forgetfulness and difficulty of communication were advantages for any correspondent who liked to be his own master. The further journalists travelled from London the harder it was for their offices to keep in touch and give them instructions (the more perfect the communications, the more complete the power of the controlling centre). In Saigon I had no telex: it was too expensive to install one in the part of the city where I lived, and perhaps not even technically feasible. I did have a telephone, but it was sometimes hard to reach other parts of Saigon let alone London, and in the seven years I was based there I spoke perhaps two or three times with the office. Instead I communicated through the telex at Reuters which, until I got a car, meant a half-hour's motorbike ride there and back, with the risk of a soaking during the rainy season. Communication, not surprisingly, was sparing.

The longer I was away from London the happier I was with this sense of being cut off, and that was the real point of the warning I was given when I first set off to Moscow. Bad communications were a secondary reason; much more important was the *Observer*'s belief that the writers on the spot should know what was important and what to write about. What was the purpose otherwise in sending them abroad? The *Observer* was a writers' paper because it trusted writers. Under such circumstances a measure of independent bloody-mindedness was essential to survival, and that at least came easily to me. As to the impetus to spend so many years of a life abroad in often uncomfortable and occasionally dangerous places I sometimes explained it to myself as an escape – from British life, at which I looked askew; from my family; perhaps from myself. None of these propositions quite convinced me. My distant uncle the Victorian traveller Robert Curzon blamed his unfeeling, spendthrift parents for the fact that he spent so many years abroad 'wandering like an unquiet spirit', but I was far enough emotionally from my father and mother not to need to put more physical space between us. Certainly there was something in myself and in other foreign correspondents that welcomed the distraction of war and revolution and the clash of superpowers. In that sense I suppose we were old-fashioned romantics, and close enough to the poet's image of the traveller who seeks out storms 'as though in storms he will find peace'. But I did not recognise in myself a sense of being driven round the world by some eternal discontent. What I did discover was the incomparable excitement of romancing new countries. They became the women in my life.

One thing puzzled my Cambridge friend Corinna when she went to work in the *Observer*'s Paris office in 1958. The *Observer* writers she met were all under forty, which she found 'odd when you consider how (let's face it) middle-aged their liberalism often is'. The paper's office in Tudor Street that I reported to three years later did not strike me as middle-aged. Certainly some of the staff were as knowledgeable as dons, but they were a good deal more worldly wise, and without a hint of donnish drabness. I had not come across anywhere more delightful than Auntie's, the pub round the corner from the office where *Observer* people gathered and conversations flickered between the serious and the trivial. There were eccentrics and there were brilliant drunks, but what everyone seemed to share was a sense of being involved in something uncommonly worthwhile. If this unusual newspaper was a club, it was the only club I ever wanted to be a member of.

The *Observer* was, in fact, a less contented place than it seemed at first acquaintance. Not long after I arrived in Moscow letters began arriving from colleagues in London worrying about the paper's mood and future. Edward Crankshaw took a moment off from the correspondence course he was giving me in newspaper writing to report that Tudor Street was 'in a state of something like demoralisation, and I find it not at all sympathetic'. George Seddon signalled his gloom by signing himself 'George Standstill'. Money problems had much to do with it. Still boycotted by Jewish and super-patriotic British advertisers because of its opposition to the Suez invasion, the *Observer* could not cope with the commercial inventiveness of the *Sunday Times* and competition from the newly launched *Sunday Telegraph*. Some years later the first rumours reached me of a search for rich patrons to bail the paper out of trouble. Someone came up with a group of Libyans; someone else suggested Saudi Arabians. The Hong Kong millionairess who made her fortune out of Tiger Balm seemed tempted to save us for a while, but then vanished back to the East. In 1975 the prize, if that is what it was, was claimed by an unusually sophisticated American oil company.

Corinna had, without meaning to, put her finger on the cause of some of these discontents when she described the *Observer*'s liberalism as 'middle-aged'. And so it was for young people like her or Peter Jenkins, who grew up after the war thinking themselves left-wing. Impatient for change, they were inclined to suspect that the Cold War and the attitudes associated with it had become obstacles to change, whereas for David Astor, the paper's editor and *de facto* owner, the Cold War remained the central issue of the age. Astor was a seductively modest man, but he towered like an oak tree above everyone else on the paper, and his view of the world was shaped by Hitler's rise to power in the 1930s and the later realisation that Stalin's Soviet Union was an equally powerful threat to the democratic countries of the West. When I went as correspondent to Washington in 1975 one of the first reports I wrote concerned revelations about President Kennedy's use of the

CIA and its various 'dirty tricks' to overthrow Fidel Castro. I suppose I sounded shocked or indignant in what I wrote, and a letter from Astor arrived soon after.

He wanted, he said, to remind me 'how matters look different in different periods of history'. Kennedy and his advisers were, like himself, products of the Thirties and Forties. They had watched fascist movements take over Germany, Italy and Spain with the support of a large part of their populations, while Western democrats did little to help their friends in those countries, either openly or when they were asked to give clandestine assistance. 'It seemed in liberal and social-democratic circles', he went on, that the West only knew how to 'play cricket' with foreign governments but 'didn't know how to help our friends by irregular means'.

> Later, when it began to be realised that the German Communists had let the Nazis get to power; that the Russians had abandoned the Spanish Republicans for some reasons of their own; that Hitler and Stalin could happily operate a pact; and finally, that Stalin's domestic system was as murderous as Hitler's and more totalitarian; the feeling began to grow – reluctantly on the Left, of course – that there was no huge difference between the two totalitarian systems, compared to the difference between both of them and the democracies.

Astor made the *Observer* a liberal standard-bearer of the Cold War because his opposition to Soviet totalitarianism was the Siamese twin of his earlier resistance to Nazi Germany. The first writers he gathered round him had profound knowledge of both countries: it was typical that my mentor Edward Crankshaw was as much an expert on the Gestapo as on Stalin's Russia. And long after the death of George Orwell and the departure from the paper of other stars such as Sebastian Haffner and Isaac Deutscher, one figure remained in the *Observer* office who embodied this preoccupation with the two totalitarian scourges of twentieth-century Europe. Few people outside the paper knew the name of Willy Guttmann, for he seldom wrote signed articles. A German Jew born in Silesian Gleiwitz on Germany's border with Poland, he was forced to leave his home town when the Nazis banned Jews from practising law. Six years after Willy left Gleiwitz a band of German convicts, led by Nazi security officers but dressed in Polish army uniforms, seized the town's radio station, broadcast a patriotic announcement in Polish, and were machine-gunned by waiting SS troops as they tried to leave. This 'Polish attack' on Germany served Hitler as pretext for his blitzkrieg against Poland and was followed within days by the Soviet occupation of the rest of the country. When the Second World War was over Gleiwitz became Gliwice in a Communist-ruled Poland and Willy Guttmann, like many other central Europeans, no longer had a home to return to.

He first worked in the *Observer* as its librarian but later became the paper's wise man, checking the accuracy of copy for the next week's edition and answering questions on an amazing range of linguistic and other topics. Surrounded by *prima donna* journalists, he was courteous, calm and a little shy, and moved about the office with the benign dignity of the much-loved law professor he might have been were it not for Hitler and Stalin. His presence was for me as vivid a reminder of the *Observer*'s purpose as any number of words written by its famous authors.

What strikes me now about David Astor's letter is its undercurrent of defensiveness. He was soon to give up the editorship, and had been bruised by disagreements with some of the paper's younger writers that welled up in the late 1960s. Members of the *Observer* staff had always had astonishing freedom, and talked as much as they liked at the long and frequent conferences that somehow drove the paper towards its next edition. There had always been arguments at these meetings, and they were sometimes fierce, but now the disagreements seemed to question the principles on which Astor based his editorship. These were the years of student revolutionaries and of belief in the approach of a convulsion that would not spare the 'middle-aged' leaders of the West. Above all they were the years of the American war in Vietnam, of hatred for Richard Nixon, and the suspicion that imperial America was as bad as, or even worse than, the Soviet Union. In the end, and almost twenty years after he retired,

Astor was proved right. By the time I came back to live in London in 1993 the Soviet Union had collapsed as conclusively as the world of illusion once constructed by my grandfather. And though some people felt nostalgia for it, no one with a knowledge of the facts supposed it could ever be rebuilt. There was no longer anything middle-aged, or controversial, about Astor's steadfast insistence on the Soviet threat to democratic countries, for the Soviet empire's flaws and the danger it had represented to the rest of the world were now plain for all to see.

It seemed appropriate that the end of the Cold War coincided with the final disappearance of what remained of the old *Observer*. In spite of its difficulties after Astor's departure – undesirable owners, dreadful finances – there were still echoes of the paper he made, not least the commitment to foreign reporting, money allowing, that reflected the belief that all five continents were a democrat's business. The Cold War had forced coherence on the world. Washington and Moscow lined up the nations behind them, and even those who wanted no part of either side were defined, whether they liked it or not, in relation to the competition between East and West. This no longer existed but instead of agreeable freedom countries more often found themselves in a Babel world without structure, a world in which it was easy to spin off into violence or misery while others, if they watched at all, did little more than shrug their shoulders. It was hard to make sense of such things and British newspapers, scared of confusing or boring the readers they were competing for, were tempted to give up the effort.

The end of the Cold War also made plain how the once innovative and daring *Observer*, like many other British institutions, could not flourish in the new world that had been taking shape, often hesitantly and with many diversions, from the 1960s on. Like all reformers, the liberal *Observer* contributed, without planning it, to the disappearance of much that it valued. As the last Whig newspaper it had championed the cause of the unfortunate and under-privileged without expecting to undermine its own values or its standing in the established world to which, in spite of its liberal ideas, it belonged.

The *Observer*'s skill at being a critic within the establishment was shown by its Pendennis gossip column, which for years gave an uncanny insight into what powerful people talked about in the privacy of their clubs and dinner tables. The paper's writers were well informed because so many of them inhabited the same world as the politicians, bureaucrats and leaders of the newly decolonised countries they reported on. Its rational optimism was another Whig characteristic. One of the hymns sung at William Clark's memorial service was Joseph Addison's 'The spacious firmament on high', an affirmation of Enlightenment confidence in a benign Creator and a human world that could, if sensibly managed, be as orderly as the movement of the planets. It was an attitude that suited the *Observer* well.

This *Observer* belonged to the same vanished world in which bank managers knew the names of even their least affluent customers and solicitors felt it their duty to help clients like my mother, who could never afford to pay a proper fee. The *Observer* might also have stood as a model of the benevolent paternalism that was attacked, and finally destroyed, by the unplanned alliance of the British left and right that brought about the fluid unpredictability of Britain at the end of the twentieth century. Working at the *Observer*, said one of the compositors who assembled lead type to make up the pages, was like living in a village; wherever you went you could stop and have a chat with someone you knew. In autumn he brought apples to the office from his garden to share them out, like any villager, among his neighbours.

The country I returned to for good in 1993 was like Babel after God punished its workers for presuming to speak in one language. There was a multitude of languages or discourses now, languages for women and minorities of all colour, belief and sexual inclination, and languages spoken on behalf of children and the handicapped (the only language no one spoke, or seemed to remember any more, was the language of economic equality: the grammar, people said, was just too hard). There was no ordering of claims; each language contained its own values that presumed equality with all the others. Small wonder many found it as hard to make sense of this new world as my autistic stepbrother Freddie, who has struggled for fifty years to put the data of his senses into some sort of useful and unfrightening order. Small wonder people sometimes feel the ground is moving under their feet, or that at moments I am reminded of that early midsummer morning in Komsomol Square when I found myself among the crowd of men and women who seemed no longer quite to know who they were or where they were going. At such moments I also remember the young gypsies I saw that morning and the lightness of their movements while everyone around them was so slow and uncertain, for here, too, chance now favours those who travel light and know no regret for the times that are past.